THE
TWENTY-ONE

THE
TWENTY-ONE

By Lauren K. McKellar

For everyone who's ever looked to the stars and wondered if they're watching.
I promise.
They are.

PROLOGUE

Grief is a private thing. It's not something I like to share with my mother and sister. It's why I never let them come to the cemetery with me. How can you be someone's rock when they've seen your cracks exposed?

I run one finger over the embossed gold words on the marble headstone. My hand stills over the date that is forever engraved in my soul: *November 21, 2014.* One short year ago. The day that changed my life.

You can protect your heart all you like. You can fold it inside bubble wrap, place it in a safe place and never let anyone near it, but the truth is, love finds a way in. We're all only human like that.

"Three months 'til your anniversary," I whisper, even though there's no one around to hear. It's a day I'm dreading.

Because the day my father died, he pulled me aside and asked of me one thing—just one thing.

THE TWENTY-ONE

"I love you, Eleanor," he said, hazel eyes gleaming into my own. "And I need you to be strong."

"I'll be strong." I sniffed and clutched his hand tight, as if my life depended on it.

Mine didn't.

Only his was in the balance.

He paused, then opened his mouth and closed it, as if trying to find the right words. "Mum and Dani ... they're not as capable as you are. Look after your mother and your sister. Take care of them. They're going to need someone like you."

I glanced over at the two of them, huddled together in the chairs sitting in the corridor. Tears stained their cheeks, and their shoulders shook with the pain of death. The pain of knowing the one person gluing your life together was going to become unstuck.

I hurt; I couldn't comprehend the idea of life without him. Life without my father. But instead of dwelling on grief, I chose to focus on an opportunity. To live life as he wanted. To devote myself to his request, and know that even though he wasn't here with me, I was making him proud.

Wherever he was.

And wherever he wasn't.

I squared my shoulders and looked him straight in the eye. "I'll make sure they're safe, Dad. It'll be my number one priority."

And it was.

Until a boy with blue eyes tore that idea to shreds.

ONE

There's nothing romantic about frostbite. No matter how many books you read, no matter how many love scenes involving a passion so fiery it could melt ice, none of them deal with the impracticality of not being able to feel your toes. Or the chances of them turning blue.

I breathe and air mists in front of my face, floating off into the empty green field before me. Well, empty except for three things. A hot-air balloon, a young couple and a picnic basket.

"It's so cold I could freeze my dick off."

Make that four things.

Zylen Blackley shoves his hands into his black tight jeans, tossing back his head so a lock of hair that had fallen over his face lands bam, right in place, as he walks over from the parking lot.

No, he doesn't walk. Zylen Blackley never walks. He *swaggers*.

THE TWENTY-ONE

"Well damn, wouldn't that be a shame? And I had my money on an STD being the one to do the job," I say, a sweet smile on my face.

"Nice one, doll. And here I thought gambling was beneath you." He walks over to my side and then whispers seductively close to my ear. His breath is hot against my neck. *Too* hot. "I guess something has to be."

"Get away." I push against his firm chest, and he steps back, a soft laugh escaping his lips. "I know you're secretly in love with my sister."

"I've known her since she was a kid," Zy says. "We're just friends, Ellie."

"Mmhmm. Friends. Who live together." I raise my eyebrows and study him. "And party together. And who will probably one day require me to bail them out of jail, together."

"Loosen up, El Bell. It'll do you the world of good."

I flip him the bird as he walks over to the ride-on mower parked next to the shipping container that doubles as office space for my boss, Colin, and climbs on board. I scowl, hating the way he looks over his shoulder and winks at me. As if that kind of thing makes my knees slightly weak, and my heart kind of jumpy.

As if.

The engine roars to life, a thick growl against the otherwise still morning. I turn my attention back to the field in front of me, and Colin, who is now striding from the balloon, leaving the couple to themselves.

He brushes past me, his briefcase in hand, and charges toward the small shipping container. His hand alternates between pushing up the thick-rimmed glasses that rest upon his nose and rifling in the pocket of his brown slacks for his set of keys.

"What's taking so long?" I ask, stamping my feet to try and keep the feeling in my toes alive. Mud splatters over the ends of my maroon Doc Martens.

"It didn't go well, Ellie. Halfway through the flight, they asked me to head back. They're having a fight," he replies, his voice raised to be heard over the roar of the mower.

I frown, and narrow my eyes on the couple again. Now that Colin's mentioned it, I can see the evidence firsthand. The guy is tall, a hood covering his head, facing toward the forest at the other end of the field. The girl, though? Her shiny brown hair shimmers over the top of her wool-lined denim jacket as she presses against his chest, her slight frame shaking. He extends a hesitant arm out to wrap around her shoulders, but she flinches it off and steps back.

"That sucks," I say. My heart goes out to the poor girl. I wonder what he's done. What's caused her all this emotional turmoil.

"It's bloody inconsiderate, if you ask me."

I blink. "Really?"

"I'm sure you want to get out of this cold just as much as I do." Colin jiggles his hand in his pocket until he finally retrieves the key to his office, unlocking the door. He ducks his head, his six-foot-seven height a stark contrast to my five-two, and steps inside.

Before shutting the door behind him, he shoots me a sly grin. "I can tell you're cold." He glances at my chest and I shudder, but ignore his sleazy line. If he weren't a close friend of my mother's, I would have quit working for him years ago.

I focus on the couple still standing in the field, right next to the little wicker basket that was once full of local goodies, from decadent cheeses, to fresh oysters, to plump strawberries to a crisp wine. I wonder how much of that the couple has consumed, or if their argument took off when the balloon did.

The fight between the couple heats up. She steps back, her hands flying left and right. The odd word travels across the field, even over the mower—"you" and "how" and "why". My mind runs wild, and I imagine all sorts of scenarios. Did he cheat on her? Lie? Forget her name in bed?

"So much for true love, eh?" Zy raises an eyebrow, steering the mower past me. He drives it just a little too close for comfort, and I step back as the beast roars and chugs toward the end of the field.

"You leave true love alone!" I call after him.

His response?

A kiss blown over his shoulder.

Jerk.

Back out on the field, the girl shoves against the guy's chest, and he staggers. His arms reach out to her, to hold her, embrace her, but she flings her hands out to the side as if to say *what am I supposed to do?*

And then she leaves.

She marches past him, her brown shimmery hair flying out behind her with the tail of her scarf.

The guy spins around, his face tilted to the cold earth beneath him. There's something so desperately lost in his stance, something so hopelessly sad—I almost feel sorry for him.

The girl stamps closer to me, her face an icy mask of composure. She's holding it together, despite the tears welling in her eyes. The sadness trying to escape her mouth.

"We're finished," the girl mutters as she walks past, heading to the parking lot behind me, and I don't know if she means with the picnic basket or as a couple.

I guess you could take it either way.

Her car, a shiny silver BMW, chirrups and the lights flash, and she opens the door and starts it up. The engine revs and the wheels spin as she tries to reverse out of the muddy park, and she slams her hands down against the wheel in frustration as it stalls.

For a moment, for just one moment, I think she's going to break.

Then she guns it for all it's worth, and the car reverses back and jerks forward, flying out onto the road.

I glance over to the field. The guy has one hand outstretched, as if somehow he could stop her from leaving with just the force of his mind and an extended arm. If only life were that simple.

Colin breaks me from my reverie when his door creaks open. I spin to see his head poking out of the office doorway. "They're gone?"

"Just one." I nod toward the man still standing in the middle of the field. He looks so forlorn there by himself. So solitary. So alone.

"Drats," he mutters, pushing his glasses up his nose. "Can you go sort that out? I don't need his bad juju around here."

I presume by *that* he means *him*—his client. The man who ordered the picnic basket from Perfect Picnics, which I painstakingly packed at nine p.m. last night for Colin to deliver this morning. Because that's what Colin, the least romantic man in the world, does for a living. He flies hot-air balloons and sells overpriced picnic baskets to those who believe in love. And in his spare time, he likes to torture me.

My hands shove into the pockets of my jeans as I stare at the tall lone figure out there. *What went so horribly wrong for you?*

THE TWENTY-ONE

I start my trek across the field, cursing with every step because the numbness is slowly creeping up my ankles. I need to get these Docs replaced. The dew creeps through the holes in the soles, turning my socks into sodden vessels, destined to freeze.

The man doesn't move to get closer to me. He just stands there, staring at the ground, his shoulders offering up quick shudders, and for a moment I think he's crying.

Dear God, please don't let him be crying.

There are a lot of things I can handle in life, but tears aren't one of them.

And heights.

I look at the big balloon and shudder. Just another reason Colin and I are so dissimilar.

I keep my eyes firmly focused on the dark soil with flecks of green patched here and there, until the edges of dull, black Docs creep into my vision. My gaze travels up denim-clad legs, over the white T-shirt and black hoodie pulled up, to a face—

That face.

Blue eyes haunt me from skin that's not tanned, but not too pale, either. His cheekbones are high and pronounced, mirroring the hard angle of his strong, firm jaw. He's hot, the kind of good looking that belongs on a campaign for some kind of men's cologne.

Not the kind of hot that winds up dumped after a romantic date of hot-air balloons and picnic baskets.

But more than all that?

He's the man who broke my heart.

And I never thought I'd see him again.

TWO

"Hi." Joel's voice cracks as he says the word. Surprise is written on his face, in his wide eyes, his rounded mouth.

"Joel," I whisper, with a slight shake of my head. How? How is he here … *now?* He has the same devastating blue eyes, but the blond hair I loved has been shaved down to his skull.

My knees float away like fairy floss, independent of my being. I grasp behind me, looking for some kind of support, but there's nothing there aside from frosty winter air and a whole world of the unknown.

And then I do what any woman who reconnects with the love of her life after a mysterious three-year absence would do.

I slap the bastard.

"Shit!" Joel clasps at his cheek seconds after my palm makes contact.

I wring my hand up and down, because damn, hitting someone in this kind of weather hurts. Still, as I see the shocked expression on Joel Henley's face, I'm vaguely satisfied.

Then my sense of Catholic guilt kicks in and I want to kiss it better.

That's all I've ever wanted to do when it came to Joel Henley. Try and make everything all right.

"I'm sorry." I step forward, then take two steps back, the irony of the movement not lost on me. "I just … wow." The word falls flat between us. "What are you doing here?"

Joel opens and closes his mouth like a goldfish, then finally forms some words. "I didn't expect to see you again."

I step back, holding my hands up. "Oh, shit, sorry. I would have called or texted to tell you I work here but—oh yeah." I snap my fingers as if just remembering. "You broke off all contact."

"I'm sorry, Ellie."

"Sorry?" I ask, three years' worth of rage firing inside of me. "Sorry you shut down all your social media? Sorry you stopped answering my calls? Or just sorry you left without a damn trace?"

And that was exactly how it had been. Sure, we'd only been seventeen, both of us still in school. But my best friend in the whole world had disappeared the year before without a damn trace. My father had just been diagnosed with cancer. And then the boy I'd grown up next door to, the one who had picked me to be on his team for school sport when no one else would, the one who had defended my reading on the bus by pretending to read along with me, the one I had lost my virginity to and fallen in love with—he'd left too.

Just like everyone else I cared about.

It wasn't as if he could have stayed—his whole family had moved to Sydney, an hour's drive away. Still, I'd thought three years of high school love meant more than that. I'd thought three years of being together meant not deactivating social media or ignoring my texts and calls.

I'd thought three years of being in love at least meant telling me he was going, and not leaving me to find out from my sister, who'd seen the truck pull out of his drive. Two days later, a *for lease* sign had appeared out the front of it.

Still, that was a long time ago. Things are different now.

Now, I look at the boy who broke my heart once more. Joel bites on his lip and studies the sparse ground, then looks up at me again. His fractured eyes widen, and different shades of blue spiral out of from his pupil. They are and always will be the most fascinating eyes I've ever seen.

"Words are never going to be enough. Especially not with you." He offers me a sad smile. "For what it's worth, I'm sorry, Ellie. I'm so damn sorry." The way he says my name sends stupid tingles over my body, and I stamp my foot. Because *damn* and *I hate you* and *everything.* "I know I didn't really … well, things were hard. I had to cut all ties with you when we moved. I couldn't …"

I raise my eyebrows and give him my best resting bitch face. "Couldn't man up and just tell me the truth? That you were moving to the city and didn't want to bother with our relationship?"

The noises around us grow louder in our silence. The roar of the lawnmower in the distance. The parrots chirping their early-morning praise chorus.

My heart, hammering in my chest.

I hate you.

I love you.

A million times I'd pictured how this day would pan out. The day when I finally ran into Joel Henley again.

Never did I think it would be like this, with him being dumped and me watching on from the sidelines. Not in a million years.

"It's complicated. I didn't know what I was doing. I was just a kid ..." He shoves his hands in the pockets of his jeans, then drills me with that gaze again. "Look, you can go. This right here—this is not your problem." Joel gives me a wry smile. Behind him, the colourful hot-air balloon mocks him with a dance, a gentle waltz in the morning breeze that's performed in direct contrast to his mood. Zy's mower growls across the field, and the scent of fresh-cut grass wafts across to us.

Silence stretches between us, and even though I'm still angry, and even though he's still a jerk, there is genuine sadness in his eyes.

"You're wrong," I finally mutter.

"I know. I'm sorry. I've thought a million times about how I could have done things differently—"

"I meant about this being my problem." I curve one side of my lips up in a smile. "I need to retrieve the picnic basket."

"Oh." Joel laughs, and and it feels good to make him smile. *Too* good.

My heart and brain war and I take a step closer, shoving my hands in my pockets. "So ... she wasn't the hot-air balloon, romantic picnic type, huh?"

Icy eyes slowly travel up my jeans, my shirt, to my face. A small, half-hearted smile graces thin lips. "No. I guess not."

I step closer, closing the gap to just a few steps between us. "Well, in my opinion, she's an idiot. I mean, hot-air balloon!" I gesture to the death machine behind him, but try to interject some light into my tone. "Champagne."

I point toward the basket on the ground. "If that's not enough to make her swoon, she has problems."

I inch around him and pick up the forlorn basket. It's weighty, as if they've barely touched the contents, and my heart goes out to the couple again.

Then I pull it back, chain it in. This boy broke my heart. And now someone else has broken his.

Fair is fair.

"I have to go ..." I wave in the direction of the lot. "So if you don't mind ..."

"Moping somewhere else?" he asks.

"Pretty much, that would be great." I laugh, not unkindly, and a twinkle reappears in Joel's eyes.

"I deserve that, huh?" he asks, falling in step beside me.

"Yeah." I nod. "Yeah, you do."

We walk, side by side, back toward the parking lot. Magpies conduct their early-morning gossip sessions, screeching from one tree to the next. The soundtrack of rural Australia.

Every now and then, I sneak a look across at him. He's still got the same beautiful face, but there's a hard edge there now, as if he's somehow more gaunt—as if life has not been kind. Tension stretches taut between us. I'm almost afraid to speak in case it snaps.

We stop when we reach the parking lot edge. I scan the dirt yard, my white sedan and Colin's blue Audi ... and the truck rumbling past on the freeway. I turn to Joel, a questioning look on my face.

"We came in the same car."

"Oh, man." I shake my head. "Rough."

"Yeah. Left me here without any way of getting home." He smiles, but this time there's no mirth in it.

"Let me call you a cab. Or ..." I suck in a deep breath, as if through a straw, my lips rounded in an *O*. "Or you could grab a ride back to Emerald Cove with me."

"Really?" he asks, his head to the side. "That'd be great, if you don't mind."

"It's fine. Where are you headed?"

"Just to the beach at EC."

"No worries," I say, all the while my head argues with me, listing the reasons this is not a smart plan.

He left you, and doesn't deserve it.

He's heartbroken.

He's still the guy you sometimes dream about ...

I push that thought down as quickly as it enters my mind. Before I can think if that's even really true, my body takes over, working on autopilot. "I'll just say goodbye." I jerk my head toward the office, and Joel nods, shoving his hands in his pockets.

My trip to the office is done with power, just in case Joel is watching. Long, determined strides. Strides that I hope say *I'm confident* and *I'm happy* and *I don't miss you* all at the same time. When I arrive at the rusty red container, I slide the door open. It's dark in here, one suspended light hanging from the ceiling offering a yellow glow. Colin's set up on his black leather desk chair, his laptop open in front of him, the bright white screen casting most of the light in the room. A filing cabinet whose colour could only be described as Manila is to his left, and a stack of paper a few centimetres thick sits next to his laptop on the shiny black desk surface. Colin hunches over the computer, his fingers furiously working the surface in front of him.

"See ya, Colin."

"Cool. You going to the Constantina gallery thing on Wednesday?" He doesn't look up from the computer as he talks, *tap, tap, tapping*.

"Yeah." I sigh, thinking of the hours of polite chitchat at my mum's art event I'll have to endure.

"I'll see you there." I know there's a sly smile on his face, even if I can't see it. "If you manage to get away from the front desk. How you do such a boring job just to help your mother is beyond me."

"It won't be that bad." *It will be worse.* The small talk. The judgmental elite. The need to watch Dani. "Anyway, I'm outta here. Have a good one."

"Going home with desperate and dateless."

I don't even ask how he knows. The office has no windows, so it's not like he'd have heard. My boss can sometimes just be all-seeing, all-knowing like that. "Nope. I'm driving him to the city."

"Gonna have sex on the freeway."

"No, I'm not, Colin."

"Don't forget to use protection!"

I slam the door shut and roll my eyes, then take a deep breath and head back over to Joel, who is not desperate and dateless or someone I plan on screwing on the side of the road.

I rifle around in my pocket for my keys then unlock the car, popping the boot and taking care not to touch the surface of the car with anything other than two fingers to avoid getting covered in the dirt that shades my white sedan. I stash the basket in the back and slam the boot shut again.

When I walk back around the front, Joel has already seated himself on the passenger side, his seatbelt firmly in place, his long legs next to the dusty dash.

I turn the key in the engine and pull out of the lot, heading to the freeway that will take us back to Emerald Cove, about an hour away from Swallow Fields, where Colin's hot-air balloon business is located.

THE TWENTY-ONE

The radio blares some incredibly loud pop-tastic music from so many years ago, and I turn the volume button down on Train's "Drops of Jupiter" to off with such force my wrist hurts. "Sorry." I shake my head. "I don't usually listen to stuff like that." *I totally do.*

I chance a quick look over to Joel. He stares out the window, a vacant expression on his face.

The car picks up speed and the steady hum of the engine swallows us up. The sun waxes its pale golden light down over the freeway that in parts is still shrouded with mist, dancing between the white trunks of the green-leaved native trees that sway as ghoulish spectres in the winter morning breeze.

"So what have you been doing for the past three years?" I ask, keeping my eyes firmly fixed on the road.

Joel heaves in a breath and lets it out with a whistle. "Study. I do communications, but part-time. And I work for one of those charity corporates in the city."

"Sounds … rewarding." *And nothing at all like the Joel Henley I used to know.*

"It is."

The rumble of the road amplifies between us. *It's going to be a long hour-trip back to Emerald Cove.*

"So … how was your balloon ride? Aside from … you know …" I say, more to break the silence than anything else.

"Ha." Joel's voice lacks mirth. "I didn't really notice, to tell you the truth."

Cars fly past us, their noise coming toward and away from us.

"Have you been up in the balloon before?"

"Pardon?"

"Have you been—"

"Sorry." *God, this is awkward.* "No. I'm ... I don't like heights."

"Heights?" He furrows his brow. "So hot-air balloon rides—"

"Yep. Terrify me." I shudder, thinking of being suspended in that tiny basket, held aloft by a simple balloon. "Did you know that 761 people were killed in flight incidents in 2014?"

He blinks. "That's a very ... specific quote."

"CNN." I shrug. "Anyway, I will not be the seven hundred and sixty-second. I happen to like keeping my feet planted firmly on the ground." I smile, indicating to change into the right-hand lane to overtake the slow-moving caravan in front of me while still keeping well within the speed limit.

"Do you know what fraction of people that is? Compared to the amount of people who fly in planes, and hot-air balloons, and space?"

I wave a hand in his direction. "Don't even try to make the number seem smaller or less likely. Colin does that all the time, and it's not the point. Heights aren't ... they're not safe. I like being safe."

My safety, and that of my mother and sister. They're the only things I have to be able to control.

"Were you afraid of heights back when we ..." Joel kills the sentence slowly, then snaps his fingers together. "No, no way. I remember we dove off the Rip Bridge together."

Images rush through my mind. Hands, tightly gripped. Air, sucked out of our lungs. The smash of water against our skin.

Then skin on skin, salt water mixed with our passion.

It's all it takes to undo me. All it takes for me to snap. "You don't get to talk about what I used to be like. You don't have the right."

"I'm sorry, I—"

"Sorry?" I spit. The car jerks as I glance at him, and I overcorrect back into my lane. "You broke my heart," I say, hurt bleeding from my mouth.

Joel stills, and looks me dead in the eye. "I left a piece of mine with you."

The line makes me melt. It's as if he has the power to take me back three years. Back to when we were happy. Back to when I didn't have to worry about exams, or my dad, or my sister.

Back to when I was just a girl in love with a boy.

"Do you remember that time we stole a boat?"

"Borrowed!" I open my mouth in mock outrage, but I can't stop my smile. "I would never steal."

"Liberated, then." Joel laughs. "Hey, can I ask you a question?"

I hesitate before replying. "Sure."

"What happened to the girl who was going to write a novel? Who was going to university to study literature and then change the world with her love of books?"

My chest expands. It's as if my lungs are too big for the small space inside of me. "I don't know what happened." *Death. Death happened.* "I guess ... I guess it was just easier to work for Mum, and then when this picnic stuff came up with Colin, I took that on board, too."

Joel frowns. "What does your dad think about that? He was always—"

"He's dead." I cut him off with blunt words. "Cancer. One year ago."

This time, Joel's hand connects with my knee. It's warm there. Comforting. "I'm so sorry."

I shake my head and give a wan smile. "Don't be. You didn't do it." It's my standard response to a statement I've heard too many times. Too many times to want to discuss it further.

We're quiet for a few minutes, and when Joel takes his hand away, I miss the heat on my leg. And then I hate myself for missing that.

We stop at a set of lights and my hand goes to the pocket of the door, searching for a distraction—something, anything to fill this weird space between us.

My hand crackles plastic, and I pull a bag of lollies up, victorious. "Snake?" I offer the bag to Joel.

He eyes it suspiciously, a smirk on his lips. "When exactly did you open these?"

Even after all these years, he knows me so well. I pause, and twist my lips. "Yesterday," I say, and silently add *or sometime last week.*

Joel gives the bag one more look then takes out a lolly, popping it into his mouth. I do the same, a long red snake dangling between my lips.

The car is quiet as I think more about Joel. About the way he used to make me feel. How he used to tie me in knots—

"Did you just do the thing?"

Joel's voice is so out of nowhere, I almost swerve. I steady my hands on the wheel and shoot him a quick glance. "What thing?" I ask around the snake in my mouth.

"With your snake."

My tongue pushes at the cherry-flavoured gelatine in my mouth. Without meaning to, I'd tied it in a knot.

Three guesses who's to blame for that ...

"I guess I did." I balance the lolly between my lips and part them, allowing Joel to see the treat inside.

"You know in high school, people would say that doing that was a sign you gave good head," Joel says.

I arch an eyebrow at him then bite down on the snake with a snap. "Oh yeah?" I chomp down on the snake, spearing it in two, then poke my tongue out, showing him the two separate pieces. "What do you think this means?"

Joel laughs, and his face changes, his lips flat-lining, then curving in a smile. "Remember that time when you made me learn all the words to the male half of the *Grease* mega mix, so we could sing at your school's talent quest?"

I cringe. "Oh God." I make a face. "Was I really that bossy?"

"To this day, I can never hear that song and not think of you."

The words hit a little too close to home. I'm so quick to fall back into an easy rhythm with him. I always have been. I roll my eyes. "What song makes you think of your ex?"

He sighs, and runs a hand up over his face, pushing back his hood. His head is shaved, as he's had it since he turned sixteen, and I want to run my hand over it, feel its smoothness beneath me.

But I don't.

Because that would be creepy.

"Vanessa doesn't get a song," Joel says in a soft voice. A voice that's just been hurt.

I pull up at the traffic lights and take the moment to really look at him. His lips draw in a thin line as he gazes out the window. There's something entirely captivating about Joel Henley. And it petrifies and thrills me, all at once.

The car behind me beeps its horn angrily, and I jolt back to reality. I flick my gaze up to the traffic light to discover it's green, and I rush to move the car forward and continue on our way.

Minutes later, we arrive at the beach parking lot. I pull over and double park, leaving the engine running.

He pauses, one hand on the door. "When it comes to us, for what it's worth? I wish I'd tried harder."

I steel my gaze against his. "Well, have a great ... life."

He nods, as if accepting this fate, and turns away. "You too."

He opens the door and the sounds and smells of the beach roll in—crashing waves, gulls crying, children laughing and squealing, despite the cool wintry air. Salt and coffee and petrol assault my senses, and I smile. This smell to me is home.

Joel hops out of the car, and I can't help but smile. In another life, another time, he would be the kind of guy I'd fantasise over. The kind of guy I could love. I once did love.

He turns to shut the door, and just when I think he's about to swing it closed, he pauses. "Oh, and Ellie Mayfield?" he asks.

"Yeah?"

"You're still the most beautiful girl I've ever seen."

THREE

"So let me get this straight," Hope, my flatmate, says, her hands out in front of her, as if she's reading them like a book. "You ran into Joel love-of-your-life Henley?" Her voice rises in pitch on the last word.

"Shh!" I hiss, my gaze darting around the bar to make sure no one has overheard. It may be a cold Saturday afternoon in winter, but Class is still almost standing-room only. Girls in too-tight jeans and boys in even tighter ones fill the lounge seats, laughing and flirting as they knock back cocktail after cocktail. I don't think there's anyone here I know, but still. Better safe than sorry.

"Sorry," Hope whispers. She takes the empty glass of wine from in front of me and turns to Lia, the third member of our group. "You want anything else?"

"Just an OJ, please," Lia says, smiling. She doesn't often drink. When your mother is a recovering alcoholic, it's not really that surprising.

"Okay, press pause on this story till I'm back with more." Hope skips back behind the bar where she works, slipping past the other two bartenders and Jase, Lia's boyfriend of two years, who owns the place.

My phone buzzes in my pocket and I pull it out, sliding across the screen to read the latest message.

Mum: Reminder about the event at Constantina this week. Need you there stuffing bags at five. Do not be late. And make sure your sister is on time.

My breath streams out of my body. Lately, Dani has been anything but *on time*. Still, I'll somehow make sure she's there. It's what I promised Dad I'd do.

It's what I always do.

Lia reaches across the table and grabs my hand, bringing me back to the present. She lowers her voice so I have to strain to hear her against the backdrop of bar noise. "Listen, I am so sorry again that I just took off." It takes me a few seconds to realise she's talking about our past. "I should never have left you. Especially when you were going through—"

I shake my head and cut her off. "It's forgotten."

Lia left our school and our town when we were sixteen. It turned out, it was because her mother was into some pretty serious shit, and she was worried we'd all find out. Well, find out more than we already knew.

That her mother had driven the two of them into a lake.

She pauses and deep brown eyes gaze at me again. "Still, that would have been rough. Your father … me … Joel …"

I flick my hand in the air, as if it were nothing. As if those weren't some of the loneliest years of my life. "The point is, you're here for me now. It's not like Joel ever came back."

Lia pauses, studying the grainy table top, then turns back to my face. "Ellie, you chased me."

I press my lips together. I didn't chase Joel like I did her. But things were different with him. He wasn't going through what Lia and her family were.

I think back to his words to me earlier today. *You're still the most beautiful girl I've ever seen.* I think back to the boy I knew so well, who'd damn well near held my hand throughout the first half of my life.

"It doesn't matter, anyway." I shrug it off. "It's not like I'm ever going to see him again."

"Fate works in mysterious ways, Ellie," Lia says, arching her eyebrows.

"It sure does." Hope slams our drinks down in front of us, her face dark and stormy.

"Are you okay?" Lia asks, ever the peacemaker. Her eyes scan the bar and settle on a tall guy sitting at a bar stool by himself. "Hey, isn't that Kyle—"

"I don't want to talk about it," Hope snaps.

"Are you sure?" Lia's tone is earnest. Care shines in her deep brown eyes, and not for the first time in my life, I'm so thankful that she's my best friend. She's just a good person. She's fought through so much and came out on the other side.

"I'm sure." Hope picks up her glass of vodka soda and takes a long sip, looking me in the eye. "So there's Joel … what else is new?"

The bell hanging from the wall chimes as the wooden door swings open. A blast of cold air assaults me, honing in on the thin line of exposed skin between my tank top and jeans. Laughter tinkles in the air, and I still. *Dani.*

I kick at the pole supporting the high table and spin in my bar stool, facing the door and Danica Mayfield. My sister.

"Ellieeeeee!" She squeals and skips over, flinging her arms around my neck.

I stiffen. She smells like she's bathed herself in bourbon.

I pull back so we can look each other in the eye. Well, I look her in the eye. She seems to be having trouble focusing on anything.

"Hey," I say, frowning. What's she doing?

"H … *hic* … hi." Dani claps her hand over her mouth to swallow down the hiccups. Somehow, even drunk as she clearly is now, she still manages to look cute. A black leather mini skirt flares out around her tanned thighs, teamed with a mauve loose knit jumper. On me, it would look as if I'd raided a costume box, but on Danica it's stylish and simple.

"What's the occasion?" I ask, referring to her inebriated state.

She shrugs. "No occasion. Just felt like a party."

"Well I think you're gonna have to take your party somewhere else, missy," Hope says, standing once more. "You're pissed. We can't serve you."

Dani stiffens and wobbles over to Hope's side. She holds out a wobbly finger as she enunciates, "Just. One."

Hope laughs and takes her finger, somehow managing to turn it around so Dani is left pointing at herself. "Just. None."

Dani huffs her way over to my side and wraps her arm around my waist. Hope and Lia discuss Lia's latest assignment as Dani whispers in my ear, "I love you, Ell Bell."

"I love you too, Dan Dan." *Look after your mother and your sister.* "You shouldn't be drinking like this, though."

"I'm a grown-up now. I do what I want."

Younger words were never spoken.

"You need to take it easy. You don't want—"

Dani jerks both hands out in front of her, as if telling me to stop. Her eyes widen, and her throat bobs.

She claps one hand to her mouth and bolts to the bathroom.

"She's not, is she?" Hope asks, but it's barely a question.

"I think she is." I turn back to the table and my two friends. "I should probably go look after her. You know. Hold her hair back and all that."

"She'll be fine," Lia says, but I shake my head.

"I have to make sure."

I say goodbye to my friends and head toward the ladies room. Only one of the three wooden cubicle doors is shut, and I rap on it gently. "Dan?"

"Go away." It's muffled, as if she's trying to hold back a sob. Or maybe some vomit.

And so I do what anyone else would do. I slide down the white tiled wall, sitting on the floor with my back propped up. I rest my hand just under the cubicle partition where my sister alternates between crying and heaving up the contents of her no doubt now near-empty stomach.

"I miss him so much."

Just like that, my heart breaks. Hearing her in pain kills me. It hurts worse than my own grief, which lurks around the base of my stomach, raising its ugly head from the mud every now and then.

"We all do, hon." I press my lips together. "He loved you so much, Dan Dan. Truly."

"I just …" *hiccup*, "… I guess it's just … I always thought he'd watch me graduate, you know? And help me decide what to do with my life. And now I've finished school and I've moved out and I … I don't know what to do anymore." This time, the hiccup turns into a sob, one that makes my chest constrict. "Does it get any easier?"

"Oh, sweetie." I shift my weight on my fingers. "Yes." I lie.

That's the thing about grief. You do what you have to in order to make the ache less.

After a while, a frail, cool hand grips onto mine. She squeezes tight, hanging on for all she's worth.

I breathe a sigh of relief.

As long as she's hanging on, I know she still cares. That she cares enough to fight the demons of grief that haunt her dreams.

As long as she's hanging on, I know she's okay.

FOUR

Being the daughter of June Mayfield comes with a series of perks and punishments.

Perk: I get to go to a lot of functions, and eat and drink things that are somehow tinier and yet more expensive than I could ever afford to pay for in real life. Plus, I get to work flexible hours. Between her and Colin, I do around four days a week, and I get paid quite well for it, too.

Punishment: Stuffing gift bags. Because truly, it has to be one of the most soul-destroying things I've ever done.

"I need one each of these flyers in the bags, plus one pen, one magnet and *one* cupcake." Mum places emphasis on the second-last word, as if concerned I might suddenly act upon my grand life plan of distributing cupcakes at random to the Sydney elite.

"Got it." I nod and pull out the chair behind the desk at the front of Constantina Gallery, where tonight's function is being held.

"Good." Mum glances at her watch and her lips pucker. "I have to get my hair done. Your sister is late." She says both with equal displeasure.

"I'm sure she'll be here in a sec. Just go." I nod toward the glass doors. Outside, the lights are beginning to dim. A grey shadow is cast over the city, and cabs and cars race past, headlights beaming yellow and white.

Mother follows my gaze, and then snaps her head back to me. "Okay. I'll be back here in two hours." She picks up her Coach handbag from the floor where it sits straight— all Mother's belongings sit straight, they never slouch— and turns to *click* her way to the door.

When she gets there, she pauses, red-painted nails on the handle. "Eleanor?"

"Hmm?"

"Do not screw this up."

I clench my jaw. As if putting pieces of paper in one hundred gift bags is just so hard to handle.

Mother opens the door and the noise of the city traffic roars in at me before the door shuts and I'm left in the concrete quiet of the gallery once more.

I take out my phone and dial Dani, but it goes straight to voicemail. Just as it has ever since I first called her half an hour ago, when we were due to start our shift. I frown and press my lips together. This isn't like her. She knows how upset Mum gets if something doesn't go according to plan.

I tap out a text, asking her where the hell she is, and begin the task of bag stuffing.

Soon, I fall into a rhythm. Flyer, flyer, flyer, flyer, pen, magnet, cupcake. Worry about Dani. Flyer, flyer, flyer, flyer, pen, magnet, cupcake. Check phone. Flyer, flyer, flyer, flyer, pen, magnet, cupcake. Worry some more.

I'm onto my tenth run when the anxiety gnawing at me becomes too much. I dial Zy, my worst enemy and her best friend.

He picks up on the third ring. "You've finally changed your mind and want to spend the night with me."

"No. Never. Ever." I roll my eyes. "Are you with Dani? She's not at work."

"Just a sec."

I hear the sliding of a door, then the line goes quiet for a few minutes. I glance over the flyer in front of me while I wait. An image of a half-naked man, muscles bulging, takes up most of the advertisement. Underneath, the words *Life drawing* are written in an elegant font, subtitled with the words *The new form of therapy*.

Why am I not surprised ...?

"She's asleep, Ellie."

"What?" I drop the flyer, and it butterfly dances to the floor.

"She's aslee—"

"Wake her up, Zy! She has to be here." Desperately, I glance at the mountain of papers I need to stuff. "I am going to be slammed trying to get this done myself."

"Okay, okay, no need to get your panties in a knot." Zy laughs softly. "Unless you need some help—"

"Oh my God, stop! Can you just get her to the Constantina, please? It's in Sydney, so you're going to have to motor."

"Okay." Zy breathes deep and long. "But you're gonna owe me."

"Bring her here ASAP." I hit *end call* before he can stipulate exactly what he expects me to do in order to return the favour.

And then?

Then I pack like the wind.

I shove papers into bags as if there were an award for it. As if this could be a national sport. There's no way Dani will get here in time to help me, but if I can get this job done, I can at least try and cover for her and save her the wrath of our mother. She needs that. Especially since she's just moved out of home, trying to prove to Mum she can make it by herself.

My thoughts flash back to the bar on the weekend. She's already so lost. She doesn't need an angry sister and mother to add to the mix.

That's why I keep packing as fast as I can, and when I'm done, miraculously five minutes before the doors open, I race out back to the storeroom and push off my jeans and tee, sliding a floral-print dress over my head. I spritz some perfume from Mum's handbag and shake my hands under my curls, hoping they look a little less frazzled bag packer and a little more event attendee.

I'm so used to wearing a mask. Ellie, the strong one. Ellie, the nurturer, who looks after her friends and family.

Now, I'm Ellie the event manager's daughter.

And Ellie the liar, as well.

"Remind me why I let you talk me into these things, again?"

I turn to smile at my flatmate and partner-in-crime. A black dress just covers the ink on Hope's upper thigh. Her painted black nails wink from her fingers as she signals the waitress currently circling the room to bring more champagne over this way.

"Because you're trying to snag one of the young, rich and wanky?" I ask, taking a glass of sparkling from the tray when the waitress pauses in front of us.

"Nah." Hope tilts her head to the side, then grabs a mini quiche from another tray that seems to float past us. "I think it's for the free hors d'oeuvres."

I giggle and take a sip of the bubbles, loving the way they seem to fizz right through my body and dissipate the strength in my knees. The taste is somehow buttery and acidic all at once, and I take another sip. Around us, the crowd swells, people almost shoulder to shoulder. Cameras flash as the press and studio photographer do their thing, and everyone seems to either have a glass of sparkling wine or some sort of bite-sized snack in hand.

There's something to be said for my mother's events. They may be boring as all hell, but at least the catering is good.

"No sign of her yet?" Hope asks, scanning the room for my sister.

I shake my head. "None. I just hope she's okay."

"Ha!" Hope snorts. "I hope she's got a damn good reason why she left you in the lurch."

"I'm sure she does …" My voice wavers as I trail off. She will have a good reason.

Right?

"Warning, three o'clock," Hope whispers, nodding to her right.

"That's my nine," I say, but look anyway. Standing there in amongst the crowds of well-dressed, overly perfumed patrons are two of the young art lovers. Dressed in suits, with hair coiffed almost ceiling high and holding glasses of champagne, they reek of money and style, with just a hint of pretentious.

They're typical of the younger crowd that attend these events. We're on the northern half of Sydney, a hub of business activity, and the sort of area where old money spawns new.

The two men, one blond with blue eyes, the other dark with gorgeous olive skin, smile, and the dark-haired man nods. It's as if they've just won the jackpot.

"Why did you make eye contact?" Hope barely moves her mouth as she talks. "It's like when you see a bear in the wild—you're not supposed to look it in the face."

"We're in Australia. We don't have bears!" I hiss, just as the blond walks forward, his steps a gentle swagger.

"Like what you see?"

I spit my champagne back in my glass. It's a miracle I don't choke on my laugh.

"The art here tonight sure is one of a kind." Hope is deliberately obtuse, and it's all I can do not to snort.

"My friend wasn't talking about the paintings." This time it's the dark-haired guy who speaks, stepping into our circle. "And I have to say, you two aren't so bad yourselves."

"Does that actually work for you as a pickup line?" I ask. A waitress inches past us, and I swap my empty glass for a full one. Using a deep tone, I mock, "Hey, I'm good looking. You're kind of okay."

The two men polite-laugh. "Fiery," Blondie says. "I like that in a woman."

"Of course you do," Hope mutters, but the two men are so busy chest puffing that they don't seem to notice.

"So what do you ladies think of the art?" the dark-haired guy asks. He points to a painting on the wall behind him, a canvas splattered in red with the words *art is life ... and death* underneath. "It's really ... complex, isn't it?"

"Yes, that's the word! Complex. With an undertone of sarcasm." Blondie nods and clicks his fingers, then turns to Hope and me. "Would you agree?"

"One hundred per cent with you on the sarcasm," Hope says, and I take a sip of wine, more to stop myself from laughing out loud than out of thirst.

"Eleanor!" Mother's shrill voice somehow rises above the crowd of *rhubarb* voices. "There you are." Mum curls her hand around my arm, a smile adorning her face. "Can I talk to you for a moment?"

"Sorry, boys." Hope nods a goodbye as Mum takes my arm and steps me away from the guys, Hope following hot on our heels.

"Hope, be a dear and run and get Ellie and I a refill, will you?" Mum asks, holding out her empty champagne glass.

Hope nods and takes the empties then disappears into the sea of people, no doubt in search of the wait staff.

Once we're a safe distance away, Mum stops and studies me, her eyes narrowed. The sweet scent of wine leaches from her breath, and I blink in the face of it. "One bag had two cupcakes," she hisses, a smile pasted on her face.

"I'm sorry," I say. "I thought I did it right." *I really did.* Then again, in my haste, it's entirely possible I got a little too liberal with my baked good generosity.

"Well for crying out loud, get it right next time."

Ow.

I straighten my shoulders and pretend it doesn't hurt me.

Mum doesn't notice. "Where's your sister? Is she still getting changed?"

I bite my lip and study the polished concrete floor. Designer shoes strut over it, milling in hubs, an ever-changing tide. "Probably." I silently add, *or possibly she's still in a car, or at home asleep.* At this point, it really could be any of the above.

"Hmph." Mum looks up and to the right, as if she's studying the intricacies of the situation. "Well, I guess it's good one of you take pride in—"

It's then that we hear it. The smashing of glass.

The hushing of voices.

All the heads in the room swivel toward the doorway where Danica stands, her hands in the air. A sheer black top and black silk skirt hang off her body, white pearls loosely draped around her neck. Dramatic curls float around her shoulders, and her deep red lips round in an *O*.

On the floor at her feet is a broken glass. A waiter stands nearby, his jaw dropped.

"I am so sorry." Dani smiles, her head tilted, and from nowhere a second white-shirted waiter appears with a broom and dustpan, tending to the mess. "I hope you'll all forgive me."

The hub of voices starts up again, and people flit to her side.

"You're not hurt, are you?"

"Those champagne flutes, so slippery."

"Really, the waiter should have been more careful handing one to you."

Hope walks up, two flutes in her hand, and elbows me in the side. We share a look.

"Poor dear. I'll go get her another glass." Mum's eyes glaze over and she takes both glasses Hope has offered and pushes past us without so much as a goodbye.

The sea of people once more part for her as she strides to reach Dani's side. When she gets there, they embrace and share the air kisses of the socially well-endowed instead of the mother and daughter they really are.

Tension tightens my shoulders. I should go and make sure Dani is okay. That she wasn't asleep late because she was sick, or anything like that.

Because that's what I promised to do.

Make sure my sister and mother are okay.

"Hey." Hope's hand cools my arm. "Let's get outta here."

I frown. "We can't." The exhibition doesn't finish for another two hours, and Mother has organised a car to take us all back to Emerald Cove. "You know she'll flip if she finds us missing."

"Do you really think she's going to notice?" Hope cocks her head toward Mum. She laughs at something Danica has said, her hand on her daughter's arm.

As much as I hate to admit it, Hope is probably right. The chance of Mum noticing our exit at all is blink-and-you'll-miss-it tiny.

"There you are!" It's a voice so obnoxious I know it's the blond-haired guy from earlier without even turning to look. "We've been looking everywhere for you."

Hope grabs my arm, her eyes wide. "We need to go," she whispers, then pauses and says, "Or we could see how far we can take this thing and try make a sculpture of his penis?"

I stifle a giggle. "Run!"

FIVE

Hope pulls me through the crowd, expertly navigating tiny gaps between people until we finally push the doors open and end up out on the street. The cold night air assaults us, but it doesn't stop us both from doubling over laughing, holding our glasses to the side to avoid spillage.

"Ladies, I can't let you leave here with those drinks." The security guard out front unfolds his arms and extends one hand, gesturing.

"Bottoms up!" Hope says, and I clink my glass with hers, and we both get rid of the remnants of our champagne before handing the empties back to the security guard.

"Can you believe it? Those guys were just ..." Hope says. She staggers down the street and I follow, eager to get out of there before anyone notices we're gone.

"Eleanor. Hope."

I freeze in my stiletto-made tracks. *Zy.*

"What?" I spin around, my arms folded across my chest.

Dark eyes flash out at me from under a mop of dark hair. There's danger in his gaze, even though he's wearing a suit. "Just be careful, okay?"

"Okay, Dad." Hope laughs, and skips down the street.

I pause, trapped in that gaze a moment longer. Goosebumps pimple my arms and I rub them, whether it's to protect myself from the cold night air or his penetrating stare I'm not sure.

The moment ends when he turns and heads back inside. I try to shake the weird feeling that's settled inside me off, and walk to catch up with Hope who has stopped a few steps ahead, rummaging through her purse.

She finally procures what she was looking for, and hands it over. "Here."

I look at the shiny foil object she's placed in my hand. "A condom?"

Hope shrugs. "The way you two were eye-fucking each other, it seems like a necessary precaution."

"Whatever!" I throw the plastic at her and she laughs, picking it up from the gutter and placing it back in her purse again as we stroll down the street.

"Where to now?" I ask. Because that's the thing about Hope. She always has a plan.

Hope pauses, and bites her lower lip for a moment. We're in the middle of a swanky part of town. Closed office buildings tower above us, and fancy restaurants with starters costing more than my shoes line the pavement. From out here, warm light and the gentle noise of glasses clinking and hushed nothings spill out onto the street.

"Aha!" She raises one finger in the air. "With me."

Eleven minutes, one dodgy cab ride and an 'are we lost/which way are we facing on the map' later, and Hope and I walk into a dark, deserted alleyway, with empty milk crates lining one side of the entrance.

"Are you sure ..." I trail off. Part of me doesn't want to doubt Hope, who is known for her expertise when it comes to Sydney's small and hidden bar scene.

Another part of me doesn't want to risk getting raped.

"Of course I'm sure." She grabs my hand and leads me to a door I didn't even notice against the black-as-shadow wall. A bouncer steps out from nowhere, checking our IDs before opening the door and gesturing to the stairwell beyond.

"Have a good night, ladies."

"Thank you." Hope and I answer in unison, then pony-wobble down the narrow metal stairs in our far-too-high heels.

As soon as the heavy black door slams behind us, one of the worst renditions of "Achey, Breaky Heart" I've ever heard reaches my ears. I still, my hand on the thin metal railing.

"Karaoke?" I narrow my eyes at Hope.

"What?" She shrugs. "They make a mean whiskey sour. And we don't have to sing."

"I'm gonna need a dozen," I mutter.

Once we reach the ground level, a lady in a cowboy hat with a check shirt and too-short shorts seats us at a table near the bar. I rest against the high-backed wooden chair and take a look around.

Wooden beams support the ceiling, with light bulbs hanging down by industrial wires. The gleaming wooden bar runs against one wall of the room, and behind it are more whiskeys and bourbons than I can count, shiny bottles of amber to brown that rise from the bar top to the ceiling. A ladder rests to one side, no doubt so the bartenders can get the top-shelf labels upon request.

Tables are littered throughout the floor space, packed with around twenty men in suits and women in dresses, laughing too loudly and talking with extra passion to ease the midweek pain.

Up on stage, an Asian man in a freshly-pressed sky-blue shirt thanks the audience and staggers off to his table, who all cheer uproariously at his performance.

"What do you wanna sing?" I ask Hope, wiggling my eyebrows.

"Very funny, smart arse," she says, flicking open her menu and then slamming it abruptly closed. "You know I don't do singing."

I place one hand over my heart. "And yet I consider it my public duty to share your gift with the world." Hope winces, and I laugh. "You know I'm kidding, babe. I wouldn't wish karaoke upon my worst enemy."

"Right?" Hope nods. "There is nothing lamer, nothing less attractive than a man who karaokes. Or a woman."

"Couldn't agree more," I exclaim, as the waitress places two small shots down in front of each of us.

"These are complimentary, from the bar," she says. "They're house whiskey, designed to help you get your night started."

I look at the small shot in front of me, then back at Hope. I don't usually drink much, but after the day I've had, I kind of feel I deserve it.

"Cheers." Hope holds her shot out, and I clink it with mine, then tip the contents down my throat. The drink burns, and then a warm buzz races through my veins, heating me up from the inside.

"Can I please get a whiskey sour?" Hope asks, as she places her empty shot glass on the waitress's tray.

"I'll just have a water." I add my empty to hers, and the waitress nods her thanks and heads back over to the bar.

The strains of Britney Spears' "Hit Me Baby One More Time" fill the bar, and the middle-aged woman on stage runs her hands down her sides. She teases at the neck of her shirt that's unbuttoned one hole too many. The mascara smudges under her eyes speak of the number of drinks she's had.

"I'm going to pee. Be right back." Hope slides off her stool and disappears toward the back of the bar, leaving me to watch Wannabe Britney oh baby-babying her way around the stage.

The waitress drops off our drinks, and I take a sip, glad to have something to do aside from enjoying this Britney rendition.

I'm so caught up in her performance, so captivated with her very obvious near-make-out session with the microphone, that I don't notice the waitress until she places one whiskey sour in front of Hope's chair, and a whiskey sour and a water down in front of me.

I frown. "I didn't order—"

"I know," the waitress interrupts, shaking her head. "It's from the gentleman at the bar."

With lips pursed, I turn my head. I scan the bar, the three bartenders working it. The couple sitting in the bar seats, all but canoodling. The girl lined up, waiting on service.

Joel.

Joel.

My eyes widen. I can't believe it's him.

Joel Henley.

Twice in one damn week.

Hi, he mouths.

Heat flushes my cheeks. *It's just the alcohol, Ellie.* I glance down at my drink, then back at Joel. *Or maybe not.*

Hi, I mouth back.

I look at him, really look at him, and I can't turn away. His icy blue eyes seem to burn into me, and I pull at the collar of my high-necked dress that's far too formal for a bar on a Wednesday, feeling very overdressed for the venue and the way his eyes strip me bare.

Joel pauses, and it seems he's just as lost in the moment as I am because the bartender waves a hand in front of his face, then says something in a voice I can't hear. My ex turns his attention back to the bartender, and my hand races for my handbag. Because holy shit! What does my hair look like? My lipstick? And is my foundation still in place, or is it looking more like a Monet painting?

I open the purse, but before I can even pull out a gloss, or a compact for that matter, I feel his presence near me. He has that much effect.

Joel Henley has always had that effect on me.

"Hi."

One word.

It's only one word, but it has me shaking.

"Hi." I slowly look up. He's there, right at the edge of my table, a small and mysterious smile twisting his lips. A white shirt stretches across his body and blue denim jeans hang low on his waist.

"Do you mind if I ...?" Joel gestures to Hope's recently emptied seat.

"Well, my friend is sitting there."

Joel looks around, as if searching. He lowers his voice conspiratorially. "Is she real?"

"Ha ha." I sardonically laugh. "She's just in the bathroom."

"Well, perhaps I could take it temporarily, then." Joel slides onto the seat, and places a glass of amber liquid on the table in front of him. "I have to admit ... I've never done this before."

I quirk a brow. "Come to a hideous karaoke bar?"

He grins. "No." He nods toward my drink. "The old 'can I buy her what she's already drinking' routine."

I let out a laugh. The words shouldn't make me feel alive, but I've had a few too many drinks, and he's really good looking, and completely against my better judgment, they do. "And how are you finding it so far?"

Darkness flashes in his eyes. "Really rewarding."

Gulp.

I swallow down more of my drink, and it doesn't taste stiff anymore. It just tastes like comfort. Confidence.

And damn, do I need some of that right now.

"What are you drinking?" I nod to his beverage.

"Scotch on the rocks." He takes a slow sip. "I know, it's an old man's drink. But at least it doesn't have a weird name. There's nothing sleazier than drinking a Sex on the Beach."

"How about a Wet Pussy?" I ask.

"Angel's Tit?" Joel asks, and I grimace. "Shit, I've gone too far. I'm so sorry, Ellie Mayfield, of the prestigious Mayfield family."

I poke my tongue out. "I'll maybe forgive you. Just this once. But don't make me sic my mother onto you."

Joel nods seriously. "I wouldn't dream of it." He takes another sip of his drink, and continues. "So what brings a fine young romance basket deliverer such as yourself to a shady karaoke place like ..." he gestures to the tables in front of us, and the lady gyrating her hips over the stage, "this?"

"I came for the live music," I say, nodding to the Britney wannabe. "What can I say? Talent is talent."

Joel nods. "Can't argue with you there. Although I gotta admit, you do look perhaps a little overdressed for the occasion."

I furrow my brow. "In a bad way or a good way?"

Joel sucks in a deep breath. Somehow, I feel as if I've stolen it. "In a good way, Miss Mayfield." He releases the air slowly. "Damn good."

Tension thickens the air between us. I lick my lips, and try to ignore the part of me that wants so badly to be in his arms again. Arms that I remember wrapped around me so many times before.

I take a sip of my drink, and it goes down so smooth. It's the kind of sip that should let you know you've had too much. It's my favourite sip, until it isn't.

"I was at an art gallery opening thing, for Mum." Joel cocks his head. "It's why I'm dressed like this."

"Oh," Joel says. "Did someone say the artwork was deep? Please tell me the artwork was deep."

"So deep." I grin. "And thought-provoking."

He nods, a veneer of seriousness washing over his face. "Could you see yourself in it? Naked?"

"Oh, yes," I agree, my eyes rolling up to the ceiling. "Is it even art if you can't see yourself naked?"

Joel raises his eyebrows. "And there you have it, ladies and gentlemen." He gestures to the invisible patrons paying attention to us. "The modern-day equivalent to 'If a tree falls in a forest ...'"

I giggle, and Joel laughs with me. His eyes change when he laughs. They're not so much icy as they are bracing. Like a cold drink of water. A flash of the ocean against the sun. Invigorating.

"Can I ask you a question?"

"Is it inappropriate?" I challenge, and it's Joel's turn to have red cheeks.

"No." He laughs. "Although I guess ... maybe it's borderline."

I give a slow smile. "Okaaaaay."

The new singer on stage reaches a particularly obnoxious high note. Someone knocks a glass somewhere, and it smashes against tiles. A voice yells 'taxi'.

"Is it weird if I haven't been able to stop thinking about you?"

All the noises stop. All of them.

Suddenly, it's just me and him.

To hell with the rest of the world.

A chunk of the hurt and pain I'd harboured for him dissipates like fairy floss on the tongue. It sparks and sizzles into oblivion.

I really like you, Joel Henley.

Hope's hand on my shoulder brings me back to life. "Aren't you the famous artist?" Her jaw drops, as if she really believes her facade.

"It's okay." I shake my head. "Hope, this is Joel. Joel, this is Hope."

Hope sticks out her hand for him to shake. "*Joel*?" she asks, the not-so-subtle subtext of *do you need me to hit him* clearly heard underneath.

"Yeah. I'm the idiot who left her three years ago," Joel says, and I can't help but smile.

"Well you got the idiot part right." Hope agrees, taking a sip of her drink.

"You don't need to tell me twice."

My cheeks burn, from too much to drink or too much embarrassment, I don't know which. I press my glass against one, desperate for the icy touch against the fire burning there.

Joel looks at me, and I feel myself falling. There's something about those eyes. Those lips. That—

"Give it up for Joellllll Henley!"

I freeze. A group of people near the front whoop and holler, clapping with their hands above their heads. A few other groups cheer too, and the man on stage, the karaoke host, looks at us, microphone outstretched like a baton in a relay race.

"You're ... doing karaoke," I say, laughter creeping into my voice. "Mr Shady Karaoke Place."

The notes of a bass guitar hum throughout the venue. The tune is instantly familiar. *Instantly.* "Summer Lovin'" isn't exactly a forgettable tune.

"No." Joel shakes his head. He pushes off the seat and to his feet, and the girl with his group of friends offers up a wolf whistle. "I am not doing karaoke."

"Well it sure looks like—"

He extends his hand, so it's right in front of me. "We're doing karaoke."

The bass line repeats itself. Britney claps, and the people in tables scattered around the bar join in.

I shake my head. "Oh no. Oh no, no, no, *no*."

Hope pushes me off my seat, and I stagger to my feet. "Oh yes," she says, just as the drums kick in.

"Summer lovin' ..." Joel sings the first line to the famous duet from the musical *Grease*, walking backward toward the stage while clicking his fingers in an overly dramatised 80s kind of way.

At first, I'm rooted to the spot. He has to be kidding me. I don't do performances in front of crowds. I don't karaoke. And I sure as hell don't cheesy couple duet karaoke, and not with a guy I—

"Get *up* there." Hope pushes at the small of my back and I stumble forward. Onstage, Joel's singing both male and female parts dramatically, causing laughter and sighs alternately throughout the venue, but his eyes are on me the whole time. And damn ... those eyes.

He keeps singing, and his voice is every bit as good as I remember. The verse finishes, and even though I know deep down that this is a bad idea, that this guy left me and our 'connection' is likely mostly in my head, this time when he holds out his hand, I take it.

He leads me up to the stage. My body turns to wood and I inch away from the centre as breath thickens in my throat. My stomach turns. I have to get out of here. I can't be here. *I can't do this.*

Joel doesn't appear to notice my mini-meltdown. He sings and dances, then shoves the microphone under my nose when it gets to the chorus.

I freeze. The light shines bright in my eyes. My heart leaps to my throat. *I can't.*

"I'm sorry." I shake my head and push at his chest, turning to leave.

A warm hand grips my wrist. The small crowd of less than twenty cheer.

When I turn, Joel's bright eyes shine, encouraging me to sing. He points the microphone toward me again as the girls in the chorus begin to sing.

"Tell me more, tell me more," I manage. The words stick like Clag in my throat, but the microphone amplifies them throughout the room. Hope wolf whistles, and my cheeks heat.

Seconds later, the microphone is back.

"Tell me more, tell me more." My voice is louder. Stronger. More confident.

Joel hams it up. He gestures for me to come closer, then spins me out with his hand. Alcohol floods my system, and the rush of being with him, the confidence it brings— it flicks a switch inside me.

This time when he walks away, his hands flipping behind his back, I follow along as if I'm one of the cheerleaders in the musical, unable to resist his charm, then

I lean forward to sing along with him in the microphone when it comes to telling more, more, more.

Hope hollers and cheers, the alcohol inside me buzzes, and I get caught up in the moment. I spin, and turn, and tease, and taunt, and Joel does exactly the same back to me. You couldn't wipe the grin off my face if you tried. Because it's totally daggy, and totally uncool, but without a doubt, it's fun. The kind of fun that seizes your chest and makes you giddy from smiling, unable to stop.

The music turns slow, and Joel steps into me, until one of my feet is trapped between his, the heat of his body almost palpable against my skin. He offers the microphone to my lips, and in those close quarters, his body sheltering my own, his lips close enough to lick, there's something sexual about the gesture. Something much more electric than just the music pumping through the speakers.

I open my mouth and breathe the words about it turning colder, and the summer ending. I make the mistake of looking into Joel's eyes.

There, I find something sad.

Something finite.

I slow as he sings his words, stepping closer still, until our bodies are a whisper from each other. My voice shakes as I sing the next line, and even though we're in the middle of a bar, all eyes on us, for the briefest of moments I hope he's going to kiss me, because those pink lips look so damn kissable right now.

The music changes, and we both gear up for the final word of the song. It's the moment that will see us kiss, or change this moment from sexually and somehow emotionally-charged to crowd-pleasing. To playing up to the audience. Somehow, I'm out of breath from the dancing, or maybe it's one too many drinks, or maybe it's the emotion of it all. My chest rises and falls at a speed not natural to me.

Joel winks at me, and it says so much. It says 'ham it up' and 'let it go' all at once.

"Nii ... iiiiiiights," we sing in nasal unison, and the choir on the backing track demands more behind us.

When the final note of the song finishes, Joel grabs my hand and raises it in the air, then jerks it down and we full-body bow to the standing ovation of a group of people I presume are his friends and Hope, who has at some point walked over to join their table.

"Give it up again for Joel and his friend," the MC announces, striding over and reclaiming his microphone from Joel's tightly clasped grip.

He takes the cordless piece of equipment away, but Joel and I still stand there, our chests heaving, our eyes locked. Joel grins, and it's so perfect that a piece of me wants to fall in it. "Bring back any memories?"

I beam in return. "One or two."

He raises his hand, and for a painstakingly long moment I think he's going to touch my lower back, my arm, my cheek.

But he drops his stray hand just as quickly, as if the errant thought caught him by surprise almost as much as it did me.

"Get a room!" Someone in the audience calls out, and it breaks any spell we could have been under. I giggle nervously, and Joel extends his arm, gesturing for me to walk ahead of him and off the stage.

We join his group of friends and Hope, all of whom aren't shy to congratulate us on our performance.

"That was amazing," a girl gushes. She grabs a beer from the table and shoves it into Joel's chest. "Here. Drink."

"Thanks, Fiona." He lifts the bottle and drinks.

I look to Hope. "Cheers, chicky." She hands me a whiskey sour and clinks my glass with her own. "Never thought I'd see you do karaoke just for some guy."

My chest flushes. I look around the room. *Is it hot in here?*

"Never thought I would either."

Silence settles over the table, and then the girl stands up and offers her hand to me. "Fiona," she says.

"Marc," a guy with short brown hair says. He has a kind of surfer vibe going on.

"Kohl," the final guy says, shaking my hand then running his own through his thick black hair. Hope almost drools.

"Ellie," I say.

Fiona's glass drops to the table where she's sitting. She snaps her neck to Joel. "*The* Ellie?"

One side of his lips rise in a smile. "The Ellie Mayfield," Joel finishes, and I pretend that my insides aren't twisting themselves in knots.

"So do you guys often come out to do karaoke?" I ask.

Fiona almost spits out the mouthful of red wine she was in the middle of swallowing. Her hands shoot to her mouth. Kohl sniggers.

"Not exactly." Marc shakes his head. "This was just another of Joely's challenges."

"Conquered in style, my friend." Fiona nods, then lifts her glass. "To Joel!"

"To Joel!" everyone echoes, Hope and I included.

"What do you mean challenges?" Hope asks.

"Ah ..." Fiona says. She pulls out a vacant seat next to her and gestures for me to sit, which I do, in between her and Hope. Joel takes a seat across the table from me next to Marc and Kohl, and I almost wish he were sitting somewhere else. Somewhere where it would be less obvious if I stared at him.

"I'm completing twenty-one challenges before I turn twenty-one," Joel explains.

I cock my head, curious. "What do you mean?"

"Well, a bunch of my family and friends set me a list of twenty-one things to do before I get to twenty-one. Sort of like ... a rite of passage into adulthood, if you will."

"Like a bucket list?" Hope frowns.

Marc nods. "Yeah," he says, "only a whole lot less ..."

"Deadly?" Hope supplies.

"I was gonna say expensive," Marc jokes, and we all laugh.

"So what kind of challenges have you had?" I ask.

"Well, this was one. Marc here set me the challenge of singing karaoke." Joel slaps Marc on the back. "Although at the time I didn't realise I'd have such an excellent singing partner to complete the task with."

"Does that mean he has to do it again?" Kohl muses.

Fiona shoots him a death glare. "I think, after the breakup with Vanessa, he can catch a break on this one."

The table falls silent, and so do I.

"So anyway," Fiona chatters on, "what about you two? Do you always come out on karaoke night?"

Hope shakes her head. "I didn't realise it was karaoke here tonight. I've only been once before, and it was late, and to be honest ..." she scrunches up her nose, "I remember it more for the whiskey."

"A lady after my own heart." Kohl holds up his glass in her direction.

"What can I say? I have good taste." Hope shrugs. "And after the function we were at earlier ..." She mock shudders, and I laugh.

"It wasn't all bad," I say, but my eyes rest on Joel, because I swear he's looking into me, looking through me right now. "We were at the opening of an art gallery. It was a work thing for my mum."

"So you attend your mum's event functions. Don't you find that boring?" Fiona asks, then flinches. "Ow! Joel that hurt!"

"Sorry," he says, but a smile twists his lips, and Fiona soon laughs along with him.

"Y'know, they're not exactly fun. But she's my mum, and it's ..." I pause, struggling to find the words to explain. How do you say *because after my father died, I picked up the pieces? I promised I'd always be there to pick up the pieces?*

I can't find the words to explain that to a group of virtual strangers. Instead, I settle for, "I guess sometimes it's just easier not to say no. I often help out her and my sister, even if it might not be what I want."

Silence falls across the table, and a particularly raucous group of guys to our left burst into laughter sprinkled with applause as one of them staggers over to the microphone.

"Sometimes you have to fight for what you want." Joel's voice is low, and his eyes dark. His words go straight to my heart.

"I ..." I open and close my mouth, unsure of what to say. The way he looks at me, it's as if we're the only two people in the room. As if no one else can hear the words coming out of his mouth.

"You can't save everybody, Ellie."

The moment ends when the cocktail waitress comes over to clear our glasses and ask if we want another round. We all shake our heads, no. It's getting near midnight, and if Hope and I want to catch a ride back to the EC with

Mum's driver, we're going to have to head back to the gallery soon.

"Well, it was very nice meeting you all." Hope shrugs on her jacket, and I do the same. Kohl, Marc, Fiona and Joel all nod and smile, and as a group we pay our tabs and walk outside where we attempt to flag down two cabs.

A yellow car with the vacant light on top pulls to the kerb, and Fiona pushes Hope toward it. "You guys go first. We'll grab the next one."

We all hug like long-lost, newly-found friends. I save Joel for last. He grips me with ferocity, and the heat coming from his body makes me feel safe. At home. I pause there in his arms, waiting for more. For proof that this connection I've been almost sure I'm feeling isn't one-sided.

Ask for my number. Please ask for my number.

"Safe travels, Miss Mayfield." His breath is warm against my ear.

I pull back slowly, and look into his eyes. His breath causes tiny clouds of mist to fog away from his mouth and over mine.

"C'mon, Ellie," Hope calls from the car. "We do not want to have to catch the train again."

I nod, and slowly pull back out of Joel's embrace. "It was really nice seeing you."

Joel gives a small nod, and I walk backward to the car. He smiles, but doesn't move to stop me. I try to push down the hurt. Is this really it? Is this the last time I'll see him?

With each step toward the car, I imagine a new rationale for the heavy sense of dejection I'm feeling. Maybe I imagined the chemistry. Maybe he told his friends about me, but it hadn't been nice. Maybe he's being sensible and giving himself time to heal after the whole Vanessa fiasco. Maybe.

My knees hit the metal of the car door and I give him one last look, then sit down and swing my legs in in front of me. I pull on the door and it slams shut. Through the glass, I take one glance back at the four of them, Fiona waving her hands dramatically as a taxi speeds past, Kohl and Marc deep in conversation about something or other. Joel still staring at me.

"You're looking at him like a lovesick puppy," Hope says to me, then to the taxi driver, "The Constantina Gallery, please."

"Right. On Main—"

He never gets to finish that sentence because the door to the taxi swings open. Joel leans into me. His chest rises and falls in quick succession, as if he had to run a mile to get here, and I wonder if mentally perhaps he did.

"What are you doing next Thursday morning?" he breathes. I can't stop the smile that flushes my face.

"Is he coming too?" the driver grunts.

"No," Joel says, then looks at me again. Mischief lights up his eyes.

"Nothing."

"Meet me at The View café at six," he says.

I cock my head. "In the *morning*?"

He nods, and the smile that accompanies his words is truly heart-melting. "It'll be worth it. I promise."

"The meter's running, you two," the driver says, tapping the glass screen that has numbers rolling across it.

My mind whirls. I'm going to see him again. And maybe this isn't the smart decision, or the safe one, especially given our past, but I want this more than anything. I want this with everything that I have.

"Okay."

As soon as the word leaves my mouth, Joel's smile gets even bigger. "You know, I think this could be the start of an epic story."

I laugh. "Get out of the cab, Joel. I'll see you Thursday."

He steps back and shuts the taxi door, clapping the roof of the vehicle in send-off. I don't stop smiling, tilting my head back to look at him as we pull away from the kerb and off through the deserted Sydney night streets.

"Something you want to tell me?" Hope asks, and I grin. Because this might be the most exciting thing I've done in years.

SIX

The time before dawn is one I like the most. It's when the old white beach house is bathed in sunlight, the early-morning rays filtered through the pine tree branches in zebra stripes. It's when the world is still before the rush of commuters from Emerald Cove to Sydney kicks in. It's when the sounds of waves crashing, birds calling, are the only signs of life.

They're not as ugly as the rest of the world.

And ugly makes me think of Joel. Because that word is everything he's *not*. My mind swims with thoughts of him, his voice, his laugh, his smile. It's been three days since the karaoke bar, and I can't get him out of my mind, even though I know I should still be mad at him for what he did.

"Summer lovin' ..." I softly sing, a smile creeping up my cheeks.

I prop one foot up on a seat at the dining room table, knotting my laces through then, prop my foot down and *bang*. The front door slams open.

"Hellooooo!"

I don't have to turn around. I just know.

"Sissy!" The unsteady thud of feet not dissimilar to a newborn pony's thud across the floor, then two warm arms wrap around my waist.

I straighten, and try not to breathe in too deeply. With the amount of fumes wafting off her, I could get drunk.

I turn around and she relaxes her grip. Mascara tracks down her cheeks like tiny ants, and her blonde hair is wild. Somehow, on her, the look is sex-tousled, not homeless, as I'm sure it would appear if I wore it.

I haven't seen her since Mum's function on Wednesday, and yet it seems as if she's been drinking ever since.

"We need to talk about last week," I say, my voice terse.

"What 'bout it?" Dani asks, then claps her hand over her mouth. "Oh … the bags …"

"What were you thinking?" I ask, shaking my head. "I had to stuff all those bags by myself, and lie to Mum about it."

Dani shrugs one shoulder then sidles up to me, wrapping her arm around my body. "I'm sorry, Ell Bell."

"I know you need the money. It's not like you're working anywhere else …" I trail off. "Anyway, don't do it again, okay?"

She shakes her head so fast and so far it might fall off. "Never. Never ever."

"And lay off the alcohol! You were drunk last week at the bar, and clearly now."

"I'm just having a little fun, Ellie. Weren't you ever young?"

It's only then I notice Zy in the doorway. He leans against the frame, his arms folded across his chest. Those dark eyes study us, and I frown. He should know better.

He's her best friend. He's supposed to keep her safe.

"Where you goin'?" Dani slurs.

"Just for a run."

"Ha!" Dani snorts, as if the very idea of exercise is ridiculous. "What for?"

"To stay fit." I take her hands and place them by her sides.

"Well, I think running is shit. Don't you, Zy?" Dani spins, and grips the chair to steady herself as momentum sees her falling too fast.

And that right there, that very moment is Dani in a nutshell. Momentum that's fallen too far. Too hard. Too fast.

"You're being stupid, Ellie. Just come hang out with us. We can have wine ... breakfast drinks!" She throws one hand in the air, her voice rising with glee.

"I'll give it a miss." I walk toward the door, and even though I try to block out those sounds, they haunt me as I go.

"You're so fucking boring, Ellie."

There.

Those words.

I baulk, then straighten my back. I can't show weakness in front of her.

They say sticks and stones can break your bones, but names will never hurt you. Whoever came up with that was wrong.

Words are powerful weapons. Words are capable of rendering me black and blue with the force of their vicious attack. They're brittle and barbed, and they never miss. It's a direct assault to the heart.

"Take care of her," I mutter to Zy as I walk past. His eyes follow me out the front door, but I don't stop and ask him for more information. I don't ask him where they've been, or what she's been doing all night.

I gave up asking a long time ago. I gave up asking when I learnt I wouldn't like the answer.

Because words may hurt me, but my sister hurts me even more.

Colin and I spend the one-hour car trip up to the Hunter in silence. My mind is a million miles from here. It's on a little girl who used to be so precious. Who'd pick flowers in the park for Mum and me, surprising us with sweet-smelling gifts on our pillows. The little girl who spent every day by our father's side from the second he was admitted to hospital, leaving him only to make more picnic lunches for the family to share.

Since he died, she's been on some kind of drinking spree. It's as if she's too afraid to slow down.

And I'm worried she might crash.

I take my phone out from my purse and tap out a text to Zy, quick and to the point.

Ellie: Please make sure she doesn't vomit in her sleep. I'll be back from work to check on her by midday.

"Penny for them," Colin says, bringing me back to the present.

I shake my head. "Not even worth that."

"Your thoughts are worth far more than a penny." Colin smiles as he pulls his Audi into the lot at the cheese factory. "That's why it's so important to me that you come and taste the cheese."

I smile. "After two years of working for you I've finally been upgraded, huh?"

"Yes." Colin's nod is curt. "Just don't tell Sharon."

"Ha!" I laugh, thinking of Colin's wife. I've met her a few times, when I've gone around to their place to pick up and drop off baskets. She's a sweet older woman with a penchant for cats and green lacy aprons, the kind of lady I'd want for a grandmother.

We exit the car and head to the cheese factory where Bruno, the Italian cheese-maker, greets us both with kisses on either cheek. Somehow, it's inherently less wanky than the cheek-kissing that went on at the art gallery the other night.

He ushers us into the cool room, rubbing his hands with glee. A smile creeps over my lips. It's hard to stay caught up in my family drama when a man as sweet as this is so obviously thrilled about, erm, cheese.

We reach the deep fridge, but just as Bruno puts his hand inside to bring out a sample, Colin interrupts. "Actually, Bruno, would it be okay if we do the sample in the garden?"

Bruno pauses, a slight frown marring his brow, then plasters that ear-to-ear smile back on his face. "Of course!"

Minutes later, I sit outside the cheese factory at a wrought-iron table-and-chairs set. The morning sun beams golden through the trees, and I shrug off my woollen jumper, enjoying the rays on my skin. I close my eyes, letting the perfection of this moment settle over me. *If only this were life. Cheese tasting and sunshine ...*

"I thought we'd make a morning of it."

I blink open my eyes. Colin stands in front of the table, a bottle of Bollinger and two champagne glasses in his hands.

"What?" I ask, scrunching up my nose.

"It's leftover stock. You know Sharon doesn't drink, and we are here for a cheese tasting … I figure, why not?" Colin sits down and places all the glassware carefully on the table. "Besides … I've noticed you've been a little stressed lately." He reaches across and places a clammy hand on my arm. "You could relax a little."

I smile, warmth settling in my chest. "Thanks."

Soon, Bruno delivers a plate of different cheeses, and Colin and I drink and snack the morning away. It's one of the most pleasant shifts at work I've had, and I smile. I can't wait to brag to Hope about my day. Compared to the usual long hours and minimal pay, this is a pleasant change.

Colin refills my glass more than his, which I guess makes sense. He does have to drive, after all. Thirty minutes, one bottle of champagne and countless slices of cheese later, my legs feel deliciously giddy, and my heart sings in my chest.

"So are you finally going to tell me what had you so uptight?" Colin asks. He stands and walks behind me, then places his hands on my shoulders.

I stiffen, my body rigid in the chair. This is unlike Colin.

"Relax, Ellie," he whispers in my ear, then starts kneading the muscles along my back. "You don't have to tell me anything you don't want to."

His rough hands scrape against my skin, the pressure intense as he massages. It's far from the relaxing activity it's supposed to be. I squirm a little in my seat, and Colin laughs.

"That kind of hurts," I say, but my voice sounds floaty and weak. Maybe I have had too much to drink. I guess I didn't eat breakfast, and I have had … I narrow my eyes at the bottles—no, bottle of champagne on the table.

"You can take it, Ellie." Thumbs press against my lower back, and I arch in protest. "I know you can."

His hands move lower. They're right above my butt, pressing and digging. His breath is hot against my neck, and I no longer care if this is Colin, a man I've worked for two years and known since I was fifteen, when he and Mum started hanging out. There is something creepy about all this touching, and I've had enough. I jump up from my seat, and leap away. Only my limbs are slow-moving and everything is hard, so I end up tumbling forward and landing on my hands and knees on the grass.

Colin laughs, a loud, braying sound. I scowl, examining the palms of my hands for any scrapes.

"Oh, Ellie." He sighs and walks over, extending his hand to help me up. I look up at him. His face shows nothing but mirth. He's the glasses-wearing, brown-slacks owning Colin, who is married, and about twenty years my senior. He colour codes his socks; he's not the sleazy type.

"That hurt." I grumble, but extend my hand and let him pull me up.

Colin cocks his head to the side, frowning. "You should have told me to stop."

"I didn't want to offend you …" I trail off and shrug.

"Well, you never could. You know I have grand plans for you, Ellie." Colin muses.

I manage a smile. This is the Colin I know. The one who plans on taking over the world, one business at a time. "Oh yeah? Life after picnic baskets?"

Darkness flashes across his face, and he stills. "You're a very talented young woman. I know you're going to make it big some day."

"Well thanks." I stretch my arms above my head, my shirt rising up a little as I do. "But for now, I'm a very sleepy young woman who'd better get home and start on the invite list for Mum's next event." *And check on my sister.* My buoyant heart sinks with a heavy thud.

"Okay." Colin stands up too, and I turn to walk toward the car only ... *tree branch. Ankle.*

Ow.

I topple forward for the second time today, my arms flailing, and then Colin is there, catching me. His arms loop under mine, his chest holding mine up.

"Sorry." I laugh and move to stand back, but he tightens his grip.

His breath is heavy in my ear. Is he ... is he hitting on me?

Then he lets go, and I pull away and inhale again. Air rushes down my throat then pours out with relief as I give another small giggle. I'm an idiot. Colin wouldn't creep on me. He has a wife. And he's friends with my mum.

My phone beeps, snapping me out of my thoughts. I fish for it in my pocket, reading the message as I stumble back to the car.

Zy: Have your sister safe in bed. She's promised to lay off the drink. For now ...

I ignore the ominous two last words of the message. Because this is the best news I've had in days.

SEVEN

Five days later, I knock on Hope's bedroom door, very softly.

Then I do it louder. Because damn it, I'm already close to running late, and softer just isn't working.

"Unless you're bringing Henry Cavill to me on a platter—and I mean on a platter—feck off," Hope groans.

I open the door with what I hope is a charming smile. "Oh good, you're awake then."

The light from the hall filters into her bedroom. Hope curls up under the blankets, her hair a dark bird's nest poking out the top of the bed. She squints one eye open and somehow manages to still perform a rather scary glare.

"Go away," she grunts.

"Can you please first tell me if this outfit is random six a.m. date appropriate?" I ask. I'd wanted to ask her last night, but by the time she'd gotten home from work at the bar, I'd been well and truly asleep.

Hope shoves her wrists down into the mattress and pushes herself up, opening the other eye. "You're lucky he's hot," she mutters, scratching her head. "Spin."

I do a full circle, and Hope nods, taking in my blue denim jeans and thick weave cream knit jumper. "Shoes?"

"Ankle boots," I reply.

"Hair?"

I frown. That's the thing about having curls. I've just spent half an hour trying to make it look casual but not so casual it's messy. "Done?" I ask hopefully.

Hope mimes drawing a tick in the air. "You have my approval. Knock 'im dead, kiddo."

"Thanks, lovely. Have a good sleep!" I faux-whisper as Hope flops back down to her mattress, and I pull the door to.

I pull on my boots and sneak out of the house, gently shutting the front door behind me.

Outside, the air bites into my skin. The cold runs bone deep, and I jog to my car, eager to get inside it and be warm again. Excitement ripples through me. It's as if nothing can bring me down today.

I turn my key in the ignition, and the car shudders, then silences.

Well, maybe a broken car could do it.

I frown and then turn it again, and it does the same thing. It's a raw, hacking kind of sound, as if the old Mazda has a cough or something. It's just not clicking over.

On my third attempt, I glance at the clock. It's quarter to six, meaning I really have to get the car moving if I want to make my six a.m. date. I don't even have time to call a taxi—in sleepy old Emerald Cove, I'm not even sure if a driver would be on at this time of the morning.

My car shudders again, and my pulse starts to throb. It's silly, and it's only a date, and I'm not even late yet, but I hate letting people down, and rekindling this thing with Joel is important to me.

So I do the only thing that seems feasible at the time.

I run.

My handbag bounces against my side as I bolt down our street, and then along the footpath of the main road. The streetlights' white beams turn everything into a shade of grey. I pump my arms and work my legs faster, faster. My jeans fight my every movement, and I curse whoever invented skinny jeans and why they're not just a little more flexible. The cold morning air rushes down my throat and aches against my lungs. My feet thud against the pavement, the only sound in this otherwise still morning.

Thankfully, I'm used to running, and soon I fall into an easy rhythm. I take stride after stride, and try not to check my watch too often. My heart thuds against my ribs, but I ignore it and push, push on to try and reach my destination.

By six past six, I'm barrelling down the hill toward the coastal café. Here there's a little more life, activity, and I can already smell the rich scent of coffee on the cool morning air. A lone figure stands outside the café, dressed in a big jacket, and I make him my target. It's the right height for Joel—it has to be him. Hopefully he's not too pissed I'm late.

I run down the steep incline toward the outdoor seating area and try to slow my feet, but the momentum I've gained is too much. I can't stop. I keep going.

Straight into the solitary figure.

Bodies collide, and an arm wraps around my waist, stopping me from hitting the pavement.

"Sorry," I say, my voice breathless from the run. "I'm late, and I ran into you, and—"

"Hey." His voice is soft and gentle. It's like a warm embrace. I turn to look into his eyes, and those ice-blue orbs somehow penetrate the black and white around us. "It's okay."

My breathing slows, and my shoulders relax. Because right now, it really does feel as if everything will be okay.

"You ran here?" Joel asks. He turns toward the counter where a rugged up older woman works the coffee machine.

"Car wouldn't start." I shrug, and follow him up.

"Flat white, please," Joel says, then nods to me, indicating I should order.

"Same, thanks."

The woman rings up our order. "Seven dollars, thank you."

I open my bag, but before I can even find my wallet Joel has already paid the lady, and she gets to work making coffee.

"Thank you so much," I say, and Joel shakes his head.

"It's just a coffee. And I made you get out here at six. It's the least I can do."

"Six past six, technically," I mutter, my eyes on my feet. "Sorry for being late."

"Hey." Cool fingers touch my chin, and tilt it up so I'm looking into those eyes again. "It's okay."

We wait for the woman to make our coffees and then walk out of the café.

Joel leads me toward the parking lot, then opens the passenger door of a gunmetal grey BMW. "Hop in."

"Thanks." I slide into the cream leather seat, and that smell that is new car and leather mixes with the coffee. I wriggle against the firm chair and all but nestle into it. These are four of my favourite scents in the world. Coffee and new car and leather and *Joel*.

Joel walks around the front of the car and sits behind the wheel, the engine purring smoothly to life. He places his coffee in the cup holder, then pulls out of the lot and onto the road. Orange lights the horizon, a burnt colour that hovers just above the ocean. It's going to be a brilliant sunrise soon.

"When did you get the car?" I run one hand over the side of the soft leather seat.

"Eighteenth present from Mum." Joel gives me a cheeky grin. "Yet another side-effect of the divorce."

Joel's parents split up when we turned thirteen, after Joel's mother cheated on his dad, then proceeded to spend the next three years buying his love, his mother a far more active participant in the activity when it came to cash versus time. "They're still playing that game, huh?"

"Yeah." He shrugs. "No matter how much I tell them it's not necessary …"

"So, where are we off to?" I ask, my gaze firmly out the window as the car drives over the bridge that traverses the point where the lake and the sea meet.

"I'll tell you when we get there," Joel replies mysteriously.

"Okay …" I trail off. "This does feel a little like a recipe for disaster, though."

"What do you mean?"

"Well, I've just hopped in a car with a guy I haven't seen in three years, and am heading who knows where. You could write a book about how badly this could end." I sip my warm, delicious coffee.

Joel considers this for a moment. "True," he says. "Although to be honest, you're not the type."

"The type?"

"The type of girl I'd have on my kill and kidnap list. For one thing, there's a paper trail that connects us. My name, email address and credit card are all on that basket booking," Joel says.

"True," I muse, trying not to enjoy the idea of there being something, anything at all that 'connects' Joel with me. "Plus, I'm a screamer. Not great kidnap material."

Joel laughs, and a sly smile twists his lips. "You're a screamer now, huh?"

Mortification washes over me. Heat flames my cheeks, and I press my forehead against the cool of the window. "Dear God, kill me now ..."

"Hey, it's good to know." He winks, and takes the exit onto the freeway to send us out of Emerald Cove.

We drive for another fifty minutes in companionable silence, headed toward the hot-air balloon field where Colin's office space is. My mind races, wondering what Joel has planned for us today. Is it a do-over of his date the other day? I screw up my nose at the thought. Being suspended in a basket over the earth sounds bad enough, let alone doing it while repeating an event Joel did with his ex just a week and a half ago. Ew.

Then we turn off the freeway and down a straight road. In the distance, metal curves slice the sky. I frown, trying to remember what they are for. We're about an hour away from home, in an area I don't go to very often. I haven't been down this road in years. Not since high school when we had a school excursion to—

The racetrack.

"So do you know where we're going now?" Joel asks, a grin on his face.

"Sure do."

"And do you hate cars and think this is the worst idea ever?"

This time he gets a laugh out of me, and I shake my head. "Well, it might not be my idea of a good time, but that doesn't mean I can't cheer you on from the sidelines."

The car jerks left. My neck jolts with the movement, my heart lurching to my throat. Wheels skid against dirt as we slide to a stop.

"Let me get one thing straight." Blue eyes penetrate mine. "You are doing this."

"No, I'm not."

"Why?" he asks, and this time there's seriousness in his voice.

"I ..." I suck in a breath. "It's just ... dangerous, you know? It's not safe."

"Life isn't about playing safe, Ellie," Joel says, and the heat in his eyes lights a fire in my belly. "It's about pushing to the limits—living on the edge."

"You mean risking your life for five minutes of thrills?"

"No." Joel trails his knuckles down my cheek, leaving flames in his wake. "It's about pushing yourself for something more."

Sometimes you see a truth in words that runs deeper than just surface level. And just when you think you've got everything worked out, your life planned and protected against everything bad, one person comes along and shatters it all in one sentence. One breath. One word.

Joel hasn't shattered me, but he's fractured a part of my shell.

And for one brief moment, I don't want to be safe.

"So, which one of you is driving first?" Marty Manson, the race-car instructor, asks, his gaze flicking between Joel and I.

"He is," I say, at the same time as Joel says "her."

We share a grin, and something dances in my stomach again. Something that reminds me of why I probably shouldn't be doing this.

He's recently heartbroken, Ellie, I tell myself, but the words don't hold the weight they did when I'd first thought them a week and a half ago at the hot-air balloon field. Now they're easily buried under a sea of *but maybe they hadn't been together very long* and *you do have incredible chemistry* and *how about all that history?*

"I'll do it." Joel steps forward, and Marty slaps the keys in his outstretched palm.

"All right, my man," he says, and gives him some last-minute instructions, which Joel nods to and takes in with wide eyes.

He does, thank God.

Because all I take in is him.

"Let's do this thing." Joel's eyes light up as Marty hands the two of us helmets. I buckle mine under my chin, thinking positive anti-helmet hair thoughts.

Marty opens Joel's door, gesturing for him to sit. Instead of sliding in, though, Joel jogs around to the passenger side and holds the door open for me. This time, the blush that creeps up my cheeks has me seriously worried about my health. It isn't natural to blush this often in such a short period of time. Seriously, this guy has me in a hot flush with just one look. At this rate, I'll be going through menopause before we finish the hot lap.

Huh.

Hot lap.

The term suddenly has a whole new meaning.

"Hop in," Joel says, and I point one leg into the car, then fold my body in. His eyes are on me the entire time.

He walks around to the other side and sits, slamming the door behind him. Marty gives him the thumbs up, and

Joel nods. The engine roars to life and Joel stabs at the accelerator with his foot.

I press my spine back against the leather seat behind me. This is perfectly safe. We've done a crash course prior to hopping in the vehicle. We're on a track specifically designed for high-speed driving, with no other cars in sight.

So why do I feel so damn nervous?

"If you want to get out, I won't hold it against you." Joel raises his voice to be heard over the throbbing engine.

Every cell in my body wants to take this opportunity to back out. To not take this chance. But despite what I want so badly to do, I hear his words in my ear. *Life isn't about playing safe.* And so I reach across and buckle my seat belt. I do it because I like this guy. I do it because the odds are in our favour, and really, this is kind of low-risk on the list of risky activities.

But mostly, I do it because I've spent the last year looking after my family and taking the easy way out.

And maybe it's time I started taking chances.

"Fuck yeah!" Joel yells, thrusting his fist in the air. I laugh alongside him, his buzz contagious.

And then?

I scream.

Because we fly.

My breath whiplashes up my throat. My body presses further against the seat, and my heart does this strange painful hiccough, where it stops working and then starts again at double time.

We speed, so fast, so fast that I can't focus on any one thing out the window. Instead, it turns into a sea of colour that all blends in one giant rainbow of light, flat-lining in shaded bars around me.

"Holy shit!" Joel yells, and when I turn to look at him slowly my head slams to the right. He grins, his cheeks stretched wide, the momentum from the vehicle's speed propelling his head back, too.

There's something so freeing about this moment— something so dangerously safe, yet all-consuming. Going fast takes the breath from my chest.

It's a feeling I've run from, but damn—it's so addictively good.

We come to a stop four laps later, and as the car softens its roar to a throaty hum, my breath finally slows, my chest rising and falling at a speed of normalcy. Joel reefs the helmet from his head and turns to me, his face alive with excitement. "Holy shit, El."

I laugh, and it's so freeing. So liberating. I undo my own helmet and rest it in my lap. "That was ... wow."

"Right?" He laughs again, and then reaches across the console to take my hand with his warm one.

"I liked it way more than I thought I would," I admit, and this time his fingers squeeze mine.

"What were you so afraid of, Ellie?" Joel asks.

You, I want to say. *I'm afraid of you breaking my heart again.*

"Come on, Ellie. Tell me."

I pause, my eyes on the road we're hurtling down with no brakes. "Life. Death." Then, after a moment ... "Falling."

He reaches over and tucks a strand of hair behind my ear.

My heart stops.

My breath stills.

"I'll promise to be here to hold you, Ellie." His words send a shiver down my spine. "I'll catch you when you fall."

EIGHT

I float to the car. No—I frolic. It's the only way to describe these silly almost dancing steps. Joy floods me, and I'm so damn happy—so damn happy—that I can't contain it. It's simply too much.

"I can't feel my knees!" I yell. I yell because Joel walks at the relatively normal pace of one step per second, back near the building entrance. I've made it to the car already.

"You know that's not a good thing, right?" he asks, but there's a huge smile on his face, and I can't help but think he has to be somewhere near as giddy as I am.

He eventually catches up and I skip over to him, throwing my arms around his neck. "We raced, Joel. We actually raced!"

He laughs, and it's all just so easy, so natural, and I'm so full of happiness and excitement and love that I lean in closer and kiss him on the cheek.

Joel stills and pulls back. Regret crashes down on me, drowning all the intense happiness that throbbed through my cells only moments earlier. "I'm sorry."

A million questions race through my mind, but the one shouting loudest is *how did I read this so wrong?* Followed closely by *what the fuck am I thinking?* This is Joel Henley. The boy who broke my heart. I'm an idiot to trust him again.

"No." He shakes his head and steps back. My arms drop to my sides. "It's not ..." He seems to search for an answer in the sky, and I wish I could see it written there too, because right now, I'm more than a little confused.

Joel takes a deep breath and places his hands on my upper arms. We're close, too close for people who are just friends, but he's the one who's made the move this time. "Ellie, you are so much more than a rebound girl." He gives a subtle shake of his head. "I can't do that to you. Not when I can already see myself falling."

"So you like me, but you don't want to use me?" I ask. "How does that make sense?"

"There are a lot of things about my life that are complicated right now." Joel lets one of his hands drop to his side, and his gaze follows it. "I just need time."

My brain ticks over this new information, processes it and stores it away. Time. He needs time. Time to heal from his past wound. Time to prove that his feelings for me aren't just false rebounding emotions. Time to sort this whole thing out.

"What happened with you and Vanessa?"

The question hangs in the silence between us.

Joel leans back against his car. His furtive glance tells me I'm not going to like the answer. "We're gonna do the whole ex thing, huh?"

I nod, my face a blank slate.

"We dated on and off for just on a year. It was never serious. I met her at uni, but none of my friends liked her much. Said she was too ... prim and proper or something."

Joel runs a hand over his head. "She broke it off with me because we're heading in different directions."

I frown. "What do you mean?"

"She wants to study overseas. I don't."

"So she's leaving you for another location?"

"I know. The irony isn't lost on me." Joel pauses and away before looking back to me. "She wasn't the one, Ellie. I never felt for her like I did for you. I just …. I need time. Is that asking too much? If we just ... hang out until ...?" Joel trails off, and he looks so hopeful.

"Of course." I smile, and close the gap between us so our bodies are near again. "As long as you let me come and join in some more of your twenty-one challenges. Because that was freaking awesome."

A grin breaks Joel's face. "I can sure do that."

The drive back to EC is relaxed, and my high from a few hours earlier has well and truly dissipated, leaving me exhausted. It's as if the adrenalin has robbed my body of its ability to function.

"What have you got planned for this afternoon?" Joel asks as we pull onto the main street of town near the beach.

"I'm just going to go help Mum pack bags for a client," I say.

"Fair enough." He nods. "You never told me why you didn't ever follow your dream. I remember when you used to hate your mother's events."

His words sting me as they did the other day. They were dreams who belonged to someone else. Someone who didn't have to look after her mother and sister. "Yeah." I shrug. "I guess … I guess life just got busy. I help Mum out at work a bit; she says it's to teach Dani and I the value of hard work, but it's not easy. Some days I feel as if I'm drowning, and all I can do is come up and hope the air will be fresh."

"You can swim, Ellie." Joel pulls the car over into my street when I point it out, and then stops outside our house. "I know you can swim."

My heart flutters, and for a moment I forget my sister, and my mother, and everything but Joel. For the first time in a long time, I want to take risks.

It's all because of him.

"Can I borrow your phone?" he asks, and I frown, but hand it over.

"Is this the official 'you're asking for my number' bit?"

His thumb moves rapidly over the face of my phone. He looks up at me, and there's something more in his eyes. A promise for the future. "No," he husks. "It's also the official 'I don't want you to leave' bit."

We sit there in silence for a moment. Me, grinning at him, even though his signals are so completely mixed, they hurt my head. Him, looking at me, his expression somewhere between hesitation and lust.

"Well, I gotta get going." Joel opens his arms and leans over to hug me.

Pine. It's the scent that hits me first. He smells like pine, even though we've spent the morning together, not in a pine forest, and there's no real reason he should. *He always used to smell like pine.*

I wrap my arms around his body and revel in how he feels up close. These arms have held me so many times— during the first school dance, as we walked home from school. My idiotic heart beats traitorously fast, despite the warnings from my head.

After what's definitely longer than appropriate hug time, I pull back.

"No." Joel's voice is strangled, and he doesn't release his grip. "Do we have to stop doing this?"

I giggle. "Hey, you were the one who said no dating ..."

"That was before you felt like this," Joel says. "Now that I've breathed you in again, I don't know that I ever want to stop."

NINE

Family dinners are a unique kind of torture my mother particularly seems to enjoy. Thankfully, she only seems to have time to get out her scalpel and handcuffs once a month. Otherwise, who knows how often Dani and I would have to endure it.

At five minutes to six, I rap on my sister's door, my knuckles smarting against the metal security screen. Seconds later, it swings open, and Zy stretches an arm behind him, welcoming me in.

"Hey Zy," I greet my sister's flatmate. "Where's Dan?"

He frowns, and folds his arms across his chest. "She's at family dinner … with you."

"No." I shake my head. "She's here. I'm about to take her there."

Zy runs a hand through his hair and looks up at the ceiling. "Shit."

"When did she leave?"

"An hour ago. She walked out and said she was meeting you at the beach."

She's just forgotten that she was taking me to dinner. I'm sure she's perfectly okay. Safe, even.

But the way she's been acting lately is anything but safe.

What if she's—

No.

I turn to Zy. "Do you know where her keys are? My car is in the shop, getting fixed."

He walks over to the side table and takes a set of keys from it, a pink, glittery star charm catching the late afternoon light. "Here."

"Thanks." I snatch them out of his hand and walk through the doorway, headed for the stairs. I'm almost at the bottom when I hear my name called, and I turn back around.

"I'm sorry, Ellie."

"It's fine." I wave him off as I unlock the car and sit inside.

And it is.

It's *my* job to keep my sister safe.

It's the one thing I promised I'd do.

I crawl through the beach parking lot, the car chugging along at a snail's pace. Tourists crowd the boardwalk, snapping photos of the turbulent sea in front of them. A group of young kids hang outside the toilet block, girls leaning up against the wooden fence palings, boys clustering around, laughing and yelling with their mates.

"C'mon, Dani," I mutter, as her phone rings out again.

I glance at the clock radio. Ten past six. Mum will be pissed if we're not there soon. She likes her dinners to run like her events. Efficiently. On time. With no unexpected delays.

My phone rings, and I flinch as the loud noise fills the small space. I press the accept button and transfer the phone to speaker. "Hello?"

"Where are you?"

Mother.

"I'm just … just stopping for petrol," I lie. My fingers tap on the wheel as I scan the park once more. Where the hell could she be? Why on earth would she—

"You're late. Your sister and I are—"

"Dani?" I frown.

"Unless you're implying I had another child at some point, I don't see who else I could be talking about," Mum says dryly.

My shoulders slump in relief. She's okay. She's at dinner already.

Then they tense. Why didn't she wait for me?

"Anyway, dinner will be served in fifteen minutes, whether you are here or not. Please try to be punctual."

The call disconnects, and I slump back in the seat. *Great.*

I drive right on the speed limit the entire trip to Mum's place, pushing it as much as I can without breaking the law. Thoughts race through my mind, the most prevalent being *I am going to kill her.* Followed closely by *Thank God she's okay.*

Dani's car rattles along the drive of Mum's estate, and I slow to a stop in the turning circle. I open the car door and pocket the keys, then race up the stairs and enter the two-storey homestead.

My feet tap over the white tiles as I walk through the foyer and head toward the tinkling laughter I hear from within the bowels of the house. It's precisely twenty-one minutes since I spoke to Mum on the phone, which means I am officially late.

"Sorry I'm late," I breathe, as I turn the corner into the room.

The long timber dinner table stretches across the room, the top a natural oak carving. Overhead, the contemporary chandelier twinkles, and Dani's golden hair shines in the soft light. Mother sits to her left at the head of the table, her hair pulled back into a French knot, and to her left sits Colin.

Despite Mum's threat, the place settings in front of everyone remain empty, except for silver cutlery and half-empty wine glasses.

"Sit." Mother nods to the place setting beside Colin, and I obediently scurry over.

"Thanks for waiting." I scoot my chair in. I flash a look at Dani, one that I hope says *where the hell were you?* "So I thought I was picking you up, Dani?" I smile sweetly.

"I got a lift in with Colin." Dani takes a long sip from her wine glass, then presses her lips together. "Sorry."

"Oh." I nod. I'm an idiot. Of course she forgot.

And I overreacted.

Just because one person was taken from you doesn't mean everybody else will be, too.

Clara, Mum's assistant/maid/chef, walks into the room, three plates balanced in her arms. She places them down in front of Colin, Dani and Mum, then nods at me and rushes back to the kitchen, no doubt having just realised I was actually present.

And then, the torture begins.

"Let's say our gratitudes," Mum starts, smiling. *Oh God. Not this fresh hell.* "I am grateful that one of my daughters arrived for dinner on time."

I stiffen. Point taken. "I said I'm sorr—"

"You are forgiven," she says.

I press my eyes shut and think of my father. Of how he'd want me to behave.

And then I open them and paste on a smile, because that was the one thing he wanted. He wanted me to help glue this family together again.

"Well, I'm grateful that I have Ellie here working for me." Colin nods. At least someone has my back. "She's the best employee I've ever had, and so hard-working."

"It's not exactly rocket science," Dani mutters, then works her jaw.

I open my mouth to reply, but Colin squeezes my knee A squeeze that goes on for just a second too long.

My skin prickles, and just as I'm about to say something, Colin moves his hand away. I look at him, but his face is just the same as ever. He's open. Friendly. The same guy who has attended dinner once a week with my family since before Dad was sick. The same guy who rushes home after dinner so he can be there as soon as his wife finishes night shift at the hospital.

He's not the kind of guy who would cheat, and certainly not the kind of guy who would hit on a young girl.

"Dani?" Mum prompts, bringing me back to the moment.

"I'm grateful that I get to work with you, Mum," she says, her words tumbling out quickly as if they're flying down a slippery-dip. I raise my eyebrows. Seriously? "It's not often your role model in business is your mother. I guess I'm just lucky mine is."

"Danica." Mum's hand rests on her heart, and she presses her eyes closed for a moment. When they open again, a thin veil of tears shields them. "That is so sweet."

"It's true." Dani shrugs three times--up, down, up, down, up, down, all in quick succession.

THE TWENTY-ONE

Clara walks over and places a plate in front of me, and I thank her as she returns to the kitchen, then start to eat the roast dinner she's no doubt spent hours preparing for us.

"It's nice that you grace us with your time, dear. I know not all my daughters have such ... academic aspirations," Mum says.

I bristle. "I'll go to uni some day ..."

"Of course you will." Colin nods.

"Either way, I love working for you, Mum, and being at uni. It's a good mix," Dani says.

"Well, it's good you feel that way, as we have the biggest event of the season coming up." Mum claps her hands together. "It's a fundraiser for Cancer Australia, and it is going to be massive—absolutely massive."

"Sounds like a good money-spinner," Colin says, taking his fork and stabbing an innocent piece of carrot with it.

"It is. But more than that, it's a cause near and dear to my heart." Mum's eyelashes flutter, as if she's at a press conference selling her story to the local papers instead of selling her story to us. The people just as affected by cancer as she was.

"Do you want some picnic baskets or hot-air balloon rides to give away as door prizes?" Colin asks.

"Please." Mother nods, sipping on her glass of red. "And girls, I'll need you both there before, during and after. This is very important to me." She pauses and turns her fork in my direction. "So make sure you dress nicely."

"What's wrong with how I usually dress?" I frown.

"You know your sister is the style icon in the family." Mum takes another sip of wine, and smiles. "Don't look so wounded, Eleanor. This is nothing new."

And it isn't. But for some reason, tonight the words hurt far more than usual.

The rest of dinner passes as it usually does, and at precisely 8:30p.m., Mum opens the front door and bids the three of us good night.

"My car." Dani frowns at me, and I shrug.

"Sorry. Mine was in the shop."

The double doors to the house close with a thud, and the white porch illuminates the scene as Dani walks around to the driver's side, her hand trailing over the roof of the car as if I could have possibly hurt it somehow.

"Good night, Eleanor." Colin smiles. "See you on the weekend." He leans in and wraps his arms around me. He smells of mint, and musk, and berries. It's an odd combination. He pulls back and looks in my eyes. Light from the house reflects off his glasses. "Don't let them bully you, okay? You stay strong."

My emotions wage war on my body. Is he a creep, or in my corner?

"Good night, Colin." Dani singsongs, waving at him from the driver's side of her car.

"Night," he waves back. "Tell that Zy of yours that I expect him to be on time this weekend."

"He's not *my* Zy." Dani rolls her eyes as she hops into the car. "We are flatmates and friends. That is all."

"I don't know who she thinks she's fooling." Colin walks over to his car, and I open the passenger door of Dani's.

"Keys." She holds out her hand, her jaw working again.

"Here." I hand them over. "You should get that fixed." I nod at the dark interior light above us, but she just shrugs, so I swipe my hand over the passenger seat, clearing the trash to the floor before I sit.

"Hey!" Dani frowns. "That's my stuff."

I raise my eyebrows at her. "Really?"

She sighs. The car engine ticks over, and I slam my door, turning to look at my sister. On the outside, she appears just the same as she did a few months ago. Somehow, though, something has changed.

Am I ... losing her?

"Dani, are you okay?" I ask softly.

She blinks, and something flashes over her face before she replies. "Fine."

"Are you sure?" I ask as the car pulls out of the drive and onto the main street.

Dani leans forward and turns the dial on the radio up. Electronic dance music fills the car. It's so loud it throbs in my chest. So loud I feel it in my soul.

When we finally reach home in Emerald Cove, I waste no time in flying from the car to the house, leaving her to whatever weird mood she's in. Something is definitely going on with her.

It's not until I'm about to go to sleep that I realise my phone is missing. I feel for it in my jeans pocket, clutching at the thin material but not coming up with anything.

I pull on a pair of sweatpants over my naked legs and tiptoe out of the house over to the car. Upstairs, lights are on in Dani and Zy's apartment. Loud music, the same electronic beat Dani had blaring in the car earlier, pounds from their window. I wince. I so do not want to go into that.

Taking my chances, I try the doorhandle and find the car unlocked.

"Thank God," I whisper. I feel around on the seat for the phone, the light from the moon my only guide as I search for the familiar hard metallic shape.

I fumble blindly for a few minutes and then, right underneath the seat, I wrap my hand around my phone. Pulling it out, several pieces of trash come with it, and I can't help my smile. Maybe Dani and I are more similar than I'd thought. We both certainly can't keep our cars clean.

My smile freezes at what's in my hand.

Along with my phone is a small bag of tiny white pills.

The talking too fast. The working of her jaw.

Shit.

TEN

Bellbirds sing in the trees, the branches creaking in protest at the wind that batters against them. I pull my jacket tighter around my body. It's protection, to stop the weather outside chilling my bones, and to stop the pain inside leaching out into the world.

I clutch the small bunch of flowers tighter in my hand until the stems dig into my palm. I hold them tight, as if they might fly away.

The walk to the grave is lonely. It always is. Each time, the path seems more desolate than before. Sure, there are people around, weeping widows and crying children, but I'm isolated. Solitary.

Alone.

I kneel and throw the stale stems from the brown cup that sits over the tombstone and shove the new flowers in, shuffling them around until they sit just so. "Banksia and thryp," I whisper, smiling softly. "Your favourites."

I settle back and cross my legs, then shift from side to side on the cold brick-paved path, trying to get comfortable.

"So …" I glance around. There are only a few mourners, scattered throughout the grounds. They're wrapped in their own grief. "So I found pills in Dani's car yesterday."

Saying the words is oddly freeing. It makes me feel better. A problem shared is a problem halved, and even if our father can't answer back, or give advice, it's nice to let it out.

"And I know I shouldn't really worry. People experiment with drugs all the time." I pause and chew my lip. Overhead, grey clouds scoot closer, the ferocious wind gusting them along. "She's not a baby anymore. I can't tell her what to do."

I swallow down the lump that's in my throat. "I just …" I purse my lips together. "I can't handle the thought of losing anyone else. But I worry that if I try to protect her, I'm just going to push her away."

I trace my index finger over the letters of his name. It's a gesture I've done a thousand times, and as usual, it provides a small river of relief rushing down my spine.

"I'll … I'll think of something. Don't worry, Dad." I press my fingers to my lips, then right in the centre of the plaque. "I won't let you down."

I sit on the couch, shoving invites into envelopes for my mother's Cancer Australia fundraiser. My head isn't here though.

My head is on my sister.

And what the hell I'm going to do about her.

"What are you looking so worried about?" Hope asks, shuffling into the living room.

"Oh!" I shake my head. I can't let everyone know how worried I am about Dani. That's my problem, and my problem alone.

Hope's looking at me expectantly. I school my features into a neutral expression. "Nothing."

"Yeah right." She falls into the couch next to me and grabs a pillow, clutching it close to her chest. "Are you sure it's not your hot date today?"

"That must be it." I grin and face her, then glance out the window. Joel isn't due to pick me up for another ten minutes, but nerves flutter through me just picturing his face.

"And so I shouldn't expect you back until tomorrow?" She waggles her eyebrows.

"Hey!" I slap her arm. "I am going to be a lady. I won't bring him home for sex on the second date."

The subtle growl of a car sounds in the drive. We both look out the window at the same time.

Hope whistles appreciatively. "Nice car."

I nod. "I know, right? His family has always had money." Slamming my laptop shut, I grab my handbag from the coffee table and stand, doing a small twirl and pointing to my blue denim jeans and navy and white striped top that hugs my curves and exposes just a little cleavage. "Outfit okay?"

Hope purses her lips, then jumps to her feet. "Wait!"

A knock sounds at the door, and Hope hollers "Just a minute" as she runs from the room down the hall, and comes back a few seconds later, black tube in hand. "Purse."

I obediently push my lips into a kiss face, and she paints some colour onto them.

"Smack."

I run my lips together as Hope holds up a compact for me. My eyes widen. She has painted hot pink lipstick on me. It somehow suits my skin tone. It's a shade that I'm completely unused to, but that I now really want to wear. "Thank you. It actually ..." I shrug. "I feel like it makes me look hot."

"Hell yeah you do!" Hope dances around behind me and slaps my arse. "Now go get 'im, tiger!"

Laughing, I walk over to the door and swing it open.

Joel wears a white tee and jeans. They're not what capture my attention, though. It's the lusty glaze that passes over his eyes as he takes me in, the way he swallows and his Adam's apple bobs.

Operation = in progress.

"Hey." I lean forward and press a kiss to his cheek, careful not to go too hard in case the lipstick leaves a mark. Up close, he smells so good, and it takes all my self-control not to lick him. Because, seriously.

Joel clears his throat as I pull away. "Hi."

Silence stretches between us, and then I point to his car. "Shall we?"

It jerks him into action, and he nods. "Yeah. Yeah, of course."

He heads over to the car and I follow him. He opens the door for me, and as I go to slide into the luxurious car interior Hope fist pumps in the window. I grin uncontrollably.

We drive off, heading out of our street and onto the main road. Instead of turning right, toward town, we head left, and I tilt my head to the side, curious. "Where are we off to this time?"

"We're headed to the university."

"Oh!" The university? What kind of a date location is that?

"Yeah." Joel glances at me, gives a small shake of his head before turning back to the road. "You look ... *wow*."

All my apprehension disappears with that one word. I practically melt into a puddle of Ellie goo on the front seat of his expensive car. "Thank you."

We pull into the university parking lot thirty minutes later, and hop out of the car. Cars typical of the average uni student surround us. Older. A little beaten up. Joel's is definitely the nicest of them all.

"So now are you going to tell me what we're doing here?" I press, shutting the door as I join Joel outside.

"Sure." He leans back against his vehicle—something I could never do with my own, as that would imply I cleaned it—and smiles. "So today, we are doing a short acting workshop, and then performing in a play."

"Ha!" I bark a laugh. There's no way he's serious. First of all, I don't act. Secondly, it's after midday. That's not enough time to learn lines or practise. Thirdly, *I don't act*.

In school, the last time I had to give a speech for some sort of debate class, I vomited.

On stage.

On the hottest guy in class.

Joel surely remembers that.

Since then, there's been karaoke, when I had booze to fuel me, but that was in front of around twenty people. And again, I had alcohol. Copious amounts of it.

Aside from that, I've been lucky enough never to have to be centre stage, a position I gladly leave for my mother and sister. After all, there's only so much limelight to go around.

Joel looks at me, his face serious, and suddenly I know. "You have got to be kidding me."

He shakes his head. "Nope. 'Fraid not. Deadly serious." He winks, and then steps closer. "You got a problem with that?"

I throw my head back and look at the sky. Of all the damn things ... "Seriously! Your last challenge involved hot laps, and even though it didn't end up being quite as bad as I'd thought, it was still freaking scary. Now you want me to go in some kind of *play*? And have people *watch*?" My voice peaks on the final word.

"Hey." Joel steps closer and places a hand on my arm. Even through my shirt, I can feel it warming. Calming. "It's going to be okay."

I give a bitter laugh. "Are you trying to find things that freak me out on purpose?"

"Of course not," he says, and runs his hands over his head. "This was on my list. And when I saw it, I thought of you. How amazing you are. And how ... how sometimes, you don't force yourself to shine."

"What do you mean?"

"I just mean ... Life is short. It's all about being all you can be. Living in the moment. Standing on the stage."

"I like my life in the wings."

"How do you know you don't like the spotlight if you've never stood in its glare?" Joel steps close, and presses his eyelids closed. "I just want you to let the world see the Ellie Mayfield I'm falling for the second time around." His eyes flash open. "Even though I know I'm not supposed to."

My breath catches in my throat and my heart dissolves. "Do you really think I can?" I whisper, even though we're alone, even though there's no other sound except the calling of the bellbirds.

Joel takes my hand. His are cool, and his pale skin matches my own. "Yes."

And with that, Joel leads me off to face my fears for the third time in as many weeks.

And I'm starting to think I might like it.

ELEVEN

The workshop is surprisingly easy. Joel has us registered, and we join eight others in the class—two students of the university, the others all outsiders, like Joel and me.

Mr Brickendorf, our teacher, does some warm-up exercises with us that are surprisingly fun. They're improvisation games that see us finishing sentences, acting up and getting lost in the moment.

Finally, we split into groups of two and the teacher hands us all our scenes, and Joel and I practise ours for the remainder of the day. It's only short, barely fifteen minutes all up, and to my surprise, learning the lines comes rather easily to me.

Still, it doesn't make me feel any more comfortable now that we're in the campus cafeteria, taking a break before we head over to the auditorium for our performance pieces. Learning lines and saying them to Joel is one thing. It's almost nice to pretend to be someone else for a change.

Saying those lines in front of a room full of people is another thing entirely.

"You freaking out?" Joel asks, as the waitress brings over a bowl of fries smothered in aioli.

I nod. "Only with every cell in my entire body."

"You were fine at karaoke the other night."

"I was drunk, on the run from my mother, and in a pub where I doubt anyone was watching, let alone sober enough to judge and watch at the same time," I say, then add in at the last minute, "And even then I was freaking the hell out."

He smiles kindly, and shakes his head. "Let's talk through it. What are you most worried about?"

I chew my lip. "Failure. Embarrassing myself. Embarrassing you. Having ... having people judge me."

"People will always judge you," Joel says simply, and he takes a fry and pops it in his mouth. "It's how you handle it that makes the difference."

"I plan on handling it by vomiting." I nod sagely. "And maybe passing out."

"Good thing I ordered an ice cream sundae after this. I think you'll need the sugar rush." Joel teases, and I laugh.

"Trust me—right now, there is way too much fear rushing through me. I don't think sugar will do anything." As I say the words, my feet tap under the table. It's true. Nervous energy crashes through me like a tidal wave.

"Well, how about we start you off small? Get you used to a bit of audience attention." Joel rests back in his chair, a smile lighting his face.

"Oh yeah?" I grab a chip and eat it. "And how do you propose we do that?"

A wicked gleam passes across Joel's eyes, and before I have a chance to stop him he's jumped on top of his chair. Half the twenty-odd people in the cafeteria turn to look at him, some with curious expressions, others ones of ridicule.

I sink down into my plastic bucket seat. *This is not happening ...*

"Ladies and gentlefolk of the cafeteria, can I have your attention please?"

Now everyone stops what they're doing, and turns to face Joel. I clasp one hand over my eyes. I have no idea what's about to happen next, but I already have a bad feeling ...

"You all need to meet the lovely Ellie Mayfield, a woman whose looks are only surpassed by her talent," he cries, and my cheeks fire up. Oh God. Oh why, why, why is he doing this to me?

"Ellie is actually a possessor of great skill. She has a talent that not everyone in this room shares," he says, gesturing widely around the room. Then, he points to the lady behind the cash register. "Madam, may I have a packet of your finest snakes?"

Oh no.

Oh no, no, no, *no*.

"If you pay me three bucks," she replies, but turns and grabs a bag that's hanging on the wall behind her.

Joel's hand flies to his back pocket, and he fishes out his wallet. Taking a five-dollar note, he hands it to the lady who, despite her earlier attitude, has decided to walk over and deliver Joel's request in person.

"Now, let me direct your attention to Ellie, who is going to do something girls worldwide aspire to do." He cracks open the bag of snakes, and pulls one out. It's long and red. The same colour as my cheeks. "She is going to tie this snake in a knot using only her tongue."

"I can do that," one of the girls near the ping-pong table cries out.

But when Joel turns to look at her, she must see in him what I see in him. That crazy beautiful face, that contagious energy that you just want to be a part of.

THE TWENTY-ONE

She shrugs, and gives a half-smile. "But let's see Ellie do it then."

Joel beams, and turns to the majority of the crowd again. "Ellie's a little bit nervous, so I'm going to need you all to cheer. Let's get this going!" His voice calls out.

One person claps.

One. Person.

One person sighs in relief.

That person is me. Looks like I won't have to do this stupid stunt after all.

"And if you all chant her name, I'll buy everyone in this room a beer!"

"Ellie, Ellie, Ellie, Ellie ..."

It's quiet at first, but soon people join in, and the voices rise as one.

"C'mon, Ellie." Joel extends his hands to pull me up to his seat. I shake my head. Everyone is looking. I'm going to make an idiot of myself.

"Please ...?" Joel wiggles the snake, and the crowd gets louder, the chants get faster. The whole cafeteria calls my name, looking at me, and yet for some strange reason, no one is laughing.

Yet.

"Ellie, Ellie, Ellie-Ellie-Ellie-Ellie ..."

I look at Joel's open face, his honest pleading eyes. I think of the hot laps. Baby steps. I can do baby steps.

Slowly, I push to my feet. The crowd feeds off my movement, getting louder and faster again, and I step up to Joel. I extend my hand, and my voice is quiet against the roar of the crowd. "Promise you won't let me fall?"

He ducks his head and whispers, "I will always catch you, Ellie. Always."

I grip his forearm and pull myself up on the chair, standing flush beside him. The closeness of his body does funny things to mine. Then he hands me the snake, and for a moment both our hands are touching, and he has this excited grin on his face, and instead of feeling like an idiot, like a fraud, like someone who's possibly about to fall off the chair and vomit, I feel—good. I'm on top of the world.

I quickly pop the snake into my mouth and the crowd goes silent. The only noise in the room is from the pinball machine and the music blasting from the café's tinny speakers.

I twist. I turn. I push.

And then ...

I pull the knotted snake from my mouth and hold it above my head.

The crowd roars. It's deafening. Some guy even lets out a wolf-whistle.

And there's this weird gooey feeling inside me that's actually kind of nice.

I jump off the seat and scamper back to my own as people come up to Joel and slap him on the back. He hands the waitress a card and tells her to put twenty beers on it, then joins me back at the table as if that didn't just happen.

I stare at him, my eyes bugging.

"Are you mad?" he asks, a cheeky grin on his face.

"No." I shake my head. "I'm actually ... I'm actually feeling kind of good."

"Then my job here is done. And when you go on stage later, it'll be just like this. Quick. Good. Only with less guys asking me how you are at blow jobs after."

I grab a fry and stab the air with it. "You are going to die a slow and miserable death."

"Ha!" Joel barks. "But not before you perform on stage tonight. Speaking of, are you gonna ask your mother to come?"

"No."

"Why not?"

I shake my head. He doesn't understand. No one really does. "It's ... I can't ask Mum for favours, or even for a bit of extra cash when I need it. She's always been so adamant that Dani and I pay our own way. That we forge our own lives outside of her house." I pause, mulling over our family situation. "It's why she asked Dani to move out as soon as she finished school."

Joel squares his shoulders. "Really?"

I shrug. "It is what it is. She's been through so much. When Dad died ... she broke down. For weeks she didn't leave the house. Dani didn't really leave her room."

He looks deep into my eyes. "You were the glue that kept them together."

The university café thrums, people drinking beers and carb-loading. A pinball machine competes with the punk band blasting from the speakers, and in the corner, a group of guys play ping-pong, the hollow clicks of the ball on the table a thumping soundtrack.

All these sounds are so much more obvious when we're quiet.

All these sounds make the silence between us louder.

"So ..." I say, trying to think of something, anything to make this weird feeling between us shift. "Tell me more about your challenges. What have you done?"

Joel snaps out of it and leans forward, and it's as if the weird moment never happened. "I guess we ran into each other when I was about halfway through," he says, and holds out his hand as he begins counting. "So I had some obvious ones—drag racing, white-water rafting, streaking through the uni ..."

"I am so glad I didn't get roped into that." *And a little disappointed I didn't get to see it.*

"Ha! I don't know if I like the thought of half the campus seeing you naked," he says, and the flirty banter is back. "There have been so many things. I had to make one thousand origami paper cranes for this cancer fundraiser thing that's done for people still suffering from the effects of the atomic bomb in World War II—"

"Wow," I breathe. Because that's amazing. One thousand origami cranes would be no mean feat.

"It was ... I don't want to sound like a total wanker, but it was kinda cool," Joel says. "Then there was making my own gin at this distillery in the city, drinking my own gin that I made at a distillery in the city—"

"Oh God," I say, imagining the quantities the challenge must have required to make it list-worthy.

"Oh God is right," Joel laughs. "I still don't think I can look at the stuff. Anyway, there has been a bunch. I'm up to number fifteen—or I guess sixteen, once you cross off 'act in a public forum'," he says.

"Who gave you that challenge?"

"My dad," he says. "He's going to be out there tonight."

Blood rushes to my cheeks. When we were younger, Joel lived with his father, a high-flying lawyer. He was busy most of the time, and I'd only see him at the odd school function. Now he was in the audience? The first time I'll see the rich Mr Henley again after all these years will be after I've *acted*? On a *stage*? In front of *people*?

"Hey, it's okay." Joel reaches across the table and takes my hand, and for a guy who's not supposed to be making moves on a girl, he's moving my heart so damn quickly. "He's not scary. I promise."

"I'll be fine." I straighten my spine. And I really want to be. Because being better, being stronger—Joel makes me feel as if I'm worth it. As if I'm good enough. "So tell me what else is left."

"I have to enter a hot-dog eating contest, go camping under the stars, ride the dodge'em cars at the spring fair, get my motorbike license and—" He pauses, looking away, then meeting my gaze once more. "And my favourite is to go sky-diving."

And for some strange reason, I have this inherent desire to do every single one of those things with him. Even though the thought of them petrifies me. Even though he hasn't asked me to, and even though he isn't even really my boyfriend.

He views life as a challenge, as a series of experiences—that's worth joining in on. Life for Joel is a ride, and I desperately want to get on.

Standing backstage, my heart is in my throat. It's stuck there, clogging my airways, and every time I hear the audience—and there is an audience, at least fifty-strong—cheer, I can't suck in air. They're going to be looking at me. Watching. Judging.

Mr Brickendorf calls our names, and Joel takes my hand. He feels so warm. Or maybe I feel so cold. I don't know.

All I know is my earlier bravado from the cafeteria has vanished, and now I'm a shaking, quivering mess.

Joel starts to walk, but my feet don't follow. They stay planted firmly on the ground.

My arm reaches the end of its extension and Joel turns around, a slight frown on his face. Then he steps closer, so close. He rests his forehead against mine and whispers those magical words that helped me so much before.

"I'll catch you if you fall."

Six words.

And yet they lace under me like a net, wrap around me like a blanket, weave through me like a song. I breathe those words. I let them consume me.

Because sometimes all we need to know is that someone will be there to do that.

I smile, and he smiles, and then we're both smiling at each other and it doesn't matter what happens out there. It doesn't matter if I make an idiot of myself. Because I have this. I have us.

"You ready?" Joel grins.

"Ready," I whisper back, and this time I lead the charge out onto the stage. I'm no longer waiting in the wings.

Out there in the spotlight, everything changes again. I feel small, so small against so many eyes, and doubt creeps in. Voices in my head. Feelings of not being good enough. Of never being enough.

Then I look at Joel, and he smiles at me, his eyes retelling their message from earlier.

I speak.

And I soar.

TWELVE

Our piece goes off without a hitch. Neither of us forget our lines, we both follow the simple blocking Mr Brickendorf laid out for us, and I don't vomit, pass out, or have to face the laughter and ridicule of the faceless audience, all who politely clap when the performance is over.

When the show is done we walk around to the front of the building, my hand still firmly clasped in Joel's. It's a place I never want to leave.

"You were amazing, Ellie. So bloody good!" He laughs, and there's a joyousness in it that's impossible to deny.

I giggle and skip a step to keep up with him, the cold night air no match for the heat in my lungs. "You were awesome."

We navigate our way back inside the building's front entrance and through the crowd, heading to the bar for a celebratory drink. When he has a beer and I have a vodka soda, we stop and catch our breaths. I can't stop the giddiness racing through my veins, though. That consumes all of me.

"Here he is," a voice booms, interrupting my thoughts, and I look up at one of the tallest men I've ever met. His face is narrow, and his thin hair greying, but those eyes—those eyes are unmistakable. They're the same blue eyes as Joel's.

I've met Joel's father twice before. Back then, he was always Mr Henley, the energetic man who drove Joel to soccer and came in to tell us when it was getting late, and when It was time to go home. Now, he somehow looks a lot older. As if more than three years have passed.

"Dad." Joel grins, and wraps his arms around his father, careful not to spill the beer in the process. "How was it?"

The older man claps him on the back and pulls away, looking Joel in the face. "You two were bloody brilliant. I don't know about the rest of them though ..."

"You're being a little biased, don't you think?" Joel raises his eyebrows, then pulls back farther again to gesture to me. "Dad, do you remember the lovely Ellie Mayfield? Ellie, this is my dad, Henry."

I put out my hand for it to be shaken, realising I have never heard his first name before. "Henry ... Henley?"

He shakes his head. "My parents had a cruel sense of humour."

"I'm so sorry." The words are out of my mouth before I have time to think them through. "I mean, I think. Should I be?"

Henry throws his head back and laughs, a big booming sound, and soon I join in. "You're all right, my dear. All right."

"Can I get you a drink or anything, Dad?" Joel asks.

Henry frowns. "I don't think you should be drinking yourself. I'm a little surprised, Son."

I look to Joel, bemused. "Do you have a secret alcohol problem you've been keeping from me?"

The mood isn't jovial anymore, though.

Now it's veritably icy.

"He's just worried about me drinking and driving, is all."

"Oh." I nod. It does make sense. But when he's only having one, and we're not leaving for another hour or so ...

Maybe there are some dark secrets in Joel's past. Maybe I'm not the only one who's hiding something from the world.

I think of the bright, vibrant, happy guy I'm falling for. I just hope whatever it is doesn't consume Joel, too.

We're almost at my place when Joel veers the car to the left and heads toward the beach parking lot.

"Please don't tell me skinny dipping is another one of your challenges." I grimace, and Joel laughs. It's melodic and rich, and completely fills the space between us.

He pulls into an empty space and eases the parking brake on. The lot is near vacant, with only a few other cars parked around us. Light from the lamp above us floods the vehicle, capturing the seriousness in Joel's eyes. "I don't think I could handle seeing you naked."

My breath catches in my throat, and I swallow down the words *do me on the car bonnet*. Because, seriously. There's only so many sexy glances from this man I can endure.

Joel turns his head to me. "Do you know any constellations?"

So not what I was thinking about. I shake my head, no.

"Me neither." He chews his lip for a moment, then lets out a breath. "My dad used to say that stars are all the souls of people who've lived before. People who we love, looking down on us."

I turn the idea over in my mind, my eyes on the jewels that glitter so high above us. If one of them was my father …

No.

"That's all very well and good, but science is science. They're planets, and comets, and moons, and asteroids, and …" I trail off as the back of Joel's hand trails down my cheek.

"Maybe stars are more than just science." The words come out near a whisper. "Maybe all that is true, but maybe it's to do with viewpoint. Maybe there's a barrier between earth and space, and each soul has a sparkle they cling to. A way they can look down on earth and find the people they love below."

Maybe.

It's something I want to believe so badly. Lately, I've been feeling so lost, and it's so damn easy to fall in love with the idea that someone is there, looking out for my family and me.

If my dad was up there in the stars, I'd want him to find me.

I miss him so much.

Suddenly, the gravity of the thought overwhelms me, and I need to get out of there, need to change the conversation topic, fast. "I … you were a star tonight. Up there on stage …"

"It was easy." He flashes me a winning smile. "I just did that old trick."

"Oh yeah?" I tilt my head to the side. "And what exactly is that?"

His eyes smoulder. "I pretended you were naked."

Oh.

His words light a fire inside me. Tension is taut as a zipline around us. The yellow lights of the parking lot wash a golden hue over Joel's face, his pale complexion. He licks his lips, and I'm drawn to them. Inch by inch, breath by breath, and oh my God, it's really finally happening, and I'm going to—

A body slams against the car window behind Joel. He whips his head around, and I widen my eyes.

"Ellie!" Dani screams, waving her hand at light speed.

Joel turns back to me, an eyebrow raised in question. "That's not little Dani?"

Disappointment sucks through my body. We were so close—so close to kissing. "Yep. That's my sister."

Joel opens the car door. Dani leans in, and even from the other side of the vehicle I can smell the bourbon on her breath. "Sissy! And … Joel!" She tries to wiggle her eyebrows, but ends up looking like some kind of facial contortionist. Still, despite it all, she manages to be beautiful. So beautiful.

Beauty's always been her downfall.

"Hey. Nice to see you again." Joel sticks out his hand, and Dani looks at it in disdain before launching herself at him. Her arms latch around his neck as she stumble-hugs him, her body hovering over his.

"Mm, you smell good, Joel." She sucks in a breath next to his neck, then pulls back so her face is close to his. Too close.

A little part of me squirms, and even though I know I'm being ridiculous, I can't help but think it. *Please don't choose her.*

"Thanks." Joel places his hands on Dani's shoulders and gently pushes her out of the car. My heart starts beating again, as if it never stopped.

"What are you doing here, Dan?" I ask, leaning forward to get a better view. The parking lot is void of people behind her.

"Just waiting for someone." She waves her hand behind her, and a gust of wind whips her long hair around her face. "He'll be here soon."

Unease twists my stomach, and I look at her, really look at her. "Who are you meeting?"

"A friend."

"Which friend?"

"Rack off, Ellie. Go fuck your hot boyfriend." She flips me the bird, and turns to wobble away on heels that are much too high for her.

"Sorry, I'll be right back." I open the car door and step out. My phone buzzes in my purse, and I ignore it, too focused on saving my sister.

I power-walk to catch her, and even though she has a head start, I manage to reach her in ten seconds, flat. My hand curls around her shoulders, jerking her fragile frame to face me.

"What the hell are you doing, Dani?" I ask. Emotion tears at my voice.

"Take a guess," she snarls, but there's a chink in her armour. The weak spot in her heel.

"Is it drugs?"

"Ha!" Contempt lines her features, and she sneers. "Poor little Ellie. You just don't understand me at all, do you?" She shakes her head. "You can't shelter me forever."

Those words break my heart. Because that's the only thing I want to do. Save her from herself.

THE TWENTY-ONE

A motorcycle roars into the lot, pulling to a stop beside us. Dani stills in front of me, and shrugs my grip off. "Go away," she hisses, straightening her shoulders and painting a smile on her face. "This is my friend."

A man dressed all in black, from his helmet to his combat boots, throws his leg over the side of the bike. He unlatches his helmet and pulls it over his head, letting loose his long, dark hair. A scar puckers the side of his lips, and his eyes are hard and grey in the dim light—eyes that have seen too many things. I don't have to look for his cut to know he's a bikie. It's written in the way he walks, the predatory way he moves.

"I ain't got enough for the both of you."

"Trust me, we ain't after a package deal." Dani saunters over and places her small arm around this big man's shoulders.

My stomach whirls inside my body, even as I tell it to relax. This is a lot darker than I'd ever thought it was.

"Hey." Joel walks to my side, his warm body a direct contrast against the cool of my arm.

"Let's go." The biker grunts at Dani and turns back toward the bike. She moves to follow him but I grab her arm, my fingers digging into her soft flesh.

"Please," I whisper. Because surely she won't. How can my own sister be involved in something like this?

She meets my gaze with her own, and there's a fierceness in those brown orbs that I haven't seen before. "It's not your choice to make."

As she walks away, I stare, unmoving. The cool wind from the sea ices my skin until I'm stone cold, from the outside in. I'm numb. This is so much more dangerous than just a small bag in a car. This is so very wrong.

"Hey."

His voice is soft, and his breath is warm against the shell of my ear.

It makes me feel something.

It thaws my *numb*.

And I run.

"Hey!" I yell, and I crash my arms around Dani's waist.

"What the fuck, Ellie?" she spits, spinning to face me.

"She can't," I breathe. The biker looks around and meets my wild gaze.

"I'm fine!" She grabs my hand and wrenches it off, but I wrap it back around her waist just as tight. Because this is my sister. I cannot let her do this.

Ever.

"Let go!" She struggles, but I become a bluebottle. Every part of me is a tentacle wrapped around her, branding her, stopping her from leaving.

The biker turns back toward his bike, and it's the motivation Dani needs. She bites my arm, her teeth sinking into my skin, not far enough to draw blood though.

That's what lets me know she doesn't really want this.

That this is a fight worth fighting after all.

Dani stretches out an arm, her body pulling against my hands still wrapped around her waist. "Stay."

For a long, long moment, he looks as if he's going to. Then he shakes his head, huffing out a breath. "Forget about it."

"No, I can explain, I can ..."

But the roar of his engine cuts her cries off. The angry noise that screams louder than the waves on the beach shore, a symphony of machine that's far deeper than anything I've heard before. The helmet clips closed, and then he flies out of the car park, the heat of the engine leaving mist in the cool night air.

When I let my arms drop from my sister's waist, her body collapses onto the bitumen. She sobs, these heart-wrenching, soul-destroying sobs that shake her body to the core and rattle my blood in empathy.

"Hey." I drop to my knees and rub circles on her back, like I've done so many times before. Like I did back then. "It's okay. It's okay."

She shudders, her small spine shaking, and then she flings her body up, sending my hand flying. "You do not get to tell me it's going to be okay," she spits, her eyes wild like a feral cat. "You promised it'd be okay before, and you know what? It wasn't."

Those words.

They cut at my soul. They eat at my heart.

"Because he died, Ellie. He *died*." A mad smile warps her features, and for once I don't see the beauty in my younger sister. For now, she's just wild, untameable—angry. "Now I'm doing what I have to do. And you may have stopped me this time, but you won't stop me again."

My heart hammers. It's fast and furious and loud, so damn loud, and even as I wrap my arm around her, even when she flings it off once more, it seems to get heavier. I retreat, my body shrinking into itself. How will we make it out of here? How can I take Dani back from the brink?

"Hey."

It's a hand on my back.

Warm. Slow.

Calm.

I turn my head and meet Joel's steady gaze. His eyes aren't judging—instead, they're calm. Relaxed. *Whole*.

"Let's get you two in the car, okay?" he says the words, and glances at me, then at Dani. He puts his hand underneath her chin, tilting it so they make eye contact. "You gonna come home with us?"

I don't know if she's as much under his spell as I am, or if she'd already decided to give up and let it go.

All I know is she stops fighting. I reach out and her body goes limp in my arms, her weight against me.

"Here." Joel opens the door to the back seat, and Dani bites her lips. She squares her gaze and studies me, and a cool composure twists her lips.

"I'm fine." She strides to the car and, with the grace of a supermodel, folds herself into the back seat.

I stand there staring, my limbs frozen solid. I can't tell if it's the night air or my own heart that's left me in this state.

I know Joel comes back for me. I see him do it, but my heart isn't there. My heart is already in the car. My heart is locked up in the back seat.

A warm hand touches my lower back. "You did a good thing, Ellie."

And it might make me weak. It might mean I'm the least feminist, most pathetic human being known to man, but for right now? His validation is enough.

It's more than enough. It's all that matters.

And when I glance up at the stars, I can't help but hope that my father feels that way, too.

THIRTEEN

When we get back to my house, Dani stumbles out of the car. I run across the road with her, and help her open the door to her apartment. Zy waits on the couch, his arms folded, a grim expression on his face.

"Where's she been?" he growls, and I shiver, his words inviting the night air to creep over my skin.

"You really don't know?" I raise my eyebrows.

"Go to hell," Dani says to me, then storms down the hall.

Zy stands, and runs his hands through his hair. "Dan, do you need—"

"You too!" Her words are punctuated with the slamming of a door, and the whole building seems to shudder.

"Where was she?" He turns those blue eyes on me, and for the second time tonight I feel shaken to my core.

"I think she was ... She's doing drugs."

"Fuck." Zy runs a hand through his hair and turns away, as if he needs space to digest this news. "Do you think it's serious?"

I shrug. "No. Probably. Yes." I shake my head and look out the window at the starry night sky twinkling above us. "I don't know what serious is when it comes to this kind of thing."

"I'm gonna sort this out." Zy's words are slow and deliberate. "I'm gonna fight this, Eleanor. You have to believe me."

I want to believe his words so badly. I really do

"Thanks." I turn to leave. Just as my foot hits the pavement, I hear five quiet words.

I won't let you down.

Joel leans against his car, his ankles crossed, staring at the sky. It's deep, and dark above us, specks of light glittered through it. His face is serious, so much so that I wonder if this is it for him—if what he's seen tonight is enough to turn him away for good.

My phone vibrates in my purse, and I quickly pull it out, seeing three new texts from Colin and one from Hope. I shove the phone away and focus on the man in front of me. I'll deal with them later.

"I'm sorry," I say as soon as I'm within a few feet of him. Joel looks at me, and I step closer, clenching my hands into fists to stop them from trembling. "I know that you probably think my family is losing it, and that the idea of a future with me is probably so repulsive to you, and my sister is so beautiful, and deep down she's a good person, but—"

Hot lips mash against mine. Hands tangle in my hair, and he kisses away every word that's yet to fall from my lips and replaces it with this exquisite, unbridled passion. His tongue demands entrance, and I open my lips and let him because it feels so good to just let go, to embrace this intense desire.

I wrap my arms around him and touch his back, his body firm against mine. He fists a hand in my T-shirt, pulling me closer.

"Joel," I breathe. Fire roars through me, and I jump up and wrap my legs around his waist, drawing him as close to my core as I can get. I rub my body against his like a damn cat on heat, but I just can't stop. I'm so hot for him. My want has become a need.

Fingers race under my shirt, tracing over the lacy bra. My nipples harden into buds beneath his touch, and I shudder as a primal urge roars through me. "Let's." *Kiss.* "Go." *Kiss.* "In." *Kiss.* "Side."

"Mm," Joel agrees, or maybe he just moans. I slide down his body and without breaking lip contact, we move toward the veranda and then to the front door.

"Keys," I breathe, pulling away to fumble in my purse. My hands shake for an entirely different reason now. I'm a live wire of nerves and tension and *sex*. And I don't want this to end.

Finally, metal finds the deadbolt. I turn the lock as Joel places a hand on either side of my head, caging me in with his body. He kisses down my neck, bites at my earlobe, and I tilt my head to the side, desperate for more. My needy body thrills at his touch.

The door falls open and I spin to face Joel again. He reaches for the hem of my shirt and then lifts it over my head, throwing it on the floor behind me. Goosebumps ghost my body and I press closer to him.

"Hey." Joel reaches for my shoulders and takes a step back. "Let me look at you."

I lick my lips. I'm not a supermodel. I know I have curves, and that my figure is hardly Dani's perfect waif.

Joel inspects me in the dim light. The kitchen door has been left open, and a yellow beam casts me in shadow. His eyes start at my feet and run up my legs, lingering over my chest. He swallows, and his Adam's apple bobs up and down.

"Ellie," he says on a whisper. "You're so damn beautiful."

That's all it takes.

I launch at him and our lips meet in a passionate frenzy once more. His hand finds the back of my bra, and—

"Well it does look like I'm interrupting."

Oh. My. *God.*

My heart stops.

Then it decides to jump ship and relocate to my throat.

Joel freezes, and when I open my eyes I see his bright blues blaring into mine.

"Colin." I manage to say, despite the fact that I'm dying a million embarrassing deaths on the inside.

"Ellie. I didn't realise you were coming home with company. Or that you had a boyfriend."

I pull back and mouth *sorry* to Joel, then turn and with what I hope is ninja speed, grab my shirt up off the floor, spinning away to put it on.

Colin stands in front of me, his lips puckered, a frown creasing his forehead. Behind him, Hope rushes into the room, her eyes wide.

"I'm sorry," she says, and purses her lips. "I tried to call. I thought you weren't bringing …"

Our conversation from earlier races through my mind. "My phone was on silent." The words are lead weights. "What are you doing here, Colin?"

He has the grace to look embarrassed, and studies the floor before raising his head in an answer. "Hope was kind enough to let me use your bathroom. I just stopped by to give you these." He points to wo boxes labelled *Sauvignon Blanc* sitting by the front door. "They're for your deliveries next week. I know your mum has that big function Wednesday, so I wanted to get in early. I didn't realise you'd be …"

"It's fine."

"Okay, well … can I have a quick word?" Colin jerks his head toward the kitchen. I nod and walk ahead of him, leaving Joel and Hope in the lounge room together.

Colin leans up against the chipped blue cupboard that lines the wall. He folds his arms across his chest. "I'm worried about your sister."

His words open a floodgate of emotion inside me. "Really?" I step closer. "Me too."

He pinches the bridge of his nose. "It's probably nothing, but I think she's involved in some dangerous things."

It's all the confirmation I need. "Let's talk to Mum—"

"No." He pushes off the counter and steps closer to me. "We don't want to worry your mum. Not when she's got this big event on Wednesday."

"So we should wait?"

"We should be there for her, kid." Colin places a hand on my arm and squeezes. It's an innocent enough gesture, but my skin prickles under his touch. The last few weeks, he's definitely become a little more touchy-feely than usual. "She's lucky she has you."

"Okay, well, good to know you know. Maybe we can chat to Mum next week." I step backward and Colin's hand drops as I paste a fake smile upon my face. On the one hand, he's a nice guy who's clearly concerned for my sister. On the other, he keeps doing these things that make my insides turn.

I walk back out into the lounge room, Colin thumping behind. "Thanks for stopping by."

"Any time," he says, then turns to Joel. "It was nice to meet you. You know, I don't think Ellie has had a boyfriend in—"

"Colin!" I protest. *We haven't had the talk yet.* "He's not my boyfriend."

"He's not?" he says.

"Aren't I?"

Slowly, I swivel on my heel to face Joel. "We haven't really had that talk ..."

"I'll leave you to it, then." Colin gives me a less-than-subtle wink and walks outside. I follow him and pull the door closed behind us, protecting Hope and Joel from the rest of the conversation.

"So the fundraiser on Wednesday, then we talk to her. Yes?" I lean in, anxious for confirmation that this is a problem with a very clear solution.

"Eleanor." Colin wraps his arms around me. The scent of strawberries chokes me. Each breath is harder and harder to suck in as he squeezes tight.

Finally, he relaxes his grip, and I step back. His hands trail around my body and—

They brush over my breasts. Just the sides, but still. It's not a natural place for his hands to fall. Memories of his recent too-friendly gestures play in vivid colour through my mind. I wrap my arms over my chest. "What the hell?"

He cocks his head to the side, a frown creasing his brow. "What are you talking about?"

"You just touched ..." I search for words to fill the blank.

"We hugged, Eleanor. Nothing more." He coughs a laugh, then shakes his head. "Have you been drinking?"

I step back. Did I imagine it? My knees are unsteady beneath me. Part of me, the old Ellie, the one who'd never rock the boat—she wants to ignore this, to let it go. To look on the positive side and give him the benefit of the doubt.

The girl Joel sees, though? The one he thinks is something better than she allows herself to be?

She's not having a bar of it.

"Get the hell out of here." I point to the street.

"Ellie, what—"

"Now," I seethe. My hand wobbles the slightest bit. Mum's face flashes in my mind. *She is going to kill me for this.*

Colin stiffens and takes a step backward. "You are overreacting, young lady." He shakes his head and turns to the street. "Your mother will be hearing about this."

For the briefest moment, fear wraps my heart in its icy talons. Then I set my jaw and roll my shoulders back. It's one small aspect of my life I'm taking control over. "Good. I can't wait to tell her my version of events."

I stamp my hands on my hips. When Colin reaches the driveway, he turns back to me. "There's still time to apologise, Ellie."

I turn and reach for the door to the house. "Yeah, there is. I'll be waiting."

Pulling the door open, I step inside. My hands tremble, adrenaline pumping through me. Joel glances up at me from the red velvet sofa.

"Are you okay?"

Slowly, I nod. "Yeah," I breathe. "I think I am."

I walk over and collapse onto the couch next to him. My heart thuds double time in my chest, and sweat sticks my arms to my sides. *This whole night is so surreal. Dani. Joel. And now ... this.*

"Did something happen out there?" Joel asks, concern knotting his hands together. "You seem stressed."

"Don't worry about it." I shake my head. "I'm just worried about my sister, I guess. That's what Colin came here for." *Or did he?*

"Does everyone always treat you like that?"

I tilt my head to the side. "Like what?"

"Like you're your sister's keeper. Her babysitter. She's a grown woman." Joel touches my arm, and even though his hand is warm, it sends shivers through me.

"I know." I shake my head. "It's complicated. You saw her tonight. She needs someone to look after her, and that someone is me."

"Tell me this, then." This time Joel leans close, so close his warm breath ghosts over my lips. "Why didn't Colin go next door instead of coming here?"

"I ..." I work my mouth like a goldfish. "I ... don't know."

And I don't. The only answer that comes to mind is because maybe he was after something else.

"Maybe you need to give Dani the chance to swim on her own. To be her sister—not just her keeper," he says.

"Ha." I bark out a laugh. "I can't just let her sink."

"Maybe she'll surprise you." Joel tilts his head to the side. "Maybe she'll swim."

I rest my head back on the couch and stare up at the white roof, the ornate latticework in the corners. My brain is working a million miles an hour. I need to speak to Mum. No. I need to quit my job. I need to—

"When do you wanna hang out again?" Joel asks, shifting his weight to the side.

I need to let this man in.

"I have this thing for Mum on Wednesday," I finally say, thinking of the Cancer Australia event.

"I'm working then anyway," Joel says, and I cock my head.

"Working?" I smile and poke at his chest. "I thought you worked for some corporation. Are they open late at night?"

"Sometimes." Darkness flashes over Joel's features. He cups my face with his hand. "I can't concentrate when I'm falling for you, Ellie." He leans close, and the fresh scents of pine and sandalwood hit me.

All the worry in my life melts away with those words, and I lean closer to him, revelling in this moment.

And when he kisses me, I am twenty-one kinds of happy.

"Post-work beach walk?" he asks, his voice breathy in my ear.

"Perfect."

FOURTEEN

It's seven a.m. when I bang against the door to their apartment. Silence greets me, and I look at my watch, cursing. She has to get up and let me in. Preferably within the next ten minutes, so I'm not late to the florist.

"C'mon," I say, pounding harder. My knuckles smart against the metal grid, and I wring my hand from side to side to try and ease the burn.

I raise my hand to start my pound again when the door swings open. Zy stands there, shirtless, his hair all sexed up, his eyes barely open. His jeans are just pulled on, the fly not completely done up, as if he just thought to dress. A nipple ring glints in the morning sun, a stark contrast to the black ink that crawls over his torso. I shiver. You'd be inhuman to be impartial to that chest.

"Eleanor, what gives with the knocking?" He croaks.

"Dani," I answer simply, and push past him into the dark house.

Inside, it smells like cigarettes, and I wonder if they're from Dani or Zy.

"She's not awake yet," Zy mumbles, rubbing a hand against his bleary eyes as he shuts the door behind him.

"She's about to be." I stride down the hall and knock on her door. "Dani, wake up!"

Behind me, Zy shuffles into his room and collapses face first on the bed before shifting his pillow over his head.

"Dan—"

"Just open the door," Zy yells, and I twist at the metal handle.

Inside Dani's room, a narrow strip of golden light creeps in beneath the blinds, highlighting the richness of my sister's soft curls. She lies in a foetal position on the bed, her sheets pulled up to her chin all child-like. As if cotton can protect her from the monsters in the world.

It's a shame it can't protect her from the monsters in her head.

"Dan." I walk over to her side, dodging the clothes littered on the grey carpet floor, and sit on the edge of the bed.

One brown eye flickers open and focuses on me, then she turns her head and buries into the pillow. I reach out and stroke her hair, letting my hands comb through those unruly curls. It's what identifies us as sisters to the general public—long, blonde curls. If only the similarities didn't end there.

"What time does the lecture start?" she asks, turning to give me both eyes' attention.

I smile. "It doesn't."

Dani pushes up and rests on her elbows, studying me. "What do you mean, *it doesn't?*"

I think about Joel and what he told me last night. How if I don't give her the chance to swim on her own, she'll keep waiting for me to save her.

"I mean, it doesn't." I spy a pink dress on the floor and pick it up, flicking it over to her. "Get up. We're going to the florist."

And whether it's from gratitude or maybe even shock, Dani doesn't question me further. She picks up the dress and holds it to her chest, then throws the sheets back and walks to the bedroom door. When she gets there, she glances back at me, a frown marring her angelic features. "I don't know what the hell you're high on, but it looks good on you."

I hug my arms around my waist, because I know all too well.

And I think it might be love.

We don't talk during the car ride to Sydney. Dani blasts music from some R&B radio station that rocks the car, and I pretend that guys singing about bitches and hoes doesn't kind of make me shudder.

When we finally pull up at the flower market, I get a space close to the door. It's almost empty at this time of day—the serious florists come in around dawn. Me being part of such a small-scale operation, I can afford to get here late. After all, flowers are only a small part of Colin's basket business.

The car shudders to a stop, and the music dies with it. Silence cloaks us, and I chance a quick look at my sister. Big round sunglasses blink my reflection back at me.

"Coffee?" she asks.

"Sure." I open the car door and Dani does the same as we walk toward the giant warehouse-style building. We stop at a vendor who's set up a coffee stand outside, and Dani orders a double-shot espresso, while I order a chai latte, because old habits die hard and I've drunk that most of my life.

We walk inside and that familiar smell hits me, a mix of every natural kind of floral scent nature can create all at once. It's fresh and rich, and hints at the exotic nature of some of the flowers on display today.

My skin prickles and I pull off my cardigan. The winter sun means it's quite humid in here. Orange blossoms to my left droop in agreement.

With every step, the question is on the tip of my tongue. How can I ask her about the drugs and the drinking? Will she open up? Will she *stop*?

But every time I go to give in, every time I consider confronting her, I think of Joel. Think of what he'd tell me to do.

And I stay quiet. Because maybe I need to be her friend first, her keeper second.

I take my pick of flowers, and a few times Dani even voices an opinion. Half an hour later we head to the car, our arms laden with nature's best.

Once the vehicle starts up, Dani turns down the radio. I raise an eyebrow in question, studying her. Waiting.

"Do you want to talk about last night?" She looks out the window.

I breathe a sigh of relief. *Finally.* "If you're ready."

They're three of the hardest words I've ever said.

Dani doesn't speak for a moment. Have I blown it? Has she seen through my pretence?

But as I pull out of the parking lot, she opens her mouth and starts to speak.

"I never meant to let it get that far." Her voice is small, distant, and when I chance a look at her, her gaze is directed out the window. "I just ... I needed the escape. To not be here anymore."

"Dan ..." I place my hand on her knee and squeeze.

"Yeah. I know. Stupid, huh?" She looks at me out from under her eyelashes.

"Not stupid." I shake my head. "Just ... you mean so much to all of us. Don't write yourself off."

She shrugs, and looks at her hands that twist over themselves in her lap. "Sometimes I just feel worthless. It's stupid, I know."

"If you want to feel desired, all you have to do is look at Zy."

"He doesn't like me like that! I don't know how many times I have to tell you ..." She pauses, and then sucks in a deep breath, whooshing it out in one go. "Anyway, I promise I'm done. I was just dabbling. It's fine. Nothing to worry about." She offers up a sweet smile.

And for now, I decide to take it.

FIFTEEN

When you suspect your sister is on drugs, every minute detail becomes mega. Every jaw clench, every finger twitch, every lingering touch on your skin.

Even the speed with which she stuffs brochures into bags comes under suspicion.

"Relax, Ellie." Dani smiles and rolls her eyes at me. "I promise I'm clean."

My jaw drops. "How did you know what I—"

She leans forward and touches my temple, right beside my left eye. "Here." Then she points to my jaw. "And here. You're an open book, Sis."

I shrug and pick up another flyer for Cancer Australia and place it in yet another bag. "I just worry."

"It's not like I'm an addict." Dani smiles. She pauses and takes one of the mint lollies that was supposed to go in the bag, unwrapping it and popping it between her lips instead. "You know how much Mum pays for this, and I don't have an extra job, like you. She only gives us enough money to get by without embarrassing her."

"You're right." One side of my lips raises in a smile. "Neither of us earn enough to support a full-blown drug habit."

For some reason, the thought comforts me, until I remember my current predicament. Colin. Work. Just another thing to add to my list of reasons to stress.

The door pushes open and Mum breezes in. Her shoes click against the tiled floor. "My little worker bees, getting things done."

"Ellie ate a lolly," Dani says.

I glare at her. "What are you? Twelve?"

Mother levels me with her gaze. "Ellie, did you really?"

I roll my eyes. "For the record, no. But I … I kind of want to talk to you about something." I pause and look at Dani. Her face is white as the tiled floor beneath us. "Actually, I want to talk to you both."

"Ellie …" Dani warns. Mum sits on the white chair between us, folding her long tanned legs.

Dani's knuckles whiten as she grabs her knees. Her eyes plead with mine to give her a chance.

It's either the stupidest or the smartest thing I've ever done, but I take it. I give her what she's asking for.

"It's about Colin."

"Colin?" Mum frowns. "What about him?"

"I think he's been … well, this sounds weird." I shift my weight from one leg to the other. "I think he's been hitting on me."

Silence.

Then Dani's laugh is so loud, it echoes around the room. She's borderline hysterical. "You think … you think …" She clutches at her chest.

I frown, and press my lips together. "What's so funny?"

Mum laughs too. My stomach twists and I bite my lip. Maybe I overreacted. Maybe he didn't—

No.

He did.

"Ellie, Colin is a forty-something man who has a wife," Dani says through her mirth. "Trust me, you're a babe, but he is so not interested."

"He touched my breasts!" I say.

That shuts them up. Mum's lips part, her frown drawn thick between her eyes. "He touched you?"

"Well, he says it was an accident. It was coming out of a hug. Like this." I lean forward and show them what I mean on Dani.

"Seriously, that's nothing. It was probably an accident," she says, and Mum nods along.

"That's hardly assault, darling." She pushes up to her feet. "Now that you've finished with your little story, I'm going to get back to it."

"I'm going to quit."

She stops walking and turns back to me. Cold brown eyes narrow, and I shrink into myself. I might have learned to stand up to Colin, but fighting your family is an entirely different matter.

"You will not accuse my longest friend of sexual misconduct." I lean forward to hear her hiss. "You can quit; get another job; so long as you're supporting yourself, I don't care. But do not test me on this, Eleanor."

The echo of her heels leaving the room throbs through me.

As Dani and I continue to stuff paper into bags, self-doubt races through me. When your family doesn't believe you, what hope is left?

"Another day, another dollar." Hope brushes some imaginary dust from the lapel of my blazer.

"Thanks again for meeting me here, and bringing me this," I say, gesturing to the white flowing skirt and navy top I'm wearing. I didn't have time to make it home to change in between setting up and the event itself.

I glance up at the well-lit venue in front of us. It's a bar in the heart of the city full of warm yellow light. The hum of voices filters out onto the pavement, as do the unmistakeable sounds of a swing band. Glasses chirrup against each other in gestures of *salute*, and the sound of laughter travels out to us.

"It's the least I can do." Hope interrupts my thoughts. "After that stunt a few nights ago with Colin ..."

"Don't worry about it." I shrug her off. If only she knew the half of it. "It's nothing major. Nothing I can't handle. And besides ... I guess it at least proved to me one thing. That Joel really is interested."

"Ha!" Hope snorts. "As if there was ever any doubt." She links her arm through mine, and gestures toward the brick building ahead. "Now come on."

I follow Hope's lead. Her black bodycon dress hugs her figure, and her steps are tinier than the ones my white tutu-style number allows me to make. We walk up to the bouncer and the bored-looking girl at the door.

"Names?" she asks, her gaze not straying from her clipboard.

"Ellie Mayfield plus one. I was here a few hours ago, setting up."

The girl scans her list then draws a big tick next to my name.

"Head on in." She gestures to the room behind her.

"Thanks."

Hope and I walk into the room and beeline for the champagne glasses that are doing the rounds. As soon as we have them in hand, my shoulders relax. It's only a two-hour event, after all. How bad can it be?

"So, things are going well with Joel, right?" she asks. Two guys walk by us with bodies that look sculpted to perfection under their streamlined suits. Hope's eyes follow them like a kid in a candy store.

"Yeah." I smile, a glow warming my insides at the thought. "Despite a situation with Dani, and Colin's interruption the other night, things ... things are great."

"You should have invited him here."

"No, he had some work thing on." I shrug. "We might meet at the beach later, though."

"Oh, moonlight beach walk. How romantic!" Hope smiles, a mischievous glint to her eyes. "So what does Mr Sex On A Stick do?"

"I don't actually know," I say, trying to sound more confident than I feel. "He's a student and he said he does work for some corporation in the city?"

"Cool," Hope says, nodding. "He—"

"You're dressed appropriately." Mother's voice sparkles as she approaches our duo. She's glamorous as always in a beige pantsuit, her red lips perfectly painted on.

"Let the air kisses commence." Hope quietly giggles, and I shoot her a mischievous smile.

"Your sister changed early and is over there. Go talk to her, please." Mother points to a corner of the room where a group of suits are clustered. Of course. It makes perfect sense that Dani is in the centre of them.

Mother leans closer, and hisses in my ear, "And make sure you drop all talk of this Colin nonsense."

"On it." I smile my plastic smile, and place my empty glass on a passing waiter's tray. My family has no faith in me. How can I smile and be on display here for the next two hours?

At least, at the end there's Joel, I tell myself. My reward. My escape from all this madness.

My phone vibrates in my purse, and I rifle through and bring it out.

Joel: What's long and hard?

I bite my lip to stop from laughing and tap out a quick response.

Ellie: I don't know, Joel. I hope whatever it is, though, that it also has mad skills.

I pocket the cell, but as soon as it's safe inside my purse it vibrates, and I pull it out again.

Joel: The time we spend apart. What did you think I was talking about?

I snort as Hope and I walk through the crowd. When we reach my sister, Dani does the standard air kiss to both Hope and myself before introducing us to her fans. "Hope, Ellie, this is everybody. Everybody, this is Hope and Ellie."

A bevy of *hi* and *hello*s greet us, and I smile politely and nod to the circle of well-dressed guys and girls surrounding her. It's a far cry from the man she met in the parking lot only two nights ago.

"So what do you two do for a living?" one of the guys asks. "Are you a student, like your sister?"

"I'm just a slave to the Mayfield empire." *Plastic smile. Just keep swimming.*

The group continues to chat, and Dani seems to keep her drinking in check. I'm just finished my third glass of wine when the microphone crackles, indicating it's time for the speeches. We all turn and shuffle toward the makeshift stage someone has erected in the back of the room, next to the bar.

"Thank you all so much for joining us tonight, ladies and gentlemen," the emcee, a man who looks to be in his mid-thirties, announces. "I'm Jim Doherty, and I'm from Cancer Australia, and I just wanted to thank you all so much for coming and donating your time, and of course, your money, to this very worthy cause."

"Should we sneak out?" Hope whispers, and I bite my lip and nod. Maybe I can even catch up with Joel early. Call on him at his mysterious place-of-work.

We push our way through the crowd, heads down, trying to avoid obvious detection. We're right at the front door when it happens. I look up to apologise to the tall man I need to push my way around and am greeted with a very familiar set of eyes. A very familiar face.

"H ... hi," I say to Mr Henley. I tilt my head. What the hell is he doing here?

He frowns as he looks down at me. "Ellie. I didn't expect to see you here."

"It's a surprise to see you too."

Time slows down. Every detail is amplified. The clink of champagne glasses. The scent of perfume. The rushing of blood in my ears.

There are a million reasons Henry could be here. He's not short of money. He could be a benefactor. He could know the owner of the bar.

But one reason makes all too much sense. It puts together hundreds of little clues that have niggled at me since Joel came back into my life.

One reason chokes me with fear.

"I can't," I say, shaking my head. I push past him, heading toward the door, Hope hot on my heels.

The emcee announces his special guest speaker.

I trip, smashing into a waiter.

Glasses crash to the floor, and the strong smell of wine filters through the space. Liquid splashes up my legs. Every head in the room turns to look at me, but I don't see them.

I only see Joel, standing on stage.

The *special guest*.

SIXTEEN

Silence cloaks the room. All eyes are on the stage. On the man I'm falling in love with all over again.

My jaw is somewhere near my stiletto-shod feet.

"I ..." Joel starts to speak, then closes his mouth. It's as if he can't find the words, and all I'm wondering is *why the hell is he up there* and *what kind of job is this?*

But somewhere inside me, I already know. It's in the weight of my heart that suddenly feels like a dumbbell as it thuds around my chest.

Because why would the special guest speaker at a cancer fundraiser be a twenty-year-old guy?

Unless that guy had cancer.

Still, despite knowing this, I hold out hope. Because maybe it's his father, or mother, or someone else he's close to. Not that that makes things any better, but it seems much more preferable to imagining that the man I have fallen so hard for could be sick.

But now as I look at him, the suit making my hands itch to take it off him, I notice things I hadn't paid attention to before. His defined cheekbones, that once I thought looked supermodel sexy, now emphasise how thin his face is. How *gaunt*. How skin I'd once thought was creamy, is now pale. *Sickly*.

"No," I whisper, and shake my head. Because please, no. Not him.

"I ..." Joel clears his throat again, and the emcee steps up beside him, whispering something in his ear. Joel shakes his head and the man walks away, leaving Joel Henley, my Joel Henley, to face the music and the microphone alone.

"My name is Joel Henley. A lot of you know me, but for those who don't, I'm going to tell you a little something about my story," he says, and a few people offer up claps of appreciation. I'm moved to the side as the wait staff clean up the colossal mess I've just made. I barely register the movement. The only other person in the room is *him*.

"I was diagnosed with cancer when I was sixteen."

The words cut straight to my heart. Sixteen. That was when he left. When he picked up and disappeared, cutting all ties.

He thought he was dying.

Still, I find some sliver of hope. Because maybe he's cured. Maybe he's been through chemo and radiotherapy, and all those other crazy treatments, and come out the other side. Perhaps he's the poster boy for cancer fundraising because look, it worked on him.

But then I think of my father.

I know the story of cancer all too well.

It's a book that wrote our family's future.

Joel continues to speak, and every time another line comes out of his mouth, it's another dagger to my heart. Words like remission. Words like returned.

Words like *forever*.

And then he says the one line I've been dreading since he started to speak. The one line that puts a taint on everything we've been through, because while I've been celebrating the birth of our relationship, he's been saying goodbye to life.

"When I first found out, my father and I moved to Sydney. To get the best treatment available. To do everything we could."

The words taunt me, teasing at the seams of my soul. No. Not him.

"We fought, and we won, and then … and then it spread to my brain."

Quiet waves of sympathy ripple around the room, then silence. You could hear a pin drop.

"And after several rounds of treatment, they worked out it was inoperable. The position it's in—you can't reach it with a scalpel. There was nothing we could do," Joel says. He lets out a breath, and my heart goes with it. "When they told me I only had another year or so to live, I decided I wanted to do more. Thanks to the good people at Cancer Australia—Milo, Jo, Cath—I was able to submit a list of twenty-one things I wanted to do before I turned twenty-one. Before I … well …" He trails off. He looks so lost for a moment. People this young and this beautiful aren't supposed to die. A woman next to me wipes a tear from her eye. "They have covered the costs of around fifty per cent of the things I wanted to do. And I had some pretty pricey items in there." Joel jokes, but it falls flat.

Hot laps.

Acting on stage.

Each memory is a ball of lead, rolling in my stomach.

"So they've helped make my last few months a bit more bearable. And that's why I encourage all of you here today to give, and give generously. Because I'm one of the lucky ones. I'm not leaving behind a kid, and I'm old enough to know that—well, shit happens in this life. It's how you deal with it that counts."

His words etch themselves into my heart. And then they break it.

The boy standing on stage watches me with wide eyes, and the girl who fell in love with him breaks inside of me. She just *breaks*.

"A big round of applause for Joel Henley," the emcee says, taking the microphone and gesturing to Joel as if he's a prize to be won on a round of *Sale of the Century*. "If that doesn't encourage you to dig, and dig deep, I don't know what will. Now, let me introduce ..."

He keeps talking, but I can't hear a word he says. Because the boy I love is running through the audience, pushing past well-wishers to get to me.

And the fear that's been swirling around in my body finally takes flight. It transforms into energy, and I run.

And hope like hell this is some nasty dream.

SEVENTEEN

The cold night air assaults me as I fly down the street. I kick off my heels when I reach the corner, grabbing them in one of my hands and turning toward the wharves.

My feet burn as I run across the gravel. Each cut is like a balm to my soul, because right now I need to feel this pain, this physical outlet for my own internal grief.

"Ellie!"

I hear my name in the distance, but I keep going, turning down yet another street. My lungs burn from the brute force of the cold night air, and my cheeks and nose are ice. It doesn't matter. None of it matters.

Shit!

I turn left around a building, and that's when it catches up to me. My body is walloped with this huge hit of despair and heartache and pain, a pain so deep it vibrates within my body. Bile lurches in my throat, and I stagger to the bin on the corner and empty the contents of my stomach. Acid coats my mouth. Tears freeze on my cheeks, and I wonder when I started crying, and when it will ever stop.

"Why ...?" I sob, my body shaking. I stagger to the corner of a building and punch the wall with my fist. The impact is dull, an echo of a pain I can't feel. A pain that's nothing compared to the ache that's welling inside me.

I cry, a raw, primal sound, and at some point two arms wrap around me. Warm. Strong.

Safe.

I hiccough my way to cohesion, and then push against his chest. "No," I choke. Though my tears, his face is somehow even more beautiful, the streetlight spotlighting him like an actor in a play. "No." It's weaker.

Softer.

Giving in.

"I'm so sorry, Ellie." He pulls me tight against his chest, so tight I feel it rise and shakily fall with every breath. He's hurting too, and somehow I hate that more. I hate that more than every ounce of pain I feel. "I ... it's why I left without a word, all those years ago. I left you, left my friends—everyone. I even closed all my social media accounts. It was just too much."

It answers a doubt that had been niggling in my mind, but now that I know the truth, I'd have rather it remained a question. Some things are better left unanswered.

There's one question burning in my mind, and I know I have to ask. Know I need the answer before I can even begin to process this monstrosity called life.

"How long?"

Two simple words.

They say so much without saying a damn thing.

"The doctors can't agree. Things were looking good, but the latest—"

"How. Long?" I seethe, but it's also a plea. A plea for him to be wrong. For this all to be a cruel, lonely dream.

"A year. Tops."

This time, when I suck in a breath it scrapes down my throat. A year? That's ... "Three hundred and sixty-five days."

My shoes drop to the ground, a dull thud that seems to come from far away, a fall from hands not mine.

"Yeah." Joel nods, and a fleeting pain crosses his features before he schools it again. And damn it, I want to be strong like him. I want to be this man, this model of good grace about what the future holds, but I'm giving it everything I have to not lie on the pavement, kicking and screaming about how unfair life is.

"Is there a treatment? A special ..."

His shaking head cuts me off. "They've tried everything. I've already had it better than most. And thanks to Cancer Australia—"

"You didn't know I'd be there tonight?" I beseech him with my eyes.

"No. I do these speaking things for them all the time. I didn't know they'd hired your Mum; she's from the EC, not the city." He licks his lower lip, and gazes down at me. "I would never have wanted you to find out ... like that."

"Or did you just not want me to find out?"

He wrestles with his answer. "I ..." He runs a hand over his head, his traitorous skin, and then looks back at me. "A part of me wanted you to never have to know. To never look at me with the pity everyone else does."

"Pity?" I ask, my eyes bugging. "So what? You were just not going to show up on one of our dates one day? And then what? I'd see your funeral notice in the fucking paper?" I shove at his chest, and he falters.

"I would have said something!"

"Would you?" I'm on a roll now. My devastation turns to anger. Anger that he didn't tell me. Anger that I don't know how to deal with this. Anger that two people in my life I've loved have been touched by this bitch named Cancer.

But most of all?

Anger that there's nothing I can do.

And nothing I try can ever change that.

"I ... it's why I tried to avoid getting involved in the first place. Why I was so hesitant, even though you're so ..." Joel steps closer. He takes my shaking fists and holds them to his face, kissing my knuckles as if they're made of glass. But it's him who's made of glass. Him who is so inherently breakable. "Ellie, I ... I think I love—"

"Don't." I sob the word out, and press one finger to his lips. They're soft, too soft. For some reason, this breaks me all over again. "I can't ..."

"I'm sorry." Tears shine down Joel's cheeks, the streetlamp highlighting them in mockery. Some are his, some are mine—all are salty evidence of this deep wound that's been cut open.

It hurts, hurts so damn much that I can't take it anymore. So I do what I do best in these situations.

I run.

And I don't look back.

At first, I expect him to chase me. Want him to, even. But then he doesn't.

And somehow, that leaves me feeling even more hurt than I had been when I found out.

Joel Henley has cancer. My Joel.

And soon he won't be around anymore.

My feet pound the pavement, tears drying as the cool night air whips around my face. Blonde curls stick to my cheeks, dance in front of my eyes, and I hurt. I hurt where my arms have rubbed against the stupid tulle of my dress. I hurt where the wind has whipped my lips.

But most of all, I hurt right in the gaping hole in my chest where my heart used to be.

I turn corner after corner, but nothing looks familiar. Buildings, apartments, pubs and shopfronts—they all blur into one unidentifiable mess. I glance up at the street sign on the corner next to me, needing some clue on how to get out of here. My hand digs through my handbag, searching for my phone. I tap out a text to Hope when I remember—my shoes are on a street corner some twenty-minute jog from here.

I thud my forehead against the red bricks in front of me. The dull ache makes me grit my teeth, but it somehow feels like release. Because no one should have to feel the pain I'm feeling without showing a scar. No one should have to hide hurt that eats up all of your insides.

I tap out a text and crumble to the ground. Dirt spikes against my bare legs, but I don't care. I feel like Cinderella, only I've completely missed the damn ball. Because it wasn't supposed to happen like this. I've shown up to the wrong event.

Somewhere farther along the dark alley, a man coughs. It's a throaty hacking noise, and on any other day, at any other time I would have got up and walked away. Today, I stay. Nothing can hurt me now.

Feet shuffle along the street and then a pair of worn canvas shoes are in front of me, stopped right at my legs. Beside them, the wheels of a shopping trolley roll to a halt. From here, I can see the plastic bags, the loose clothes—most likely everything this man owns. It's the caravan of the unfortunate.

"I don't have any money," I say, only my voice is so hoarse from the raw bursts of emotion that I barely get the words out. The stench of human waste filters through my nose, and I pray that he's not about to pee on me. Because there's not a lot that would make me feel worse than I do right now, but I have to admit that that would be up there.

"'Ere."

A hand with dirt-lined nails passes down a bottle inside a brown paper bag.

I eye it for a moment, thinking what a stupid idea this is. How dangerous drinking something out of this man's hands could be. He could have some kind of contagious disease, have spiked it with some kind of date-rape drug, or even pissed in it, for all I know. This is definitely not a safe move.

Then I think what safe has done for me so far.

I clasp the bottle with both hands and bring it to my lips. I tip my head back, and the strong scent of whiskey assaults me even before the liquid hits my lips. It burns my tongue, brings a fire back to my throat, then heats my chest and my stomach.

I drink long, and I drink hard, big gulping swallows that speed through my body. The cheap alcohol mixes in my gut, and my stomach lurches.

It's all the indication I need to stop. I wipe my lips with one hand and raise the bottle toward my saviour. A round face shadowed by wiry grey hair looks down at me, eyes a wicked black in the dark. "'Ave some more."

I swallow, and look at the bottle again.

My knees are starting to feel ... numb.

God, I want to feel numb.

I bring the bottle back to my mouth, but just as I do, the whiskey rebels against my body. Excess saliva coats my mouth, and I drop the bottle, stagger to my feet and hurl into the nearest bin for the second time tonight. It's acidic. It stabs at my throat.

THE TWENTY-ONE

But it's still got nothing on my heart.

"Fuckin' weirdo." The homeless man picks up the bottle and shuffles down the street, pushing his trolley full of belongings.

For some reason, that makes me laugh, but there's no mirth in my outburst, just a kind of lunacy.

A taxi pulls up to the street corner and Hope flies out, the door left open behind her. She wraps her arms around me, even though I probably smell like spew, and whiskey, and heartache.

"I'm so sorry," she whispers in my ear. She pulls back and studies me. I dread to think what she must see. Messy hair, reddened nose and cheeks, and eyes that even a panda would find offensive. But for some reason, she doesn't leave me there in the middle of the street. "Come on."

She links her arm through mine and walks me to the waiting car, where she ushers me inside. I slide across the leather seat and latch my seatbelt through.

"She spews in here, there's a cleaning surcharge." The cabbie points to a sign above his head that details all the information anyone could want to know about the kind of fees one might pay if they dirtied his car.

"Got it. Emerald Cove, please," Hope says, and then puts her hand over and squeezes my knee.

My phone starts to ring, that damn "Drops of Jupiter" song, and it makes me want to cry all over again. When I was outside with Colin the other night, Joel must have assigned that song to be his personal ring-tone. Who else would it be?

I hit cancel, then turn my phone off. I can't talk to him right now. It hurts too much.

In a soft voice, Hope says, "I know this sucks, honey. I know." She bites her lip, and then looks me square in the eye. "But I promise, it's going to get easier. Better."

I nod, but my eyes are vacant, my head a million miles from here.

Because it's not going to get easier.

I just don't see how it could.

EIGHTEEN

When my father died, I didn't stop. I kept going. I had to look after my sister and my mother. I had to organise the funeral and be strong.

Now? Now, I don't stop, but I'm not really here, either. I'm lost. I'm so far gone, I don't know how to find myself again. Because the man I love is going to leave me.

For the second time in my life.

He calls, at first every ten minutes, then every hour, then twice a day. I don't answer. I have nothing to say. Nothing will ever be able to quite articulate *I'm sorry* and *why* and *it's not fair* all at once. And that's not even covering the big one.

Please don't go.

Cancer is a vicious bitch, and she's already taken the man who was once the most important person in the world to me. She plucks out her victims and gnaws at their being, eats at their soul. They're chosen without rhyme or reason, and just when you think you have the nature of it down, that you've beaten the beast which controls you—

Snap.

She breaks you in two.

You breathe your last breath.

I don't want Joel to end up like that.

And that is the crux of it. I'm a horrible person. I'm going to Hell. Because I've already been hurt so much that now, the idea of willingly putting myself back into a situation like that again? Loving someone who is going to die scares the ever-loving shit out of me.

In romance novels, the heroine always does anything for love. She'll throw herself under a train if it means being with the man of her dreams.

I want to throw myself under that train. I'm just petrified that after I do, no one will be around to scrape me up off the tracks. I'm the one who always picks up the pieces. I can't break again.

And shutting him out of my life now will be easier than losing him later.

I throw myself into work, stuffing paper bags as if my life depends on it. When I show up to work at the hot-air balloon field an hour early, Colin raises an eyebrow, but he doesn't say a word. When I place the baskets in order then stumble as a wave of grief hits me, he stands and holds me close.

I don't feel the nausea I did days ago.

I don't feel a damn thing.

One week later, I'm shut in my room. I haven't left it to do anything aside from work. My body is a constant fight between *how can I keep loving him* and *how can I walk away?* I'm tired, so damn tired of fighting. So damn tired of it all.

Hope and Lia have come and gone, both trying to get me to talk, to deal with it all, but it's not that simple. This isn't just another romance novel. This is the story of my life.

Then my door swings open, flying back to hit the wall. My head jerks up from where I'm reading on my bed.

"Get your arse up."

Dani.

"I don't feel—"

"I'm not taking no for an answer." Dani strides over to me and pinches the corner of my shirt as if it's dirty laundry. "And change. We're going clubbing."

I look up at her. Clubbing is the second-last thing I feel like doing right now.

The last thing is leaving the house.

"I'm not clubbing with you." The words sound foreign to me, my throat hoarse. Maybe it's because speaking isn't something I've done a lot of recently.

Dani huffs out a sigh and flops down beside me on the bed. "You are clubbing with me." She pauses, then picks up a strand of my hair and lets it fall limply to my back. "I don't know who you are and what you've done with my nerdy sister, but this"—she gestures up and down my body with her finger—"simply will not fly. I get it. The guy you were dating is dying, but guess what? Shit things happen. You have to deal with them anyway."

I rub across my eyes. The lids are heavy, so heavy, and all I want to do is sleep. "I am dealing with it."

She shakes her head. "No. You're doing what you did with Dad."

I blink my eyes and shoot up from where I've been lying, my book falling to the floor. Goosebumps prickle on my skin. "What do you mean?"

"I mean, you're shutting off. Closing down." Dani shakes her head. "Come out with me. We'll have a few drinks, hang out … just get out of the house. It'll do you a world of good."

The words sink in around me. It's the last thing I feel like doing.

"Come on, Ellie." Dani reaches out and gives my arm a squeeze. "I know you're strong, and this is your thing, but … how is being strong working out for you so far?"

They're all the words it takes to rip me out from between the sheets.

"Four tequila shots and two vodka sodas, please." Dani slams a fifty down on the counter, right in front of her cleavage revealed in her super low-cut top, and I raise a brow at her. I don't ask how she got the money. For once, I don't want to think. I don't want to be responsible. I just want to *be*.

Is there anything so wrong with that?

"Coming right up." The bartender gives her a wink and walks away, collecting some glasses as he goes

"Isn't that a lot?" I chew my lip. I want to forget, sure, but I'm not a big drinker. I don't want to end up in hospital.

Hospital.

Where Joel will end up.

Where Joel will die.

"Actually, forget I said anything." I paste on a smile, just like I pasted on some bright red lipstick and smoky black eyeliner a few hours earlier. According to Dani, if you look good, you feel good.

I'm just waiting for the second half of the promise to kick in.

"You are going to have fun tonight, missy." Dani pokes me in the ribs, a wicked glint lighting her eyes. "They say the best way to get over a guy is to get under another one. So …"

"I think they also say that's the best way to get an STD." I poke my tongue out, but manage a laugh.

"Whatever."

Four shot glasses thud against the counter, and the bartender places four wedges of lemon and four tiny packets of salt, like you'd get at a fish and chip shop, on the wooden countertop. He twists the top off a bottle of tequila and starts pouring from high above the glass, his arm muscles bulging underneath his tight black tee. Stubble lines his jaw, and he has that whole Mediterranean sex god thing going on.

You know. If you like that kind of thing.

If you're not hung up on a guy with soul-destroying blue eyes.

"So what brings you ladies out tonight?" he asks, as the liquid falls into the final glass.

"My sister is broken-hearted." Dani looks prettily at me, and then bats her eyelashes at the bartender. Her pupils seem funny, as if they're smaller. Or maybe bigger. I frown. Is that a drug thing?

The bartender responds by pulling out a fifth shot glass and filling it with tequila, too. "Well then." He raises his glass. "Commiserations to the poor sucker who doesn't have a hottie like you in his life any longer."

Dani rips open her salt packet and licks along her hand, never breaking eye contact with the bartender. For just a second, his suave veneer drops as her tongue meets her skin, but he covers it up and brandishes a cocky smile again.

My sister pours the salt onto her hand, then takes mine and pours salt along that, too. Thank God she didn't try to lick it. I might have died.

We both lick our salt. It's grainy and intense on my tongue. I hold my glass and get ready. I guess this is it. This is what it's like to grieve normally.

"To Ellie." Dani raises her glass.

"To Ellie." The bartender brings his glass to ours, and when they connect, a sliver of tequila runs down the back of my hand. The other two bring their glasses to their lips, knocking the potent liquid back, but I just stare at mine for a moment. Is this really the best idea? Is drinking going to make Joel any less on my mind?

His eyes, burning into mine.

His lips, crashing against my skin.

Memory flashes into my mind in vivid Technicolor, and it's all the prompt I need. I take the shot and knock it back. I relish in the burn as it slides down my throat. I crave the pain that flames through my lungs.

Some things you'll always remember.

They're what I'm drinking to forget.

I slam my glass back on the counter and take the next one, not pausing to suck on the lemon wedge or restack my salt.

"To the truth." I knock the alcohol back, and it burns just the same as the first. It burns in a way that lets me feel something that's not just heartache. And for that, I am eternally grateful.

For that, I think tequila is my new best friend.

"Two more!" The glass lands on the counter.

Dani giggles and does her own shot, placing it down beside mine. "Easy, tiger. You don't want to burn out too quickly."

She's wrong.

That's all I want.

Still, I take the vodka soda when the bartender hands it over, and Dani leads me deep into the crowd of people moving on the dance floor. Sweaty bodies slide against sweaty bodies, hips pressing against hips, hands running over backs, bums and boobs. The music is seductive with a thrumming bass line that pulses through my body.

Joel.

His laugh.

"I'll catch you if you fall."

"Hey!" Dani yells into my ear, her hand hot on my shoulder. "Forget about him. You got this."

I pull back and look into her golden brown eyes that glint against the flashing strobe lights. Her face, so similar to my own, bears a soft smile. She raises her glass, her hand steady. "We have each other. That's enough. Remember?"

My own words to her echo in my ears. I said that so many times when Dad first died.

I suck up the vodka soda through my straw in one long hit. It doesn't burn like the tequila—I barely taste it at all. All I know is that when I'm done, my knees tingle. My hips tingle.

And I'm one step closer to numbing the pain.

"Go Ellie!" Dani grins and knocks back some of her own drink, then starts moving her body to the music. I join her, and soon we're dancing in amidst the sea of people.

The words to a familiar song become me. They writhe through my body, pull up my emotions and suck me dry. Soon every *I love you* is my I love you, soon every *I hate you* is my condemnation of the boy who broke my heart. The boy who stole my life.

Sweat sticks my tank top to my back, and my zip-up leather pants feel looser around the waist. For the briefest moment I wonder if it's so damn hot in here I've lost weight, then heat presses to my back. A frisson of electricity fires over my arse, and my hands fly back to clasp my zip.

It's done up. *Now.*

I spin around. Zy stands there, a self-satisfied grin on his face.

"Really?" I fold my arms across my chest, then stop when I see his gaze drop to where I know my cleavage peaks out of my top.

"Just making sure these other guys didn't see …" *Please don't go into details.* "Your black lacy G. I got your back."

I press my eyes shut, and a part of me dies.

And then, *dies.*

Because that's all it takes to shock you from the present to reality. One little word.

One little heartache.

"Go dance with my sister." I flick my hand and gesture Zy toward Dani, a scowl twisting my lips. Dickhead. What an obnoxious, self-entitled, egotistical—

The beat of the bass line changes to an upbeat Taylor Swift number. *Shake It Off.* Oh! I love this song.

I bounce my body up and down, my movements reflecting the lyrics, and for some reason Dani laughs at me, but I make like Tay-Tay says and shake it off. I don't need her judgment. I don't need her pity.

After a while, Dani raises her hand to her mouth in the unmistakable symbol for *more drinks,* and I nod and follow her obediently to the bar. We wait in line with Zy and a throng of others, five-people deep, and when we finally muscle our way to the front, it's an achievement. I pull my credit card from my wallet, the one I used to monitor oh-so-carefully, and slam it on the counter.

"Nine tequila shooters, and three vodka sodas," I say.

The bartender, the same one as before, furrows his brow at me, and leans in closer, as if he can't hear me.

"I said, nine tequila—"

"We're after nine tequila shots and three vodka sodas, please." Dani smiles, her jaw ticking, and it seems she must speak his language because he nods and gets to work preparing glasses.

"What's wrong with him?" I ask. The bar bears the entirety of my body weight. Somehow, I'm all chest, arms and head. How did that happen? When did I lose weight in my legs?

"Take it easy, Eleanor." Zy's hand rests on my arm, and I flinch.

"Hands off, you." I brush away his fingers, but they're not there. Were they ever? Did I imagine him just touching me?

Zy's hands fly in the air beside his head, and I keep a close eye on them. *I'm watching you, hands.*

"I'm just saying, take it easy. I don't want you getting hurt." His face clouds with a shadow of darkness.

Sickness lurches in my stomach. Anger lurches in my throat and I open my mouth, prepared to spew it all out, to retch it all over him when—

"Ellie, right?"

I spin around.

She's tall. Brown hair. Brown eyes. Pale skin.

You'd think she'd be so ordinary, but she's not. She has this fight for life burning deep within her.

And a best friend whose heart is entangled with mine.

"Hi."

She nods at me, and narrows her eyes. "It's Fiona."

As soon as the name rings in my ears, I know it. I know it as well as I know my own birthday. As well I know my own address.

"You're seeing my friend, Joel." She tucks an errant curl of chocolate hair behind her ear. "Well, you *were* seeing."

The words cut me like a knife. Even though it was a choice I made, it hurts so bad.

"We're camping at the Basin tomorrow," Fiona yells

in my ear. Her breath is hot—everything is hot. I pull my tank from my sweaty body. God, it's hot in here. "You should come."

I balk. "I can't."

"Why not?"

"Hey, your stupid friend"—Dani pokes Fiona in the chest—"broke her heart, you dumb bitch."

Fiona raises her eyebrows, and her gaze runs from Dani's toes to her face, to her jaw clicking, back and forth, and back. "Okay, lady," she says. "Maybe try chewing some gum or something." She ruffles in her handbag and produces a pack of Extra. "It might stop you from chewing off your face."

"Fuck off." Dani flicks the pack and sends it catapulting through the air into the throng of sweaty, writhing bodies to the side of us. "I'm outta here."

She grabs Zy's wrist and then mine, and charges toward the dance floor.

I want to go. With every cell in my body, I want to follow my sister, because out of everybody I know, she is an expert when it comes to forgetting. She truly understands what it means to escape. To feel good.

And even though Fiona's words tick all the warning boxes lodged in my brain for drugs and danger and dumb-arse decisions, I follow.

Because I'm tired of playing the big sister for once.

We find a spot on the opposite side of the club, right next to the emergency exit doors. The three of us form a loose circle here, where the air is a little easier to breathe. Where everything is a little simpler to digest. We jump, we laugh, and for one tiny moment I'm not just a girl whose ex-boyfriend is going to die, or who's looking after her sister.

I'm Ellie Mayfield.

THE TWENTY-ONE

And I'm kind of enjoying that.

We dance, and when Dani asks me to come to the bathroom with her, I know exactly what it means. And even though I'm gone, so far gone that I can't quite feel my legs and all my thoughts blur into one big, beautiful rainbow of thought, I know I don't want to go with her. I know I want to remain on my own.

Zy looks at me then at Dani, as if trying to decide who he should stay with. I shake my head, laughing. Of course he should go with Dani.

He leaves, and I raise my arms up in the air and swirl my hips to the music, loving the way it owns me. How this DJ somehow understands every iota of emotion travelling through me at this very moment.

The song changes, and a sexier, dirtier beat vibrates through the room. I scoop my hips low, my hands travelling up my thighs, over my hips, up my waist.

And then, they're not my hands.

They're not my hands at all.

Lips press against my neck, and I'm so tightly strung. The sensation sizzles across my skin, and it reminds me of everything I want. Everything that's been burning within me for too long.

My arms reach up and wrap around his neck, his smooth skin. I grind my body back, loving the contact of skin against skin. Of man against woman. I inhale, and the scent of sweat and spicy aftershave hits—

This is not Joel.

It's not so much a realisation as a reminder. Because did I ever really think it was?

I spin around, and my hands run across short spiky hairs on the back of this man's neck. His face is pockmarked from acne, his eyes the wrong blue, his jaw the wrong set. His frame is bigger than Joel's cancer-ridden body.

Everything about him isn't Joel.

And yet, there's a part of me still hearing my sister's words from earlier. Wondering if the best way to get over the boy I thought I'd love forever is to get under another one. If life truly is that black and white.

The boy leans forward, and a whiff of vodka pauses my breathing before he passes my face and hits my ear.

"You're hot."

His breath is warm. Clammy, like a rainforest.

And worse? It smells like tuna. Cat food. Intense, fishy, and uncompromising.

From our up-close-and-personal position, I see the sweat marks that stain his white T-shirt.

Still, I try not to push him away. Because he could be what I need. He could be my salvation.

His hands wrap around my waist and he thrusts his hips toward mine. The jolt of our private parts making contact isn't so much an explosion as a train derailed. It's painful, clumsy, and not at all where you want it to go.

Sadly, my admirer doesn't seem to realise. "Yeah," he whispers into my hair, circling his hips. Much to my irritation, I can feel his growing erection blossoming against my thigh. A good indication of how short he falls, both in the height and the turn-on department.

He leans forward, his blue eyes locked with mine. I'm definitely boozy, but I'm starting to see the funny side of this. After all, he's managed to do one thing successfully tonight—convince me that going home with a random is the worst idea my sister has ever had.

I lock eyes with his, waiting for him to provide whatever other fascinating insight into my life he might have—

Lips crash against mine.

Big.

Warm.

Wet.

It's as if someone doused a lump of jelly in hot water, rubbed a frog's butt all over it, and then pressed it to my face.

I pull my hands up to shove against his chest and push him away when I'm jerked back, hands on either of my shoulders pulling me against a warm, hard chest.

"Fuck off," Zy growls. I turn to look up at him as he pushes me behind him and faces off with the guy who had tried to kiss me.

"Hey, man." The guy's hands fly in the air. "She started it."

"Don't take advantage of girls who—"

I tug on Zy's shirt. "He wasn't. I'm an idiot. I …" The room spins before me. I grab onto Zy's shirt again, this time to stop myself from falling.

He turns to me and grabs either arm, holding me up. "Are you okay?"

And in that moment, I know.

I know that kissing someone isn't going to make this go away. I know that hiding from it won't change anything either.

And I know that I'm going to be sick.

And I am, all over Zy's black skate shoes.

NINETEEN

The drive to the beach is deceptively easy. I spent a week trying to avoid him. Four days throwing myself into work to keep him off my mind. One night trying to forget he ever existed.

But when push came to shove, when I woke up feeling shady as all hell and hungover as a bitch, finding him was the only thing on my mind. Finding him was the only way I could think of sorting out my headspace.

Joel's always been able to get inside there. And I hate and love that all at once.

And that's why I park the car at Emerald Cove beach and reach over to the passenger seat for my handbag, then head toward the long bushwalk that leads to the top of the cliff and then down into the Basin beyond. It's a popular tourist attraction around here—people travel from the big smoke and even interstate to do the scenic walk, known for its whale-watching opportunities and idyllic private lagoon campsite.

I power-walk through the scrub, thankful that I wore my Docs as usual. Bushes scrape past the bare skin of my arms, but I push through. Push. *Push*. Because that's what I do now when I want something.

Insects buzz around my face, and I swat them away. I pull out my phone to try and call Joel, to check he's still at the campsite, but a dead screen stares back at me. I forgot to charge it after my big night out with Dani.

Zy put me in a cab shortly after I got kicked out for my little dance floor vomit incident, but he and Dani had decided to stay on.

Did she make it home okay?

I shake the thought away as if it's just another insect, and keep on walking. Of course she did; she's an expert at surviving. Besides, I left her with Zy.

Sweat dampens my skin, sticking my curls to my forehead, my white peasant shirt clinging to my sides. The trek uphill is steep, and my cheeks heat with every step. My limbs are weary from the physical effort it takes to climb this hill, and when the path opens up into a clearing, I lean up against a tree and wipe a hand against my forehead. Maybe I should have brought some water. Or worn less clothing.

But not once do I think I shouldn't have come.

Because no matter how hard this is, how so damn painful, I can't live without Joel. Not while he has another second in him. Not while my heart is so tied up in his.

It's the energy I need to keep going, and I push off the trunk and power up the hill. My arms swing by my sides, and when I pass the lookout at the top of the hill forty minutes later, I don't even slow down to admire the view.

As the path twists and turns and heads south, my pace picks up a little. I rush, and roll through a rough section, nearly turning my ankle when it skids on a rock. Branches lash against my skin leaving sharp stings in their wake. I run and I run, and it seems like hours before I reach the clearing at the bottom, but it's only been minutes.

I double over, my hands on my knees, my breath coming hard and fast from my mouth. A stitch cramps at my side, and even though I have no doubt I look like absolute shit, I don't care. Because right now, I need him, more than I've ever needed anything before.

As I stagger through the campground, happy families stop to look at me. One mother grabs her toddler and pulls him close to her side, as if he can catch my insanity from sight alone.

Then, I spot them.

Three multi-coloured tents are set up in a corner where the bush meets the still blue lagoon. I recognise Kohl's crazy hair first, the tightly wound curls bobbing up and down as he makes his way over to an Esky for a drink.

I steel myself, grit my teeth, and make my way over. It's time.

At the campsite, two guys recline in fold-up chairs, beers in hand. They laugh and talk loud, something about football and whose team is best. Fiona walks out from behind a tent in a super teeny-tiny bikini, and her jaw just about hits the dirty campsite ground when she eyes me. The boys spin around and take me in, their voices trailing off to silence.

It's nothing compared to Joel, though.

He walks out of the man-height tent, a smile in his eyes. "What's going on? What happened to ..." He trails off as soon as our eyes connect. The tension that frissons between us is palpable. He steps out of the tent and clears his throat. "Ellie."

Even though my cheeks are on fire, somehow this simple look from him manages to light the flames anew. And that's when I know. No matter how many obstacles are between us, I'm going to make every moment count. Because I can't walk away now.

Not when he's the best thing I have.

I should explain why I'm here. Tell him how scared I was. How scared I am. How when things got tough, I ran away from the pain, but I came back and chose him.

And that's the thing. The very crux of the matter.

It doesn't matter about the rest.

"I'll always choose you." The words leave my mouth and I run, slamming my body into his.

Joel doesn't hesitate. He wraps his arms around my waist, pulling my hips to his, our chests flush against each other. Our kiss is needy and desperate, two mouths searching for some sense of sanity in this crazy world, and a fire roars through me that's so different from the heat I normally feel. This is thrill. This is passion. This is *alive*.

"I love you," he breathes between our kisses, and my teeth bite against his lip as he turns parts of me on I didn't know could feel so damned erotic simply by being in close proximity to him. His hand grasps underneath my shirt and he walks us backward into the tent he just appeared from, shutting the zip behind us.

Within minutes, my top is off, his shirt is on the floor, and he steps away, breathless. *Breathless because of me.*

"God, you're beautiful."

After my hangover this morning, after all I've done, I should feel anything but. But this is Joel Henley. And everything he says makes sense.

Slowly, I reach behind me and unclasp my bra, exposing my chest. I bite my lip as the lacy material falls to the ground, and I'm completely exposed to his gaze.

"Ellie ..." His breath shudders, and he gives a small shake of his head. There's nothing but pure desire in his gaze, and it's a love story I could get used to. It's a story I want to complete.

Outside, the sound of some rock band blares from a stereo. Fiona yells something about swimming, and I know they're not going to come in. Because this moment is ours and ours alone. It belongs to us.

This time when our lips meet it's slower, more controlled. Joel's hands fumble with my fly and I fumble with his, and when his hands win the battle with my shorts and they fall to the floor, he rushes his hand to me and I writhe against him, alive with need. I'm no longer safe Ellie, Ellie in control, because the things he's doing to me turn me inside out and then some. Every cell in my body burns with desire, and I go from desperate with want to dangerously on edge. And then I combust all around him. All over him. Simply from his touch.

"God," I breathe, my head back, my knees week.

Joel just smiles and takes my hand, leading me to the blow-up bed in the back of the tent. He shucks off his jeans, and I take his cock in my hand and work it, thrilling at the way it hardens at my touch, at the way his eyes roll back in his head, at the way just a flick of my tongue can elicit the sexiest moan from his mouth. It turns me on again, more, and then I'm hungry, insatiable, and I pull him down to meet me on the mattress, pushing him to his back.

As he hits the navy blue pillow, Joel looks at me, a smile teasing his lips. "I like this side of you."

Heat rushes to my cheeks, and I freeze.

"Hey." He sits up and places a hand on either side of my shoulders. "It's so fucking hot."

His words, so carnal and full of some kind of raw truth, set me off again. Our mouths meld and our teeth connect as we fight for our elation. Every ridge, every line fills me, and I'm heady with lust and life and love.

This isn't slow and controlled passion—it's fast and it's furious, and we ride toward release as if it's life or death.

And I guess, in some way, it is.

TWENTY

We're a sweaty, heady mess. I know I must look like shit, but nothing in the world could take me out of this embrace. Nothing in the world could make me want to lose the closeness I feel lying next to this man who to me, is everything. Who I never want to let go.

"If you don't come out in five minutes, we're coming in. Kohl left his wallet in there, and I need pizza," Fiona screeches from outside the tent.

Well, maybe something.

"How can they get pizza delivered out here? We're an hour walk from a road," I say, shaking my head.

"Water taxi."

"That must cost—"

"More than I care to think about, but that's Fiona for you." Joel shrugs. "Her family has money."

I silently curse. Looks like the moment is over.

"We should get dressed, huh?" Joel pushes a strand of hair back from my face. I look up at him, into those stormy eyes. The tent casts his face in a red hue, and for a moment I have this irrational thought. We could stay here forever. I don't want to go back into the outside world. Once we leave this security bubble, everything is going to be real again.

And damn, do I like the fantasy we're building instead.

"Do you think if we found the wallet and threw it out they'd leave us alone?" I bite my lip.

"Ha." Joel grins. "I love the idea, but I think we both know the line about the wallet is a thinly veiled excuse."

"Okay." I press one more kiss to those soft, sinful lips and then grasp the sleeping bag that's on the floor next to us to my chest, letting it shield my body. I stand up, holding it in place, but just as I turn to walk away, Joel gives it a tug, and the slippery material slides through my fingers.

I should feel naked and exposed.

But the look in Joel Henley's eyes tells me he sees something I don't see. That he sees me as a whole lot more than a girl who's a little conscious of her curves.

"Don't ever hide your beautiful."

Melt.

I give a coy smile and pick up my underwear, wriggling into it, then pull on my shirt and shorts. I pick up Joel's jeans, and make as if I'm going to throw them to him. I weigh them in my hand, as if determining their worth. Then, "Nah," I say, holding them out behind me.

"Oh?" Joel laughs. "You want to play that game?" He scrambles to his feet, a predatory glaze in his eyes. He stalks toward me, and a chill runs over my body.

I take two steps to the back corner of the tent, not breaking eye contact, wanting to know what he'll do when he reaches me.

"Are you sure you want to do this?" Darkness flashes across his eyes, and my breath catches in my throat. Both yes and no war within my mind, and I open my mouth to speak.

Fiona beats me to it. "Starting the countdown! Thirty. Twenty-nine. Twenty-eight. Twenty-seven ..."

I laugh, and it breaks the tension that cast its net over Joel and I. His stance loses some of its threat and he wraps his arms around me, one large hand pinning my wrists together while the other secures his denim.

He leans his head down and rubs his nose against mine, Eskimo-kiss style. "I love you, Ellie Mayfield."

"I love you too, Joel Henley."

"Nineteen ... fuck it, four, three, two, one!"

In lightning speed, Joel pulls his pants on and buttons the fly, spinning to face the tent flap as the zipper buzzes its way to the ground.

"I didn't interrupt anything, did I?" Fiona sticks her head inside, looking both ways.

"Oh you did." Joel walks over and gives her a mock punch on the shoulder. "But it's nothing we won't pay you back for when we're loud later tonight."

"Tonight?" I frown.

Joel turns back to look at me, and those eyes have me. Because when he looks at me with those steely blues, he could ask me to do anything and I'd be there with bells on.

"You have to stay, Ellie." His lips glisten in the low light. "We're not finished yet."

Hours later and the five of us sit around a campfire eating pizza and drinking beer that isn't cold enough to be good, but isn't warm enough to be bad. Grease drips from my fingers all down my chin, and my hair is twisted in place with a pen I found in the bottom of my handbag. It's the least glamorous thing I've done in a long time, and I absolutely love it.

"So Ellie, tell us your story," Fiona says, as she grabs a slice of the pepperoni.

"Oh, no." Kohl groans.

"Not this again." Marc rolls his eyes. "Now is probably a good time to mention that we all hate Vanessa. Like, hate her. Like, want to throw her off a cli—"

"Dude, lay off my ex," Joel says softly. A slight flame of jealousy licks at my soul, but I quash it down. He's with me now. We were meant to be. I turn to Joel, the question I'd asked so long ago burning my lips again.

"She left me because of …" He runs his hand down his slight frame. "Y'know."

Cancer. I take his hand and squeeze it. *I made the right choice.*

"I don't hate her." Fiona sighs, then gives me a look. "She just never wanted to do anything fun. Always was too afraid about getting her hair out of place."

My hand flies to my curls before I realise what I'm doing, and I tuck a stray strand behind my ear. Fiona's shrewd gaze narrows. "Her story isn't a happy one."

I swallow and look away. Tales about Joel's ex are something I don't need to hear. "So tell me more about the story thing. What is it?" I ask.

"Fiona believes that everyone has a grand life story. Something that sums them up, with a beginning, a middle and an end," Joel says, and takes a big bite of pizza. Cheese strings from his lips to his hand, and it's all I can do not to lick it away and break the connection. Joel licks his lips, and then catches my eyes. Lust fires between us like a shell from a cannon.

"They do. You have a hero, and a goal, an obstacle and a resolution." Fiona doesn't notice our eye fucking and continues on. "Take Kohl here for example. His story starts with a girl who broke his heart. The middle is when he overcomes his personal challenges and finally falls in love again, and the end will be when he marries the love of his life. So really, his is a story about Kohl, who wants to find true love, but his heart has been broken so badly that he's afraid to put it all on the line."

"Get stuffed." Kohl flicks a piece of pepperoni at her, and she ducks.

"So everyone has a love story?" I ask, my head to the side.

"No." Fiona slows her chewing. "Some people's stories are action. Some are too much action." Her face darkens and closes off for a moment, and I have a feeling there's a whole lot we don't know about this girl. A whole lot of secrets being kept behind her shiny black hair.

"Like my story," Joel says, and from the grateful look Fiona shares with him, I wonder if it's just as much to save her as it is to continue the conversation. "My story is all about life."

Fiona places her hand on his leg. "Joel ..."

He shrugs. I glance around the circle. All three give him that look. Silence falls over us. And suddenly, I see why he kept that secret from me. Why he wanted to stop this from happening.

Even though I feel the same as they do, even though I don't want to face the fact that the man I love is dying, I have to do it. For Joel.

I suck in a deep breath. "So yours would be a story about Joel, who wants to live life to the fullest, because he's only got a certain amount of days to do it in."

As the words leave my mouth, three stunned faces glare at me.

And one face that speaks of nothing but love.

"Hell yeah." Joel leans in and kisses me on the lips, and even though he tastes like pepperoni and I probably taste like onion, it's all okay.

In fact, it's better than okay.

It's everything.

When our lips part, it's to a cacophony of catcalls and wolf whistles. My cheeks fire up again, and I press my hands to them, no doubt smearing grease all over my face.

"So ... who wants to go for a midnight swim?" Joel asks, a dangerous glint in his eyes.

"Oh hell yeah!" Fiona leaps to her feet. The boys clamber up around her, and she looks back at me, challenge clear in her gaze. "You coming too?"

I look out at the still, black water in front of me. It's the kind of dark that seems to go on forever, that inks right through you. Small boats float a little way off shore, their spires stabbing ominously into the air. A chill breeze passes over the campsite, and I huddle closer to the fire.

The moment I look up, I see Joel staring back at me.

Making every moment count has never felt like this.

I stretch to my feet. "Of course." I meet Fiona's gaze and give a wicked smile. "I was just wondering if clothing was optional or not."

"I love this chick!" Fiona loops an arm around my shoulders.

"Clothes on, ladies. I cannot watch Joel fuck someone in the water." Marc flips us the bird, rips off his shirt and dives in the lake. The resounding splash fills the campsite.

"Let's do this!" Fiona rips off her shirt and shorts so she's clad only in matching BONDS underwear and then runs toward the water, Kohl not far behind.

"You know you don't have to if you don't want to ..."

Before Joel has even finished the sentence, my shirt is over my head, my shorts are on the sandy campsite floor, and my hand is extended for his.

Because that's the way I want to do things now.

Together.

Sometimes, life isn't fair. Getting up at five a.m. to make it back in time to sort out my baskets for the day isn't fair. Worrying about how I'm going to try and keep my sister from trouble isn't fair. Falling in love with a boy who's going to die isn't fair.

And yet somehow, we don't get a choice in it. Joel doesn't get to choose whether he lives or dies. And even though it hurts putting my heart on the line like this, even though it's simultaneously the bravest and scariest thing I've ever done, I do it anyway.

Some things are worth the risk.

So even though air mists around my face and I feel as if I slept in a salt jar, I give Joel a light kiss on the cheek, careful not to wake him, and push up from the bed we're sharing. As I take a step, a hand wraps around my ankle and I still, looking down at him.

"We still need to talk," he whisper-croaks, and I nod.

Because yesterday was fantasy.

Today is reality, the hard part of our story.

"I know." My hair falls across my face and I don't move to brush it away. It provides me with a little shelter. It shields me from what I'm worried he'll see in my gaze— a fear of falling. Fear of falling too hard, too fast.

"I'll catch you, Ellie."

And just like that, I feel I can manage again.

I blow him a kiss, which Joel catches and places against his heart, and it's so corny I roll my eyes. Then, when his eyes close one more time, I do the lamest thing I've ever done. I take his T-shirt from where it rests on the floor and hug it to my chest. Right now, I just want to take a little piece of Joel home with me.

I start the long walk back to my car, back to my life, back to reality. The sun is just winking out over the horizon, so it's not hard to see the nuances of the path. The air is so crisp and chilling that it somehow makes me feel fresh, as if I haven't just had wild monkey sex with the man I love, swam in a saltwater lagoon and basically moisturised my face with pizza oil without taking a shower in between.

When I reach the lot, my car doesn't have a ticket, despite being parked in the spot much longer than would legally be allowed. I took a chance. I took a risk.

And everything worked out.

Now I just need to work out how I'm going to deal with the rest of life with Joel.

Still, as I drive back home I feel as if nothing can drag me down. My phone is plugged in on charge, music blaring out the car speakers. I'm in love. I'm happy. And there's still a chance the doctors could be wrong. Doctors are wrong all the time. And sure, Joel says he's done chemo and all that medical stuff, but maybe he could try an organic diet. Less pizza and beer.

More sex in tents ...

My head is so far in the clouds that when red and blue lights fly past me, a silent wailing, I barely give it a second thought. I do my cursory pull over as they pass, then move back onto the deserted road, heading for home. Everything is so perfect. Everything is looking like it could be all right.

And then all at once, it comes crashing down.

The red and blue lights illuminate the skin on my hands.

The men run inside.

Run.

I pull up outside my house. Somehow, I stumble from the car, the door left open. Without looking inside the building, I know exactly which apartment these men are going to. Exactly where they're headed.

An officer puts out his arm, trying to stop me from entering the stairwell. "Ma'am, you can't—"

"Move." The voice isn't mine. I don't scream at policemen. I don't swing their arms out of the way and barrel up the stairs, despite being told not to.

But somehow I'm in the stairwell, taking the concrete steps two at a time, then flying down the corridor where the door to Zy and Dani's apartment is wide open.

"Dani!" I scream, barrelling inside.

In front of me, three men and a lady in blue hover over a prone figure on the floor. Bags and a board lie to their side, and they're speaking in short clipped tones, efficient and official.

In the middle of it all is my sister.

She's still.

Too still.

"No," I whimper, and clutch at my shirt. It's stiff from exposure to life, and I feel so stupid, so damn idiotic for thinking this didn't matter just a short few minutes ago. How can I be here, messed up from too much pizza, swimming and sex when my little sister ... my little sister ...

They say sticks and stones can break your bones but words can never hurt you.

They're wrong.

True pain can only be inflicted by words.

Words like "Resuscitate."

Words like "Gone."

I crumble to the shag-pile carpet floor. My knees smart as they make contact with the wool, and then a hand is on my shoulder, trying to get me up, trying to get me away.

"Ma'am, we need you to—"

"Eleanor." Arms wrap around me. Cocoon me. Save me. "She's the ... she's her sister."

"I'm sorry, but we still need you both to wait outside."

"Okay. Okay. I got this. Eleanor, can you stand?"

They're all just words running through my head. Dialogue in a book. Meaningless. Because that's my sister lying there on the lounge room floor, and I can't handle that.

"Come on, Eleanor. I got you." Two hands shift under my armpits and then lift me to my feet. My knees fall out from under me, but Zy somehow pulls me to him so he half-carries, half-walks me out the door and down the stairs.

When we reach the grass he lowers me down, sitting with me. He smells of smoke, and booze, and all things bad. All things that could be partly responsible for what happened up there.

"Bastard!" I slap at his chest. "How could you?"

Zy clutches his chest through his black T-shirt. "Eleanor, I didn't know."

"What happened?" Agony rings in my voice, and I'm speaking far too loud, and the crowd of early-morning walkers and neighbours who have gathered at the police vehicles gaze over at me. Their stares make me angry, even though they shouldn't. Even though I know better.

"We were at a party. I wanted ... I wanted to leave. She wouldn't come home with me, so I left her out."

Torment scrawls across Zy's face, and even though I want so badly to hate him right now, to blame him for what happened, I can't. He's already doing enough of that himself.

"I woke ..." He chokes, and I flash my eyes to him. Steely brown eyes look back at me, angry, trying to tamp down the hurt he so obviously is feeling. "I woke up to get a water, and she was in the living room ... like that."

"Hey." I place my hand on his arm. "You ..."

I don't have the words to finish that sentence because just then, the paramedics take Dani on a board down the stairs into the back of a waiting ambulance.

"Dani." I scrabble to my feet and limp over to the car, but once again I'm met with resistance. "I'm her sister, please," I beg, but the look on the policeman's face tells me everything I need to know. It's pity and hesitation all at once.

"No ..." I shake my head slowly, then race back and forth. "No, no, no."

"I need you to—"

"NO!" I scream.

The ambulance doors slam shut and the siren starts up, a chilling morning prayer to an otherwise quiet street. It races off, gravel flying from under the wheels, and the sucker punch in my stomach transforms into an internal bleed.

I double over for a moment, leaning on my knees. How did this happen? How did life go from getting under control to even worse than I'd ever imagined?

"Ma'am, they've taken her to Wilfred Barrett Hospital. Are you okay to get there yourself?" A paramedic from the second ambulance shadows me. I look up, unsure how to answer. Because no. I am not okay.

"I'll drive." Zy's voice is flat and emotionless, and I look up at him and nod. I don't have the energy to form words.

He walks over to my car, and I follow behind. When he turns the engine, I voice the words I've been most afraid to ask. "Has someone told Mum?"

He gulps. "She'll meet us at the hospital."

And so begins the longest short drive of my life. The whole trip, only one thought races through my head.

I'll never be forgiven for this.

TWENTY-ONE

I haven't been in a hospital since Dad died. As soon as I step foot in the linoleum-floored building, memories smack me in the face with the intensity of a 747. There's a jetliner's worth of heartache I've hidden in this building, and I'm only realising it just now.

Zy walks up to the desk and does all the talking while I stand slightly back. I smell things that remind me of my father. Antibacterial. Instant coffee. I hear things that remind me of him. Beeps. Murmured voices. Shoes squeaking against clean floor.

"Come on." Zy grips my hand and zombie-walks me to the hard plastic chairs. I do what I'm supposed to do. I sit.

Even though I'm paralysed with fear.

Even though this is the last place I want to be.

I open my mouth to speak, but my tongue feels thick, heavy. "How long?"

"They don't know." He steeples his hands at his nose. "They're doing everything they can. She's ..." He doesn't finish the sentence.

He doesn't need to.

A beep comes from the bag Zy's holding, and it's only then I realise he's been grasping my handbag this entire time. He's such a picture of masculinity, all big, broad shoulders, tattoos and piercings, that the image somehow seems so very wrong. I laugh, and he gives me a strange look, as if maybe I've lost it.

Maybe I have.

I take my phone out and swipe across the screen.

Joel: Can't stop thinking about last night. When can I see you again?

Joel. Somewhere in between my driveway and the emergency department, I forgot all about him. Forgot that there's another person in my life who will soon end up in a place like this.

Acid coats my mouth. I bite down on my lip as hard as I can, so hard I taste blood. It's a salty sweet release of the pain I want to feel.

"Hey." Zy shakes his head. "Don't do that."

Obediently, my lip pops out of my mouth. Zy takes my phone and looks at the screen. "Joel, hey?"

I don't answer. I'm trying to focus every part of my body on my sister pulling through this. Surely, if I concentrate hard enough, I can make it happen. I can will her to stay alive. To keep with me.

Right?

"Is he your boyfriend?"

"Mm."

Please just fight. Keep fighting. Push. Keep pushing. *Breathe.*

Keep breathing.

The clip of heels across the floor mixes with the floral scent of Chanel perfume. I lift my head to see my mother strutting through emergency, somehow managing to look as if she just stepped off a catwalk. She makes eye contact with me and gives a slight arch of a perfectly manicured brow, then goes to the nurse at the reception desk before coming back to join us.

She crosses one panty-hosed leg over the other and clasps her hands together, a resounding noise that echoes throughout the room.

Keep breathing.

"Where were you?" She narrows her eyes at me.

I shrug.

Keep breathing.

"Hello? Answer me." She jabs at my shoulder, and I try to pretend I don't feel it. I don't have energy to feel.

Keep breathing.

"Leave her alone, June. She's in shock." Zy. My unlikely protector.

"Well at least she's in the right place. Should we get someone to treat her for that?"

"For fuck's sake," Zy says.

"Nurse." Mum's on her feet, calling across the room. "We need something for—"

From the corner of my eye, I see the doors to the hospital swing open. A man in scrubs walks out. He has a clipboard in his hand and a cool, calming demeanour, his expression not giving a single thing away. "Mrs Mayfield?"

As one, Zy and I rise, even though it's not either of our names that were called. Mother clips across the floor to the doctor and I shuffle my feet, barely moving one in front of the other. I want to slow this moment down. I want to delay what this could mean.

Right now, uncertainty is a gateway to hope.

THE TWENTY-ONE

By the time I reach the man, he's already shaken hands with Mum, and turned to face Zy and me.

"My daughter and Danica's friend." Mum gestures to Zy and me.

"I'm Dr Jones." The doctor nods, but doesn't extend his hand to shake. "Danica is going to be okay."

All the air releases from my lungs in a *whoosh* so powerful the papers in the doctor's hand ruffle. She's going to be fine. Danica is going to be fine.

The words repeat themselves in my brain. I haven't lost her.

Not any more than I already had.

Words from the man's mouth echo in my brain. *Activated charcoal. Intubation. Rest.* Then finally, "She'll be able to go home most likely tonight, provided she keeps improving."

"Should we go and come back?" Mum cocks her head. *Should we go and come back.*

All my life I've played it safe. I run from confrontation; I don't run toward it.

But when she says those words, something inside me breaks. And I don't know if it's ever getting put back together again.

"Can't you just be here for your child for one day?" I spit.

"Eleanor." Mum's eyes widen, the unspoken reprimand clear in her gaze. "We can talk about this in private. *Later*."

The doctor clears his throat, and Mum turns her gaze back to him. I don't, though. I keep my eyes glued on her. Guilt churns in my stomach. Why didn't I say something? Why didn't I just tell the truth about what I suspected sooner?

"Is this sort of behaviour normal for her?" the doctor asks. "We need to talk about follow-up care and—"

"She does not have a problem. Whatever this is." Mum gives a little laugh, as if the very idea is absurd. "I will talk to her about it though. Of course."

It's just about as much of her bullshit as I can take. I turn on my heel and walk back toward the plastic chairs, slamming my body down into the nearest one. A few moments later, Mum sweeps past, arching one of those beautiful eyebrows at me as she goes. Zy still stands where the doctor left him.

Slowly, he walks back to me, sinking into the seat beside mine. "I think it's time to tell the truth."

My heart is heavy in my chest.

Because I know deep down he's right.

It's a truth I've been running from. A truth that reveals I've failed at my task. They say the truth will set you free ... won't it?

So why does the truth feel so damn wrong?

Mum walks over and sits beside me. "I know you think this is all my fault."

I shake my head and gaze up at the roof. "No. It's mine." I swallow the metallic taste down. "I knew she was doing drugs. I should have said something. I should have—"

"Anyone could see she was having problems, Ellie," Zy says. "June, you saw her at your events. She was drunk half the time. You had to know that."

Mum sniffs, and a slither of vulnerability weakens her gaze. Underneath it all, she's just as scared as I am. As we both are.

"I just ... God." I rest my head in my hands. My stomach aches at the thought of the *what if*s. "I should have told you."

The sounds of heels clicking away echoes in my mind. Each step sears my soul.

Joel's phone goes straight to voicemail every time I dial. I shake my head and glare at the screen, as if that will somehow make the damn thing connect. As if that will make a difference at all.

"Is this the time I should be saying 'maybe he's just not that into you'?"

This time, my glare is directed at Zy. "I think it's more likely that he's just not that into charging his phone, given that he's camping down at the Basin."

"Fair enough then." He offers a wry smile. "I think we should talk to her. Tell her to stop. Together."

"Like a united front kind of thing?" it makes sense. After all, so far I haven't had much success solo.

"Absolutely." Zy props one foot up on the seat next to him, then pulls out his phone and starts streaming some football game. We sit there in silence for the next little while, Zy no doubt wondering who's won, the Tigers or the Knights.

Me wondering how the hell I'm going to convince my sister that this time, she has to stop.

Ten minutes pass, and Dr Smith is at the doors again. He beckons us forward and lets us know we can see her now, giving us the room number and directions to help us find her.

The walk to Danica's room is long. I'm rushing and slowing, stopping and starting, desperate to see her and terrified of it.

Finally, the curtain is pulled back—

And there's my sister.

She's so small in the big white hospital bed. Her golden skin is somehow pale, as if the sun has been sucked right out of her, along with the contents of her stomach. As if all the light left within has been dimmed.

When she sees us, her eyes don't fire with her usual exuberance. Instead, she gives a small wiggle of her fingers hello, a weak smile curving her lips.

"Hey."

And all the composure I've been working so hard to keep, all the walls I've erected to keep me safe from hurt, break.

I run to the bed and wrap my arms around her neck, squeezing her tight. "Thank God you're okay."

Her hair smells like vomit, and Dettol, and her body shakes ever so slightly under my grasp. It's just another reminder of how frail this girl really is. I give her a tighter squeeze, as if that will somehow help hold her still. "I love you so much."

"You're hurting me," she says, but her voice is muffled by my shoulder.

"Shut up." I pull back and look her in the eyes. This time a little hint of the usual Dani sparkle is there. "You're ruining the moment."

She manages a laugh and I pull away, clasping my hands in front of me. Dani's gaze travels from me to Zy, then back again. "Where's Mum?"

Oh.

"She's ..." I work my jaw, trying to find words to fill the empty space that follows.

"Ha!" Dani snorts, shaking her head. "I guess I have to actually have a terminal illness to warrant that kind of attention."

I lean forward and squeeze her shoulder. "She's coming back. She just had a thing to do."

Dani shakes me off and levels her gaze at me. "I guess this event isn't important enough for her to attend."

It's a statement I don't have an answer for.

Shuffled footsteps from the hall, the beeps from the machines, the whirring of telephones—they all create this symphony that reminds me where we are. And just how far we have to go.

Zy nudges my arm, and once again I look for words that aren't there. I know what he wants me to do. What he wants me to say. It's just now, here in the moment, the words are as elusive as they've always been.

"Ellie has something she wants to talk to you about."

This time, I spin and glare at Zy. He shrugs, and pushes me forward again.

Dani looks on curiously, and I smile. "*We* have something we want to talk to you about."

"You two? Together?" Her eyes widen. "That's a first."

"There are some things we can agree on." Zy folds his arms across his chest, and I see the brief look of fear flash over Dani's features. Zy isn't the serious type. For him to be here with that kind of attitude, things really must be intense.

I look over my shoulder, checking to see if anyone is near, but we're alone. "You need to slow down. Stop drinking. Stop … taking things."

Her lip wobbles for a split second and then it stills. "I have this under control." She laughs, but her laugh is too tight. Too tense.

"You can't keep doing this. I think you need help, maybe rehab—"

"Rehab is the last thing I need," she hisses. She leans forward, and the machine above her head flashes faster, her heart rate spiked.

"Then how come you're in hospital, huh?" I challenge, trying to keep my face level on hers and not the panicked machine above her.

"I was just blowing off some steam." She shakes her head and flops back against the pillows, as if the whole thing exhausts her. "I'm fine. Honest."

Zy steps forward, gesturing up and down her prone body. "Fine, Dani? Because this doesn't look fine to me. This sure as shit looks like you're in hospital because you're running from your problems. *Again*."

Maybe it's the fact he's always so gentle with her, or perhaps it's the fact that there's a coldness in his eyes that frightens even me.

It breaks Dani.

Tears roll down her cheeks. "You don't understand."

"So tell us!" I spread my arms wide. "Tell me. Tell Zy. Just tell someone, Dani. Because you can't keep going on like this."

I turn and march to the door. Every step I take hurts. Every step I take feels like a step toward my sister's funeral. Because right now, I'm doing exactly what Mum did. I'm walking away when times get tough.

It's the only ammunition I have left in my case.

I reach the door to the room and still, certain she'll call me back. That we'll go back to being sisters who care for one another.

She doesn't.

She doesn't say a word.

TWENTY-TWO

When I walk up to The View café three days later, Joel leans up against his car, two takeaway coffees already in hand. My body aches from weariness. It's been three days of research. Research on the best rehab places in Sydney. Research on natural therapy cancer treatment. My eyes sting from staring at screens for far too long.

Joel passes one coffee over to me and pulls me close for a hug. I sink into his embrace. The smell of coffee and man and *him* washes over me, and I want to breathe it in forever. I want to bottle it up right there and then.

We hop in the car and start our drive out of Emerald Cove.

"So, how has your week been?" Joel asks.

I glance over at him, my lips twisting as I consider telling him. I haven't mentioned it in the brief texts we've exchanged since we last saw each other. It seems so trivial to bother him with something like that when he has more than his fair share of problems to contend with.

His hand drops from the wheel and reaches over to my leg. He tucks it under my thigh, and shoots me a quick smile before looking back at the road. "Tell me."

"Well ..." I search for the right words. "My sister ... she overdosed the other day, and wound up in hospital."

"What?" Joel flicks his head to look at me, and the car swerves with him. My heart leaps in my throat, but I don't panic. I don't grab for the wheel, or try to control things beyond my doing. I just let it be.

Joel jerks back into an overcorrect with a sheepish smile. "Sorry," he says. "So what happened?"

I shrug and look at the fields flying past as we head onto the freeway that leads out of town and toward the hot-air balloon field. Green and browns blur as we pick up speed, the grey sky overhead casting a melancholy shadow over the earth. "She just ... I don't know if it's because she's only just dealing with Dad's death, or if she's sad, or if she's just ... I don't know. At first I thought she was experimenting. Being 'cool'. But hospital ..." I shake my head. "I told my dad I'd look out for her. I can't handle letting him down."

"You won't." Joel's words come quickly. I look across at him, and his expression is deadly serious. "You could never disappoint him. You have to realise that."

"But I told him I'd—"

"He was sick, Ellie." Joel's brow creases, but he quickly shakes it off. "I'm ... I'm angry he put so much on you."

"He was dying."

"He was wrong!" Joel roars, and my eyes widen. "How dare he make you feel as if every sin your sister commits is on your head? How dare he?"

"That's not what he meant!" I fume. Anger burns in my chest and I can't quash it. "You don't get to say things like that."

Joel opens his mouth to speak, but no words come out. Instead, his face twists in a grimace. His hand falls from the wheel and the car veers left. My heart hammers, my breath lodged in my throat.

"Joel!" I scream.

One second is all it takes. He grabs the wheel with two hands, his eyes wide, his back rigid.

My breath comes short and sharp. My heart thuds so loud I hear it over the talkback radio softly sounding from the car's speakers.

"Sorry."

His voice is so quiet, I'm almost unsure he spoke.

"Are you … okay?" I ask, my voice wavering.

"Yeah. I just …" He rubs his hand at the bridge of his nose. "Sorry. I'm fine."

But something tells me he's not fine at all.

Just shy of an hour later we drive past the hot-air balloon field, and I give a small sigh of relief that quickly turns to panic when we pull into a driveway a few blocks up. A giant white sign greets us as we pull in.

A giant white sign with a picture of a girl with her mouth open.

Jumping out of a plane.

"Uh-uh." I shake my head. "No. No way."

Joel pulls in to park next to one of the cars in the lot, and turns to face me. "I know you said you were afraid of heights, but I thought since I was going anyway …"

"That you would try and force me into it?" I place my coffee down in the cup holder and my nails dig into the leather seat, just in case Joel decides to try and pry me out of the car and throw me into the plane.

"No." Joel shakes his head and smiles. "Of course not. But I'm diving today, and I'd love to do it with you."

He bats his long lashes at me as I unclip my seatbelt. "No. No way. No how. And also? Worst date idea ever."

Joel laughs. "It is kind of horrid, right?"

"Yes!" I agree, hopping out of the car. The dawn light stretches across the parking lot, that warm yellow gold colour that highlights every peak and trough of brown country earth. "I'll come in, but there's no way in hell I am jumping out of a plane today. None. Zero."

Joel just gives a small laugh, and we walk toward the tall building together. A plane sits behind it on a runway that stretches off into the distance.

My mind whirls at a million miles a minute. What the hell was he thinking? I don't like heights; he knows this. And yet, despite that, he's brought me to a sky-diving centre.

And not only that, but isn't he sick? Is this really safe?

When we reach the building doors, Joel turns to face me. He reaches out and clasps my hands in his. His hands are soft, gentle. *Kind.*

"Still not jumping out of a plane," I say, before I can get far too lost in those damn eyes again.

Joel laughs. "I have a confession to make."

"Go on." I narrow my eyes.

"We're not here to go skydiving."

Before I can ask anything further, Joel turns and walks into the building, the door sounding a chime as he opens it. I scamper in after him and stand beside him at the desk while Joel speaks to the lady there. He fills in some paperwork, then takes my hand. A huge grin stretches his face, and there's a boyish excitement to him.

"Come on." He pulls me past the desk and down a corridor till we reach a large space. The roof opens up, and there's a glass enclosure in the middle of the room. Suspended in mid-air are two people in ridiculous onesie costumes, all blue. They balloon about their bodies as an invisible force holds them horizontal in the air as if they're impersonating superheroes.

"What the hell?" I turn to Joel.

He's still smiling, and when he turns to face me, I catch the force of his joy. "Indoor skydiving. It's on my list," he says. "I know you said you don't like heights now, but I thought maybe this would be a good middle ground for you. I don't want to sound like I'm trying to counsel you, or change you, or ..." He heaves in a breath. "I just think you're so much more than you let the world believe. Life's too short to spend being afraid. I know you can take on anything. This is just a small step."

I let his words sink in, stew in my brain, and even though heights terrify me—*terrify*—I feel as if maybe I can do this. After all, my efforts to keep my family safe so far haven't exactly succeeded. Out here, in the middle of nowhere with no one but Joel to see me fail—what have I got to lose? After all, the divers in the ring in front of us don't appear too high off the ground.

The machine changes gears, the engines turbo charged, and the two divers shoot up toward the roof of the building.

Crap.

What the hell am I getting myself into?

Before I can overthink it, I swallow and turn back to Joel. "Yes," I say. "I'll ... I'll do it."

"Are you sure?" His face is serious. "I don't want to force—"

"I'm doing this." There's conviction in my voice, and it seems to shut Joel up. He nods and turns, heading back toward the reception desk, and I follow him.

"She's in," he says to the teenage girl behind the desk.

She smacks her gum and looks at him, then at me, and I can just tell she's wondering how the hell I landed here with a guy like that. "I'm gonna need you to sign here." She spins a clipboard around and points it toward me. "You guys are about half an hour away."

After signing up and changing into the ridiculously unflattering flight gear, Joel and I sit on the chairs to the side of the chute. We watch as a young boy gets in and flies, and seeing this small human who can't be more than three or four spinning happily in the air helps calm my nerves somewhat. After all, if a toddler can do it ...

We receive a briefing from a flight instructor, and then it's time to go in. We have the option of going separately or together, and I'm just about to say I'll do it by myself when fear kicks in. It lurches in my belly and claws its way through my body. My heart hammers at my chest, and I don't know what the hell I was thinking when I said yes because it seems as if every pulse of blood sends a screaming, resounding *no* to each part of my body.

"You don't have to do this," Joel says softly. "I know I kinda sprung it on you—but this is your call. Really."

I swallow, thinking of everything that has happened this week. I need to change. I need to do something for *me*. *Badly.*

Mutely, I nod, and follow him toward the tube. Just before we get there, Joel turns back to me. He clasps my hands in his, a gesture I'm becoming all too familiar with, and says, "I believe in you."

I give a nervous giggle. "Thanks."

He shakes his head. "No, Ellie. If at any moment in there you're doubting it—know that I'm not. I know you've got this."

I open my mouth to reply, but the instructor interrupts the moment with some safety information. He briefs us again, giving the rundown, and then it's happening, and the air is a wall of vertical movement in front of us. And Joel is flying.

He wavers for a moment, his body not quite maintaining the Superman-like posture required, but then he straightens and he's doing it. A giant smile warps his face, his cheeks round and almost wobbly as the air presses against them.

The instructor smiles at me, I purse my lips. Now that it's right here, right now, I don't know that I can do this. I don't know that I can—

Don't think.

Just do.

I run forward and launch, my arms outstretched, and the air captures me, lifting me buoyant.

In an instant, my heart lurches. The ground wavers beneath me. My heart leaps to my throat, and my legs kick out, my body flipping. The air thickens, and I can't breathe. I need out. I scramble toward the door with my arms, but the world spins, turns, or maybe I am. All I know is I'm lost. And I'm scared. And I hate this, hate it more than anything. My chest rises and falls ultra fast. I'm not in control. I need to be in control. *I can't do this.*

A feeling worse than fear, worse than dread, consumes me until it's everything I am. I'm going to die. The ground is so far away.

And then there's Joel.

One hand grips my own, tight in its grasp.

Blue eyes bore into mine, and there's so much peace in them.

The rise and fall of my chest slows. My legs scrabble about, and Joel gives a gentle smile, a small nod. It's as if he's saying *you can do this. You got this.*

I take a deep breath and remember his words from before. *I have this.* It takes every ounce of my strength, but I close my eyes for a moment, focusing with all I have not on the empty air beneath me, but on my body, and what it's doing. I concentrate on each limb, every muscle, and try and force them to relax and just seep into this activity, into this sensation.

When I open my eyes again, Joel smiles at me. And I know without even looking at him that I'm doing it. That I'm flying.

I'm freaking flying!

I laugh, but I can't hear it above the roar of the engines, and from the look on Joel's face he's laughing along with me. Weightlessness propels me, and it's so light and freeing. I can't believe I've gone from despair and worry to this beautiful sensation of peace. Of flying.

When the instructor motions that we can go further up, making the hand symbols to ask if we want to, Joel looks at me. Regretfully, I shake my head. I want to, so badly, but the reality of the fear that hit me just a few minutes ago is still fresh on my tongue. I don't want to push it.

Joel doesn't miss a beat. As soon as I shake my head, he reaches out for my other hand. We hold hands and float on air, pushing the limits but not breaking them entirely, and in that moment, I know.

I'm better than the scared, careful girl I've been. I have the feeling that I can do anything.

And I never want to let go of that.

TWENTY-THREE

Adrenalin runs through my veins as Joel parks the car outside The View and we walk to the beach. Storm clouds scud over the ocean, painting the waves a dark grey-green.

We sit on a bench, and even though I've just had one of the most amazing moments of my life, even though I've finally pushed myself to really try, we have to talk.

It's as if pushing myself to take that risk has shown me how much I have to lose.

And how much fun falling really is.

I nestle into Joel's side and he wraps his arm around my body. "So ... tell me what happened."

Joel's chest heaves up and shudders down, as if the weight of the world is compressed against it. "Well ... when we moved to Sydney, all those years ago. When I deleted all my social media? That was when ... when I was first diagnosed."

My brain ticks at a million miles an hour. How must that have felt? Discovering you had such a horrid illness at such a young age ... I shudder.

"I just couldn't face the questions. The best surgeons were all in Sydney, and I ..." He turns to face me. "I was young. Embarrassed that you'd see me at my worst. That something bad would happen and I'd ... die." The word is quiet. "I didn't want you to go through that with me."

"That wasn't your choice to make." Anger flares within me.

"It was, Ellie." His words come quick. "I know you're mad, and I know that hurt, but it was me. My body. My choices."

I tighten my grip on the bench, but nod. It doesn't make it okay, but who am I to say I would have done it differently?

"They tried all the therapies—chemo, radio ... Dad even wanted to try hypnotherapy."

"Really?" I frown.

"I know." Joel laughs, but there's no humour in it. "But eventually, I beat the odds. They couldn't find it anymore. It looked like I was ... free."

A seagull calls overhead as it floats on the breeze, bouncing toward the waves. That's free. It's strange to think of the word in terms of a human. A human who is now dying.

"I ended up going to TAFE and finishing school there, then I got into uni. That's where I met Fiona and everyone. They didn't know about the cancer thing, and I didn't want them to. It just ..." He shakes his head and runs his hand over his skull. "It's not who I am. Or who I was. I don't want my past to define me."

I nod slowly, thinking of Dani earlier in the week. Is that what she's doing? Living life to the fullest so the past doesn't define her?

"Then six months ago I had to go back in for a check-up. I'd been having headaches—nothing serious, but I think somewhere deep inside, I knew." He pauses and looks me dead in the eyes. "I think somewhere inside we all know when we're dying."

I touch his arm. "Don't say that."

He shrugs me off. "The cancer is back. They did another few rounds of chemo, but it didn't work. It was too aggressive. Impossible to operate on. They told me that even though things seem okay now ... I only have ..." He blinks, and a tear trickles over his cheekbone. My heart aches seeing him like this. It aches knowing the pain he's going through. "I only have one year to live."

I press my lips to his cheek and taste the salt there. "Hey," I whisper. My hands find either side of his face and I look him in the eyes, so close to my own. "You don't know that that's a fact. I'm sure there are things we can do, like ... like a natural diet. Have you tried a natural—"

"I know, okay?" Joel's gaze is fiery. I flinch, and drop my hands. "I'm okay with it. I just ... I've led a good life. A great life." He pauses and turns to me. "I just didn't count on meeting you again. Things with Vanessa were casual. Safe. With you ..." He shakes his head. "I didn't count on falling so far."

I wrap my arms around his neck and bury my face there, just breathing him in. Hoping I can breathe him in for much longer than just the next few months.

Joel takes my shoulders and pulls me back to look me in the eyes. "And if you need to leave ..."

Staying isn't safe. It's the biggest risk I've ever taken. It's indoor sky-diving, hot-lap racing, drinking too much and falling too fast all at once.

"I'm not going anywhere."

Loving Joel Henley hurts.

But it's totally worth the ride.

Work drags. I started at six a.m. and spent the entire day thinking about getting home, preparing for Mum's next event, then hopefully seeing Joel afterwards.

"You're in a good mood, then," Colin says, as I line up the empty picnic baskets in his office in record speed.

"Just trying to get out of here on time." I give a wan smile.

Colin places his hand on my shoulder and steps close to me. Too close. I stiffen and move back, but he tightens his grip. "Have an early mark, Ellie."

His words are nice, but his body language is oh-so wrong.

I frown and slowly step backward. "Thanks."

"You're not being funny about the other week still, are you?" Colin shakes his head. "I thought we'd gotten past it."

"I just … I have to go." I turn on my heel and leave. I have to quit. I have to find another job and leave this one behind.

As I walk to the car, thoughts of work fill my mind. Maybe I can actually do what Joel said. Maybe it's time I pushed myself, applied for university, and—

I'm just about to open the door when a lone figure jogs toward me from the still running motorcycle that's now parked alongside the lot. "Wait!" Zy calls.

"What?"

He crosses the lot and stops in front of me, his chest heaving, big puffs of mist clouding his face. "It's Dani."

Tilting my head, I study the overcast sky. "What now?"

"She didn't come home last night." Zy shoves his hands in his jean pockets. "Do you ... know where she is?"

"Shit," I mutter. The pounding in my head that seems to be a regular occurrence when my sister's name is mentioned starts up again. "No idea."

"I tried calling, but you didn't pick up."

I shake my head. "My phone's on silent. Why are you only telling me now? Why did you wait?"

Zy shoves his hands in his pockets and looks sheepishly at the ground. "I … I only got home this morning myself."

Cold air rushes through my lungs.

Dani is gone. I just hope it's not too late.

"We have to go look for her."

Zy nods. "I'll check Sandy Cove."

"I got EC." I throw my body into the car, turn the key and start the engine. I grab my phone from where it's sitting in the centre console and clear Zy's missed calls, then hit dial, plugging my headphones into my ears. "Call Dani," I instruct Siri, and soon the ringing starts.

And then, after a while, it stops.

So does my heart.

"Redial."

My fingers clench and unclench the wheel. My knuckles are bone white.

Minutes speed by, and I watch as the clock ticks over, but still my sister doesn't answer or call me back. My stomach does a funny twisty thing and I wonder not for the first time why I ever let her leave the house without me. Why I somehow thought having her and Zy move in across the road from Hope and I would keep her safe.

I race out of the parking lot, then head onto the freeway. Silence eats the space in the car. It's the white noise of fear. Because *what if it's happened again?* What if I haven't managed to keep her safe?

Half an hour later, I take the exit to Emerald Cove, and my head aches with a pain so severe, so intense it's hard to see. Black dots crowd my vision and I shake them away.

"Come on, come on," I whisper. My knuckles grip so tight on the wheel, they're white.

Reaching the beach takes a total of fifty-eight minutes. Ten steps from my car. Four typed out, not-sent text messages to my mother where I go to tell her that Dani is missing, then take it all back. One lonely metal bench overlooking the ocean, freezing my legs through my thin denim.

She finally answers the phone on the tenth ring, her voice sleepy. "Yeah?"

"Dani, thank God," I rush, biting on my lip. "Where are you?"

Pause.

"I ... I don't know."

I press my eyes shut and inhale, the salty ocean air filling my lungs. When I open my eyes, everything is the same. Stormy skies, fierce ocean, and me.

"Do you need me to come and get you?"

More silence fills the line, so thick it could choke. Then, after what feels like hours tick past, I hear one tiny, muffled word.

"Yes."

It's all it takes. It's all it's ever taken.

"Look at your phone map and text me your address, babe. I'll come now."

A hiccough that could be a sob comes through the line, and my heart breaks. It really does. Because watching her float away like this is so damn hard.

I hang up the phone and wait for it to vibrate with her location. Two minutes later, a text comes through, and I walk back to the car, phone in hand. Instead of feeling relief that she's found, tension lines the muscles in my back. Finding her is half the battle.

I text Zy and tell him things are under control, then I drive to the address Dani gave me as fast as I can. Where normally I'm safe, with her I take risks. She needs me too damn much.

Fifteen minutes later, I pull up out the front of an old rundown house. Tiles are missing from the roof, and couches line the veranda, battered and stained beyond salvation. Danica Mayfield sits on the concrete front step, her knees huddled to her chest, her long, blonde hair straggling around her shoulders.

She shakes.

I've never seen someone look so broken in my entire life.

I open the car door and her head snaps up, as if she didn't hear me pull over. She pushes to her feet, meeting me halfway across the too long lawn, and when I open my arms she falls into my embrace, her tiny shoulders shaking as she sobs.

"Hey." I rub my hand soothingly on her back. "I'm here. I've got you."

We stand there and she cries, full body sobs. I sometimes worry she might break. She's so fragile. So damn small.

"You her ma or some'n'?"

My gaze shoots to the balcony. A guy stands there, shirtless, arms folded across a pale, weedy chest. A cigarette dangles from his lips, and demons haunt his face, the ghosts of hallucinations past.

"Well?" He prompts. Attitude curls from his mouth with the cigarette smoke.

"Or something." I shift so my arm is around Dani's shoulders and shepherd her to the car. She doesn't look back—doesn't make eye contact with the guy once, despite the holes I feel he's burning into our backs.

I open the door and she collapses into the seat, an unset Jell-O of the girl she once was. My hand is on the handle to the driver's side when he calls once again.

"She'll be back."

It's not a question. He turns and strolls back into the house, flicking the cigarette to the concrete porch beneath him as he walks.

My stomach sinks.

Those three words are the threat I fear the most.

With every kilometre we drive from the house, tension tightens in my stomach. My hands grip the steering wheel, nails digging into my palms on the other side.

"We need to talk about this." I force the words. They're from a script I've performed before. It's one my sister hates.

"I don't want to." Her tiny voice answers me.

I slam my hand against the steering wheel. The plastic smarts my palm, and I give a small shake of my wrist as if I can jiggle the pain off. As if life works like that.

"Relax," Dani says, but her voice is so quiet that I have to strain to hear it above the chug of the old car.

"Relax?" I spit, shaking my head. "I just picked you up and you were crying, Dani. Crying. Less than a week ago you were in hospital because of a fucking overdose. What are you doing?"

A sob hiccoughs from her chest. "I'm so sorry, Ellie. Thank God you're here."

"Now," I mutter, shooting her a dark glance.

"Always." Dani leans across the console and places a hand on my knee, giving it a squeeze. "I know you've got my back, Eleanor. And I'm so grateful for that."

The words are a reminder to me. *Look after your mother and sister.*

"No more drugs. No more drinking. No more—"

"I got it. No more." Dani's voice is shrill. "I won't do it again."

I have no doubt she means that. Until she doesn't.

"You just ... you can't just go off-grid. You need to stay in touch. Let us know what's going on." I glance over, but she's staring out the window. I stop at our street, waiting for a break in traffic to turn up the road. "Even Zy was worried."

"Ha!" Dani snorts. "When isn't Zy worried?"

"Are you kidding me?" I raise my eyebrows. "Zy is supposed to be a bad arse. He's not supposed to do things like worry. He's supposed to be the reason we worry about you in the first place."

The traffic clears, and I swing the car right and up the steep incline that opens our street. At the speed of a turtle wading through quicksand, we crunch into the gravel drive of the house I share with Hope. Zy sits on our front stoop, his hands resting over his knees. He stares at the ground, as if it somehow holds the answers to every question he's ever wanted answered. When he looks up, relief is painted clear across his face.

Before the car completely stops its roll, Dani opens the door and runs up the drive. I pull up the hand brake, and even over the grating noise I hear one last sob as she wraps her arms around Zy's neck, her golden hair flying out behind her.

They speak in soft murmurs, and I deliberately tune them out. Instead, I unclick my own seatbelt and get out of the car, opening the boot to the three baskets waiting for me to take them inside. A quick check of my watch and it's after two—I'm going to have to hurry if I want to shower before Mum's event tonight.

I grab the baskets and walk toward Zy and Dani, still locked in an embrace, staring at each other. He wipes a tear from her cheek, and she buries her face in his neck.

"She was at some kind of drug house, Zy."

He pulls back and looks at me then to Dani, concern shining from his eyes. "What?"

"It was an accident. I'm so sorry." Dani huddles into him, her shoulders shaking. "Please don't hate me. Please …"

I walk closer and place the two baskets on the ground. "I've looked up a few rehab centres. Maybe we can—"

"No!" Dani jerks back. Her eyes dart from left to right, a wild animal cornered. "I won't. I'm already seeing the doctor this week as a follow-up from hospital. Please just … give me one more chance."

"We've given you last chances before, Dani." My tone softens when I speak. "It's getting harder and harder to believe."

She pauses, licking her lips. Her eyes flit to the picnic baskets before us. "Remember when you said you thought Colin hit on you, and me and Mum didn't believe you?"

"What?" Zy eyes me.

I nod. "Yes?"

"Whoa, whoa. Let's talk about—"

"I have it under control, Zy." Then, to Dani, "Go on."

"Remember how that felt? To not have people believe you?"

I narrow my eyes. "Go on."

"I'm saying I'm going to do this. Believe me. I just need one more chance."

I walk up the step to the veranda and fiddle with my keys. With one hand on the door, I look over my shoulder. "Dani?"

"Hmm?" she asks, a smile twinkling in her eyes.

"Please. Please, just ... just make it the truth this time."

I open the door and push inside, yelling out a hello to Hope. I go to plug my phone in to charge, but it rings before I even pull it out of my pocket.

I glance at the screen, seeing Joel's number, and warmth floods me. My Joel. The one thing going right in this world. The man I love.

I swipe right to answer. "Hey, lover."

Heavy breathing bursts down the line.

Straight away, I know. My heart switches to double time. My pulses thuds urgently in my neck.

"It's Fiona," she says, a croak in her voice. "Joel's been taken to hospital."

TWENTY-FOUR

My feet thud through the corridors of the hospital. The sound echoes along the halls, rubber against lino, a racing *thunk* in time with the beat of my heart.

Some things in life are ingrained in you. An innate knowledge of right and wrong. A sense of communication, and expressing how you feel.

The way to the oncology department is ingrained in me.

After all, I came here every second day for one whole year.

As if blindfolded, I run. Tears gloss over my eyes and blur the filthy looks nurses give me as I tear through the department, past the different desks and surgeons as fast as my legs will carry me.

When I finally reach the wing, I slow. My breath aches in my chest, blood pumping through my body as a result of the race I just lost.

You can sprint all you like; sickness beats you in the end.

I round the corner and shudder to a stop. The room is right in front of me, the letters written to the side of the door in big block figures. *318.*

With one hand to my heart, I try to slow my breathing. I swipe at my eyes, pressing away the tears. This is a weakness I can't afford to show him. I have to be strong.

"You got this," I whisper to myself, then walk into the room.

It doesn't feel like a normal room in a hospital. Then again, it has Joel in it. Was I ever expecting anything less?

Fiona, Kohl and Marc sit squashed into two chairs. They have a deck of cards out and are playing some kind of poker, from what I can tell. Joel's dad, Henry, stands to one side, talking on his cell phone. His eyes are the first to make contact with mine, and he gives me a small sad smile. It says he's sorry I know and he's glad I'm here all at once.

None of them hold my focus, though. My focus is on the boy lying in the hospital bed.

Seeing him here develops a film of memories in my mind. The clinical sound of machinery. The deathly white of the hospital sheets. The way a body that you know is so big can appear so small when confined to a thin mattress on wheels.

His eyes both lighten and dim when they see me, and when he finally does speak, the smile I know and love—and I do love it—isn't there. "Hey."

One word.

It stills the laughter coming from his friends' table. Even his father pauses mid-sentence.

All eyes are on me as I walk into the room, my hands shoved into my pockets. "Hi."

"I think I'll go get a drink. You guys coming?" Fiona places her cards face-down on the table.

"I'm not really thirs—" Fiona hits Marc over the top of the head, cutting him off. "Sorry, got it."

"You guys don't have to ..." I trail off as they depart the room. Even Joel's dad leaves, and soon it's just Joel, me, and the machines pumping fluid and God knows what into his body.

"So ... about that whole twelve months thing ..." I try and make a joke, but a sharp pain stabs me in the stomach and a sob catches in my throat.

Joel presses his eyes shut, as if it's too much for him to watch, then sucks in a deep breath, his chest rising and falling under those stark white sheets. "*Predicted* twelve months." His voice is hard, cold. I know right then and there that this isn't the Joel I made love to at the lake. This Joel is an entirely different beast all together. "But sometimes, shit happens."

I reach out and take his hand, stroking my thumb over the top of it, but he doesn't make any effort to engage with me. His hand is a dead weight in my own.

"I know it sounds stupid, but there's still hope. And I hear there are new tests being done in—"

"Stop!"

I flinch and jerk my hand away, as if his word struck me across the face.

Remorse lines his features and he purses his lips, then shakes his head. "I know you're only trying to help. But I've had treatment before, Ellie. This is ... this is it for me."

The tears that have been lurking behind my eyes all day break loose. I sniff to try and hold them back but still those suckers break free, running down my cheeks. All thoughts of being strong for Joel fly right out of my head as the grim reality of the situation kicks in. Something's eating him alive, whittling away at the mechanics of his brain. Day by day, minute by minute it's sucking at the marrow of his soul until his very life force runs dry.

He's not going to fight this.

I think of the list, of the twenty-one things, and I know.

He was never going to fight this.

He's fought it before.

Cancer won.

A sheen mists over Joel's eyes, and somehow that's so much worse than crying myself. He's supposed to be the strong one. He should be happy.

But how can he be?

What do you do when your happily-ever-after has an expiration date?

I reach over to wipe away his tears, to try and dry his face, but he stills, rigid as a board under my touch.

"Don't."

"I'm sorry," I whisper, and fold my arms around my waist. There is no handbook for this. No guide to tell you how to help a person in life-ending pain.

We sit in silence, and Joel looks out the window. The view is of another wing of the hospital, a cream rendered building that towers over this one. Windows with reflective surfaces shine back at us, showing us the purple of this building and the red of the sky as the sun sets. It's a staid view. Mundane.

It might be the last view Joel ever sees.

"This is just ..." I pause. "This is fucked. You taught me never to give up. To push myself, and live in every moment. And now, here you are."

"Dying?" he asks, a bitter laugh in his tone.

I shake my head. "About to start the sequel."

Finally, Joel's face breaks into the easy smile I know and love. He manages a soft laugh and shake of his head, then he holds out his arm, shifting his weight to one side of the bed. "C'mere, Ellie."

My stomach twirls as I slip off my shoes and slide up onto the bed to lie beside him. His arm wraps around me, and I rest my head against his shoulder. It's a tight fit, but I'd stay here for eternity if I could. If it meant not leaving Joel, no sacrifice would be too much.

"So I've ... I've had a feeling for a few weeks," Joel says. He kisses the top of my head, and he smells so good, his lips so warm, that it's hard to believe he's sick. Hard to believe this is it. "I've been sick a few times, and getting kind of dizzy."

"Like the other day, in the car?" I ask, my mind flashing back to our time on the way home from the indoor skydive.

Joel snorts. "You're never gonna let me live that down, are you? You almost kill someone once ..." He shakes his head. "Anyway, so then I've become more and more tired. Too tired. Unnaturally so."

I clap my hand to my head. "I didn't notice …" *How did I not notice?*

"I know what you're thinking, and no, you're not," he corrects me. "How were you to know?" He shrugs, and my head shifts with the movement. "How was anyone to know …"

The words float between us. His deep breathing is oddly soothing, and I find myself timing my breath to be opposite to his. As if somehow I can suck in all his sickness and breathe fresh air back into his lungs. If only life were that simple.

If only love were that easy.

"They say it could be a month—maybe less."

Somehow, hearing it from him is so much more real than hearing the words from his father or Fiona.

"This morning, I collapsed. Just couldn't walk. And that pain ..." He pauses, and I press a light kiss to his cheek. "It was vicious. Like a savage dog let off its lead, tearing at my head. Hacking and biting and just ..." He grits his teeth, and something flashes over his face—it's as if he's lost focus entirely. "Fuck!" he yells, and slams his hand down on the table beside the bed. The cards jump, and one floats to the floor, dancing as it falls, a mockery of the anger looming in the air. "I fucking forgot what I was saying."

Joel turns his body to the window, shielding me from his pain. He hasn't spoken the words out loud, but it doesn't take a genius to know that this beast controlling his life is affecting his brain, too. He shares his mind with a monster.

A few minutes pass, and even though I know Joel wants his space, I fight it. Because that's what he's taught me. Some things are worth fighting for. And Joel Henley is definitely one such thing.

I loop my arm around his waist and spoon my body up against his, pushing up the bed a little so my head rests right above his shoulder. I press a kiss to his neck, and it smells so good, so much like pine and beach and *Joel* that if I close my eyes, for just one moment, I can forget we're in a hospital. I can forget my soul mate is dying.

"So I started a really great book this morning," I say. It's a lie. All I started this morning was an action plan on how to find Dani, but I can't tell him that. It's not what Joel needs.

Joel needs fairytales and happy endings, and I don't know that Dani is one.

It takes him a while, but finally his body shifts, his head turning back to me. "Oh yeah?"

"Mmmm." I nod, and I launch into the tale of a book about love and laughter and taking chances, pushing life to the limit. There's no truth to my words, no real book on which to base this plot. I'm just making it up as I go along in the hope it distracts him from the horrible truth facing him right now.

At some point, the red light outside dulls to a cool purple, and the white lights overhead flicker on. Food trolleys clatter down the hall, and nurses chat in other rooms about the five-star dining the hospital provides.

I push up to my elbows and go to speak, but when I look over my shoulder, Joel's already asleep.

I take one of the cards, the King of Hearts, and I begin to fold. First I rip it into a square, then I fold it in half again. It won't pop out at the end, so I search the drawers in the bedside table until I find a piece of thinner paper. This time, I complete all the steps until I have the perfect paper crane. I place it on the pillow next to his head and, after pressing a kiss to his soft, cool lips, I leave.

Only my heart stays in that room with him.

TWENTY-FIVE

The week passes by in a blur. I call up Colin and let him know I have to work around hospital hours. I don't have time to focus on finding a new job right now. I just have to be there.

I have to be there for Joel.

And when I'm not being there for Joel, I'm trying like hell to keep my sister safe.

It's a Wednesday afternoon when I take Dani and stop in at the hospital to see Joel on our way to Mum's. It's not going to be long enough, but Colin had me packing baskets all day, and I figure any time is better than none. I just try not to think that every time is one time closer to the end. Every inhale is one breath closer to the last.

"Are we going to be long?" Dani asks, her feet thudding down the hall beside me.

"I told you, you can wait in the car." I shrug as if it's no big deal, and thank God she doesn't call me on my bluff. Really, there's no way I'd let her wait there. Not when I can't guarantee that's where she'd stay.

I stop at the ATM on the way to Joel's room, withdrawing my money for rent to give to Hope. I shove the notes into an empty slot in my purse, then start to walk again.

We turn the corner to Joel's room and I pause for a moment, looking back at my sister. "Please, just be nice. Okay?"

She rolls her eyes, as if it's the ultimate insult. "He's dying. I'm not a complete bitch."

I ignore her callous tone and turn back, paste a smile on my face, and walk into the room.

Joel lies on his bed, the television above him flicking through pictures but no sound coming out. To his right is a table with a jug of water and a glass, as well as a bunch of flowers. More flowers are planted on the mantelpiece above him, and there's even a *get well soon* balloon.

It doesn't look cheery.

It looks like a funeral parlour.

As per usual, there's a group in attendance. Today it's Fiona and a girl I haven't seen before. The afternoon sun streams through the window giving Joel's skin a golden glow. A glow he needs, because colour by colour, he's changing. His face isn't cream anymore. His eyes aren't as blue. Bit by bit, he's slipping away.

"Ellie!" Fiona smiles, and jumps up from the chair to come and hug me. She pulls back and looks at Danica. "Hi. We met at the bar that time. You were off your face."

"Whatever." Dani pushes past and claims the chair Fiona just vacated. Fi mouths the word *sorry* to me, and I shrug it off. It's not like I can argue otherwise.

"Hey! Where's my kiss?" Joel asks, a small smile crossing his lips. I all but knock Fiona out of the way and hurl to his side, placing a hand on his cheek. Up close, he's even paler than he looked from the door. Goosebumps travel down my arms as an inky dread washes through me. *He's leaving.*

As quickly as it comes, it goes away. I have to be strong. I have to be strong for Joel.

I lean in to give him a chaste kiss.

"Seriously?" he murmurs, then cups his hand at the base of my neck, pulling my face close. When our lips meet, his are needy, full of desire. They part and his tongue seeks entrance to my mouth. Heat flares within me, and my hand reaches for his waist, his body that I still somehow crave, even though I know he's so broken.

His fingers fist my hair and he nips at my lip. Desire teases between my legs and for one moment, one small, tiny moment, I forget where we are and imagine us back in the tent at the lake.

"You're in a hospital, remember?"

Dani's words bring me back to the present, and I pull back. My cheeks flame as I gaze deep into Joel's eyes, our lips only separated by an inch. "Hi," I say.

"Hi."

My hair curtains us off from the world. Joel grins up at me, and there's so much love in his eyes.

"Hi," I say again, a giggle bubbling up inside me.

"Hi." He laughs, and presses a small kiss to my nose.

"The young lady here might have a point."

The voice reaches my ears, and I pull back more completely this time, turning to face an older lady who's just walked in. Instinctively, I reach for Joel's hand, twisting his fingers in mine. "Sorry," I say, smiling. "I'm—"

"Ellie Mayfield." The woman interrupts and folds her arms across her chest. She isn't smiling, but I'm not exactly breaking out the milk and cookies, either. "I'm Candice Armstrong. Joel's mother."

I blink, recognition flooding back to me. "Of course. Ms Armstrong." I smile, but she doesn't correct me. There's no *call me Candice* here.

I look to Fiona for support, but she just bites her lip and screws up her nose as if to say *I don't know.*

"She's only here for a short while, when her schedule allows," Joel says, apparently not feeling anywhere near the level-ten awkward I am.

"Joel." She scolds, a *V* forming between her brows. "I love you."

"But only during visiting hours?"

The question hangs awkwardly in the room. A steely gaze shines between Joel and his mother.

"I'm sure your mum …" I trail off, looking for words to fill the empty space. "I'm sure she means well."

"I did quite like Vanessa, but I'm glad you found Ellie again," Ms Armstrong says. *Ouch!* Talk about a veiled compliment. "You seem very happy together."

Joel squeezes my hand.

"They are."

I blink. *Dani?*

"He loves her, and she loves him." She pops her gum and leans back in the plastic chair, her gaze out the window. "It's sickening, really."

"Well …" Mrs Armstrong shakes her head, then looks to the door. "Perhaps I should go."

"Thanks for visiting," Joel says.

Mrs Armstrong leans over to kiss his cheek, then straightens. She nods at me and leaves, and I settle again on the side of Joel's bed, the rays from the sun glinting golden against the hair on my arms.

"Thank God she's gone." Joel grins up at me.

"Is that the first time she's come?" I whisper in his ear.

He shakes his head. "Third." Joel pulls back to make eye contact. "I don't know if she's scared of me dying, or just can't find the time, you know?"

When I nod, he nips at my lobe and then sucks it into his mouth, his soft lips sending a thrill through me.

"C'mon, guys, save that for after public visiting hours." Fiona rolls her eyes.

"What's new?" I ask Joel. It's code for *how are you feeling and what's been happening* all in one.

Joel takes it all in his stride. He pulls one of my blonde curls and watches it spring back up, a smirk playing on his lips. "Well, I've watched a whole heap of porn, and—"

"Joel!" Fiona groans.

"Just watched some TV. Took some drugs. Stared at this boring-as-batshit view." Joel gestures to the plain cream building blinking at us out the window.

An idea winks into my mind, and I nod. "It does kind of suck."

"Just a little." Joel smiles, and then looks over to my sister. "How you doing, Dani?"

"Good." She doesn't look up from her mobile phone where she's tap, tapping away.

"Going to any parties tonight?" He tries.

That causes her to still. She raises both eyebrows at. "You're gonna have to try harder than that."

"Worth a shot." Joel raises his hands in the air, and I laugh.

We talk some more about all the important things— love, life, and the accuracy of *Sons of Anarchy*. After twenty minutes, Dani gives me the eye and I say goodbye.

But even though my body leaves the hospital, my heart stays right on that hospital bed.

And I wonder if I'll ever get it back again.

It's dark when Fiona, Kohl, Marc and I sneak into the hospital room. The curtains are drawn, blocking the outside world and the early rays of sun.

Joel snores, a deep steady rhythm that has me secure in the knowledge he won't wake while I prepare his surprise.

The nurses were on board with my plan, if a little sceptical, and a lot concerned that I would be responsible for the clean-up. Which of course I would.

As we work, I fall into a soothing kind of rhythm. There's so much going on—with Joel, with Dani, with work—it feels nice to focus on something menial and labour-driven for a while. It's bliss to escape my head.

It takes us two whole hours, but after a lot of tape, ties and lung power, we're ready. I shut the door to the hospital room, thanking my lucky stars not for the first time that there's currently no one else sharing this space, and suck in a deep breath.

"Oh Joel," I sing from the door. The others are beside me. Fiona bounces on the balls of her feet.

Joel shifts on the bed, but doesn't open his eyes.

"Sexiest boyfriend in the wo-orld," I sing, and this time, even though his eyes remain shut, a smirk plays upon his lips. That one small gesture sends blood pumping to my heart.

"Are you here to give me a morning blow-job?" he asks sleepily.

"Get your mind out of the gutter," Fiona barks.

Joel's eyes fly open—and that's when we spring to action.

Fiona switches on the blue spotlights that send streams of cobalt light against the walls and over to the window which has been covered in blue crepe paper.

Marc walks over to Joel, who's looking at me with a quizzical expression on his face. "What's going on?"

"You'll need this." Marc clips a helmet over Joel's head, and it looks so thoroughly ridiculous I can't help but laugh.

"What?" Joel asks, touching the helmet as if unsure if it's real.

"You're bored of the view, right?" I say, hoping to distract him from what Kohl is doing.

"Uh-huh." Joel nods.

"We know you can't exactly jump out of a plane." I suck in a breath. Here's where it could all go horribly wrong, and he could be terribly offended by my idea. "So we thought we'd bring you the next best thing."

Joel opens his mouth and asks something, but I don't hear it. Kohl flicks the switch on the generator and the room erupts into chaos.

An industrial fan blasts into life, a mechanical roar filling the room. The air is strong and directed right at Joel's bed. His head falls back against the pillow, though I suspect it's more from shock than the strength of the wind. The flowers on the shelf above him press toward the wall, and some even lose their petals.

That's not why we did this, though.

On the floor were five hundred white balloons, each with the number twenty-one on them.

And when the fan starts up, they go flying.

At first Joel laughs, batting them away as they near his face. He frowns, shaking his head, and smiling at us all in turn. Marc turns on the second fan so the balloons whirl from left to right, suspended in the centre of the room.

Then, it clicks. Joel looks over to me and holds out his arms, balloons knocking into them from left and right. "C'mere," he yells, and I laugh because he got it. I knew he would get it.

I dance across the floor to the bed. Fiona grabs Kohl's hand and spins him around, dancing in this sea of white and blue. Marc joins them, all three laughing.

I bat balloon after balloon and finally reach Joel's side, my lungs aching from laughter. Joel's breath is hot on my ear when he says, "You gave me sky-diving."

I smile, nodding as the white balloon clouds tuft around us, the wind presses back our hair, and the blue light from the window is reflected around the room. It's a far cry from the real thing, but it's made Joel happy, and in these final weeks, that's all I could possibly want.

All I could possibly need.

TWENTY-SIX

It's my day for Dani watch, and even though I'm trying to be patient, even though I'm trying to be sympathetic to her needs, I can't help but resent it.

Every second I spend sitting in this car, waiting for her to walk out of the college gates, every second I sit between her and Colin during family dinner that follows after, every second that slows me getting to work and then packing the picnic baskets is a second more I could be spending with Joel.

And you can count the seconds he has left.

We're still only on week two of his predicted four-week outlook, but they've said things can change at any time now.

It's strange—it's a logical fact I know oh-so-well. I've been through it all with my father. But there's this stupid voice inside me that refuses to believe this could be it. Maybe they've got it wrong.

The boy in that hospital bed isn't sick. Sure, he isn't as strong as he used to be, and he is sleepier than normal, but he's still so alive. It's just so hard to argue with that.

The clock ticks over to three, and I gaze left and right, searching for the familiar blonde curls over the sea of other heads exiting the building. School finished ten minutes ago but still there are stragglers working their way out of the buildings, clustering around trees next to bus stops.

None of them are my sister though.

After another ten minutes, I give in and call. She doesn't pick up, and that familiar sick sense of dread I have when dealing with her kicks me in the gut.

I check my watch for the fourth time this afternoon, cursing when it tells me the truth. It's five to four. Two hours before visiting time ends. Three hours before I'm supposed to be at work, at Colin's.

I get out of the car and slam the door behind me, leaning up against the metallic blue sedan, and dial Zy this time.

He answers on the third ring. "What's up?"

"She's not here."

Silence.

"Shit."

"Do you have any idea where she could be?" Worry clips my tone as I crane my neck, hoping to see her dawdling out of the building.

"I don't know, maybe—"

"Ell Bell!"

The two words turn my blood cold. I turn to the left.

Danica.

She stumbles down the concrete path, blonde curls flying in the wind behind her. A guy who has to be at least ten years older than her has his arm around her hip, part helping her walk, part groping her boobs.

"That's my bodyguard." Dani points to me with a shaking hand. Her pupils are dilated, her jaw clenching and unclenching.

"Is that ..." Zy trails off, reminding me I'm still on the phone.

"Yeah." I sigh. "I'll call you back."

I hit *end* on the call and pocket the phone, folding my arms across my body to protect myself from the chill that's descended, despite the spring warmth What has she done?

I blink back the tears that threaten to fall and press my thumb and forefinger to my nose. *Please don't let this be happening. Please ... not again.*

"This is my sister, Eleanor." Dani wraps an arm around my shoulders, affecting an English accent when she says my name, and then laughing hysterically.

The older man laughs too, shoving his hands in the pockets of his denim jeans. His denim jacket cloaks his body snugly and there's a sinister look in his gaze, and I have a feeling he's seen far more with those steely eyes than I ever want to glimpse in a lifetime.

"Your sister owes me money. You got it?" he barks.

I blink and jerk my head back. "Pardon?"

"She owes me. She said you'd—"

"Can you please lend me two hundred dollars, sis?" Dani hisses the *s*. "I forgot my debit card."

Anger burns inside me. "Dan, I don't have that kind of money."

"You don't want to fuck with him," she stage-whispers.

"It's only two hundred." The man shrugs as if it's no big deal. As if he thinks perhaps I'm not living week-to-week in a shack, employed for minimum wage by a creep and my mother.

"Do you take direct deposit?" I ask, and am rewarded for my smart-arse comment with a death stare.

"The only direct deposit I'm interested in is the kind I can make in your sister's—"

I hold my hands up in apology. "Got it. Sorry."

I open the car door and open my wallet, turning my arse away from the couple when the guy whistles. It's clear he thinks this is hilarious.

I find the partition with my rent in it and slide the notes out, my hand shaking. "Take it," I whisper.

I don't look at him, though.

The whole time, my eyes are glued to my sister.

"Take it all."

"Yeah." He grabs the cash and walks away, leaving me and my sister alone.

I storm inside Mum's house, Dani hot on my heels. I turn to face her, anger burning through me. "This has to stop, Dani. It's not a joke any more." And as much as it makes me feel like a little kid, I utter those three last words. "I'm telling Mum."

"I'll pay you back," she says, her voice quiet. "I promise. I'll get it for you tonight."

"Where?" I shrug. "Do you think Mum will lend you the cash?"

"I won't let you down, Ellie. Just chill. I've got this," she says, her words coming at a rapid speed, and strides down the hall toward her old room.

I walk into the living room and head straight to the fridge, pouring ice-cold water into a glass. It numbs my throat on the way down, and I wish it could numb my heart.

My phone vibrates in my pocket, and I pull it out to check it. *Joel*. Probably wondering what time I'm coming to the hospital later tonight. My thumb hovers over the accept button, and I'm just about to pick up when Mum walks into the room.

"Eleanor. You're early. For a change."

For some reason, those three added words are all it takes. The anger and hurt, the guilt and regret that have been roiling around inside of my gut since the day Dad died all spew forth from my mouth, as if someone has opened the gates and now there's no stopping it. "I got your daughter here on time after some druggy demanded money from her." I step closer to Mum, my hand clenching around the glass tumbler I hold.

"Money?" Mum frowns, as if the very idea is so unlikely it offends her sense of self.

"Money." I confirm, and glance up the hall, as if afraid she might hear. "We need to get her help, Mum. We need to make this stop."

She shakes her head, but I see the doubt in her eyes. I pounce on it like a hungry animal. "She's got a problem. This isn't a one-off. This isn't twice. This is at least three times she's done it." My mind flashes to the man I love in the hospital bed. "Life is too short, Mum. She could die."

The word sends a shockwave over her. She clutches at her heart, then thins her lips. "You better—"

"No!" I throw my hands out. "You better stop blaming me for this." Tears well in my eyes, and I shake my head. The weight I've been carrying with me for the last year cranks up a notch. I stoop under its burden. "I have done everything I fucking can."

Mum nods, and turns to the hall leading to Dani's old room. I follow, my feet leaden on the tiled floor.

When we reach the closed door, Mum turns to look at me. Her raised brow speaks volumes. It says hope and heartache and everything in between.

Then she opens the door.

Colin's gaze flies to us. His arm is around Dani's shoulders in what should have been an innocent gesture.

It's where his other hand is that isn't.

Fondling her breast.

TWENTY-SEVEN

The first time I hear my mother swear isn't in a hot fury. It isn't in excitement, or glee. It's in exactly the same manner as she does everything in life.

Cold. Calculating.

Cruel.

"What. The. Fuck."

Colin flies from Dani and brushes down his shirt, as if wiping off evidence. "I don't know what you think you saw."

Mum changes from worried caregiver to protective mamma bear in an instant. Smoke all but fumes from her nostrils as her fists clench by her sides in a gesture that screams fury. "You were touching my daughter."

"I can … it's not what it looks like." Colin babbles to Mother, his arms outstretched as if pleading.

I glance at Dani.

She tucks a handful of pineapples, fifty-dollar bills, into her jeans pocket.

A stone of realisation balls into the base of my gut. *She needed the money …*

Dani shoots me a smirk and it says volumes. It confirms the fear I've had ever since Colin started trying to push boundaries with me.

Maybe it was because he was paying for something more with my little sister.

Colin claps his hands together, almost in a beg. "I'm sorry, I—"

"Get the fuck out." Mum points to the door. Colin's gaze travels from my sister to my mother's hand, and his normal soft pink pallor turns a deathly shade of white.

"I …" He swallows, and glances around the room. "I don't know what you think you saw, but …"

"Whatever it was, it was too much. Go. Now."

He doesn't need further encouragement. A hot arm brushes past me as he races out of the room.

I press my eyes shut as a million thoughts race through my brain. It's hard not to ask Mum if she believes me now.

It's harder still not to shake Dani and ask her why she lied. She so obviously knew Colin was a sleaze—why did she laugh? Let Mum think I was making things up?

When I open my eyes again, my sister is sitting on the bed, hugging her knees to her chest. Tears streak down her cheeks, as she looks out the window, as if somehow that might hold the answer to all her problems.

I hold my breath, waiting for my mother to unleash. Waiting for her to rail against my sister, as she's berated me so many times. Waiting for Dani to get what she deserves.

"It's okay, sweetie." Mum walks forward and sits beside her on the bed. She pulls Dani's shaking body close to her own and strokes her hair, the long blonde ringlets that stick to her back. "It's okay."

"Mum, she took money." The words fall from my lips before I have time to think.

Dani sobs harder, her frail shoulders shaking.

Mum's head whips from my sister to myself and back again. She gives a small, almost imperceptible shake of her head. "She wouldn't do that, Eleanor."

My eyes bug out of my head. "Seriously?" I raise my hands in the air in question. "Why don't you believe me?"

The only answer is Dani's gentle sobs, and Mum's soothing *there there*s.

I bite my lip. My sister is in trouble. I want to go over, to hug her, to make sure she's okay, but a part of me thinks of Dani in the car this afternoon. Dani who took my rent money to help pay for whatever drugs she bought off that junkie. Dani who is letting a close family friend touch her in exchange for cash.

That Dani needs help.

And by sheltering her from the storm, I'm not protecting her. I'm exposing her even more.

All my actions of the past few months come back to slap me in the face. Finding the drugs. The trip to hospital. Covering for her at work.

All of that was me enabling her to slide further and further down this slippery slope.

A slope I could have stopped her falling on.

"You should go," Mum whispers, and they're all the words I need. "Let me deal with this alone."

I turn on my heel and I leave, running from the room, down the hall, out the house and into my car on the street. I sit there, staring at the place I called my home. The place where I grew up.

The place where my sister and mother now talked, consoled—without me.

All I ever wanted was to keep my family close. Somehow, I've torn myself apart from it, and I don't know how to fix this.

I grab my phone. There are four missed calls in total, all from Joel and all within a few minutes of each other. My stomach lurches as I start the car and pull out of the drive.

The streets are quiet, thank goodness, and as the phone rings I pull out onto the main road, my headlights beaming against the pale yellow early evening light. The phone rings out, and anxiety tightens my grip on the wheel. Why wouldn't he answer?

Why did he call so many times?

Fear chills my skin. I blast the heater, and hot air puffs my arms and legs, but it isn't enough to warm the cool creeping over my heart.

"There are at least two more weeks," I whisper to myself, but the words ring hollow. Because this time a month ago, there was one more year.

Life can change at lightning speed. A storm is coming, and I don't want to get hit.

I swallow down the extra saliva that's coating my mouth and stop at the traffic lights, staring at my traitorous phone. No new calls from Joel. I'm almost afraid to dial again, because if he doesn't pick up, *what does that mean?*

I know with terrifying certainty that I'm not ready for him to die. I'm just not.

With a shaking hand, I hit redial. The sound of my phone ringing takes up all of the space in the car. It's a hollow repetition that burns against my heart.

The lights turn green and my car jerks forward.

The phone rings out.

It's then that I make a decision. I've lived my entire life by the rules—I need to break them for once.

My foot slams to the floor. I speed toward the hospital. I drive like a woman possessed, racing through amber lights and sitting above the speed limit. I'm hyper-aware of everything around me. The way the sun sets, a pale pink hue ghosting across the horizon. The sound of the Avett Brothers song on the radio. The hot, hot air that mists across my face. The sour taste in my mouth.

As I steer the car through the final roundabouts to the hospital, a movie of this afternoon plays through my mind. Dani. Colin. Mum. *Joel.*

My head hurts, and I touch the place between my eyes. Deep lines crease there and I try to smooth them away with my hand.

I pull up outside the hospital and park my car in the ten-minute waiting bay. Because I'm going to go inside, kiss my boyfriend, and then come back down to the car and park it down the street, in the proper bay, once I know he's okay. We'll laugh about this as I recount my actions to him over the phone. How paranoid I am. How silly I was to be so worried.

My key slides out of the lock and then I'm inside the hospital, trying not to run for the elevator. I press the up button and the doors open straight away, as if this moment was meant to be. As if the universe is working to keep me on schedule.

The elevator shoots up to the third floor, and when the doors open I stride down the corridor, a smile plastered over my face. Joel doesn't need to see how worried I've been. He doesn't need to know of the hurt playing through my mind.

Just as I turn the corner toward his room, my phone vibrates in my pocket. I pull it out and read his name and smile. Perfect timing.

I reach the door to room 318 and round the corner, a spring in my step. "Hello?" I sing in a playful voice, hitting *answer* to his call as I walk inside.

Only it isn't Joel calling me at all.

It's his father.

And he's a mess.

Joel's father is the picture of grief. His normally combed grey hair is tousled, as if torn out of shape by desperate wringing hands. His eyes are red spider webs, and his skin splotchy, as if someone has spattered pink and white paint all over him. Two fingers press to the bridge of his nose while he holds a cell—Joel's cell—to his ear.

His eyes lock with mine, and he slowly pulls the phone to his side.

In that moment, I know. My whole life is about to change.

Numb fingers hit *end* on my mobile, and I stow it back in my pocket. With all my strength, I move one foot in front of the other. One foot in front of the other.

When I'm at his side, I wrap my arms around the frail older man who looks as though he just lost a part of himself.

And maybe he did.

"Ellie." He breathes the word into my hair. His arms wrap around me as if he's drowning and I can somehow save him.

I don't tell him I can't swim.

I can barely save myself.

After a few moments, he pulls away, swiping at his eyes even though there are no tears. He shakes his head and shudders in a breath, then lets it out between rounded lips. "He ... he's asking to see you."

Hope dances in my chest and I press my eyes shut, praying for just one short moment. He's asking to see me. That means he's alive. That means—

That means he wants to say goodbye.

I push my shoulders back and look Mr Henley in the eye, then nod. He steps to the side and I walk forward, but it's not my body taking these slow steps. It's not my eyes that latch onto Joel, lying still in his bed, the machines around him somehow looming more ominously than usual. And it's not my knees that crumple beneath me when I fall into the chair.

I'm somewhere else. Removed. Detached.

This isn't happening to me. This cannot be real.

The girl who isn't me clasps Joel's hand, and it's colder than normal. I rub it between my palms, trying to warm the life back into him, as if I'm two pieces of kindling and can spark a flame within him. That's all I want. That's all I've always wanted. For him to keep fighting. For him to fire up.

"Joel," I whisper.

Slowly, oh so slowly, his head turns. Two eyes blink open, and then those blue orbs are locked with mine. Only, there isn't the usual power behind his gaze. Half his energy has been sucked away by this cancer.

The door cricks closed behind me, and I glance over my shoulder to note that Mr Henley has left the room. I only look for the briefest moment, though. Right now, every second I get to stare at those eyes is worth all the money, all the security, all the safety I have.

It's everything.

"Hey, sexy." I smile, and trace a finger down his cheek. He rests his eyes shut again, a small smile playing on his cracked lips. "Do you want a water?"

His head moves left to right, and he opens his mouth the tiniest bit. "No. Thanks."

"Okay." *Take the water.* Want *the water.* "You don't have to."

He huffs a laugh, and then wracking coughs shake his body. They make the machine above his head beep that little bit faster. When he falls back to the pillow, peace once more creates a mask over his face.

It's then and there that I know.

Joel Henley is dying.

He's dying right in front of me.

And there's not a damn thing I can do about it.

"I don't want you to go," I whisper. My bottom lip shakes, and I sniff. Tears prickle at my eyes, and I hate this. I hate that I'm crying again, and that this is the end, and that I didn't even see him much today. I hate that I didn't dress in something nice, or bring a nice gift, and that I haven't prepared the perfect things to say to give him courage in these final moments.

Most of all, I hate that he's dying.

And I don't want a tomorrow without him.

"I'm not afraid," Joel croaks. I reach out a hand and squeeze his fingers between mine. Tears well in my eyes, and an ache that's physical swells deep inside me.

"How can you not be afraid?" I ask, my voice breaking over the last word.

Joel gives a small smile, a weak grin, and looks at me again. "See those constellations, out there?" His head tilts slightly toward the window, and I nod. "The one that's burning brightest? The ..." he coughs, and I tighten my grip. "The first star?"

I nod, yes.

"That one's mine. I'll look for you in the stars, Ellie Mayfield." He brings my hand to his lips and gives it a tender kiss. "I'll always find you there."

My heart hurts, the kind of ache that feels like a wound ripped open. It's all-consuming, and I bite my lip. Creating more pain holds the tears back. It keeps the agony at bay.

"Not ... going," he says, but every word seems to cost him. A frown mars his forehead, the only indicator that he's in a lot of pain, but I know him. It's enough. "Tell me ... how ... your day was."

I toe off my skate shoes and lift the blanket up, then slide into the bed beside him. One arm rests over his chest, and my other sits under my head, holding it up so I can look upon him. I press a kiss to his forehead and pull back. He's ice on his hands, but fire in his cheeks. That one person can feel two extremes seems completely at odds to me, but I don't say anything because there's no one to say it to. There's just Joel and me, and a heap of white balloons.

"Tell," Joel croaks.

"I didn't do anything exci—"

"Tell."

There's a finality in his tone that isn't to be argued with. Typical Joel. As stubborn as he dies as he was when he lived.

Was.

No. Not yet.

Is.

Even though my heart focuses on him, I let my mind float over the events of the day, sharing them. "So, things went to hell at home," I say. Joel's eyes flare with a tiny hint of light. "Dani owed money to some drug guy. And I think she's been hitting on Colin ... maybe using him to get money ... I don't know." I let my breath rush out. "Mum already knew she had a problem, but I think telling her today—now she believes it. Even if I don't know what's going on inside her head."

"You told her ... truth."

I nod. "I know. It seems the truth isn't as liberating as I'd thought it'd be."

Cold fingers grip my own, and they're strong, so much stronger than I thought they'd be. His grip is tight and I feel my shoulders untense, and every muscle in me slowly uncoils as if on a spring. Because he's got me. He's catching me as I fall.

"You're ... you're a strong person." Those fingers squeeze my hand, but his words squeeze my soul. "She'll ... she'll come 'round. You don't need me. I know you've got this."

I stare out that unchanging window. Car headlights reflect off the glass in the other building—little specks of white against deep black panes. Doubt still plagues me. How does he know? What if she doesn't speak to me for weeks? Months? Years?

What if Joel dies, and I'm left here ... alone?

The finality of the situation settles over me like a heavy blanket. Terror seizes my body and tightens its grip. I pepper kisses along Joel's forehead, down his cheek, over his lips. "Please," I whisper with fierce intensity. The tears I've fought so hard to keep locked up well and trickle slowly down my cheeks. It hurts. It hurts so damn much. "Don't leave me."

"I'm ... not." A shaking hand traces over my lips, and I kiss it, determined to shower him with affection. To let him know with every ounce of my being that he is loved—he can't go yet.

My thoughts must show on my face, because hot lips brush against my cheek. "I love you, Ellie Mayfield." Those eyes lock with mine, and he is all I see. This boy. This face.

That heart.

Warmth swells inside me. This moment, right here, right now—it's where I want to be. I let all thoughts of the rest of the world evaporate into the night sky. I am here. I am with the man I love.

Only death can't take these precious moments away from us.

"I love you, Joel Henley."

Brown lashes fan across his cheeks as his eyes flutter closed, and soon his breathing settles into a shallow rhythm. I move my elbow from under my head and rest upon the pillow, watching him sleep. I want to commit this moment to memory. I want to etch this view so fiercely into my brain that nothing will ever erase it.

And with everything I have, with every cell in my being, with every pulse of blood around my body, *with every breath of air into my lungs*—I pray.

I pray that he makes it through.

And that if he doesn't, he takes me with him.

TWENTY-EIGHT

"Ellie."

Fingers wrap around my arm. The voice isn't familiar—feminine, soft.

I tighten my grip around Joel's waist, melding my side to his. Perhaps if I press hard enough, I can mould myself to him. Imprint him upon my body as he's been imprinted upon my soul.

I don't remember falling asleep, but at some point I must have. Now, tiredness cloaks my body in a mist I can't fight through. It's nice being asleep. Nothing can hurt me here.

"Ellie, I need you to wake up."

That same voice again. This time, the fingers give a little squeeze and a pull, and I fight the wave of sleep that's crashed upon me and blink my eyes open.

Joel's face is the first thing I see, and I smile, leaning forward to kiss his cheek. This time it's cool, and I thank the lord. Surely this is a good thing. His fever has broken.

"Please, can I get you out of the bed?"

I turn and see a nurse standing there, lines creasing her brow. I give a small smile. I don't mind moving. This gives me the perfect opportunity to repark my car. Avoid getting a ticket.

A man in a shirt and jacket enters the room, and for the first time I realise it's still night. The corridor outside is bathed in a bright yellow light, and outside thousands of stars sparkle in the sky. They twinkle like tiny jewels in a deep, dark crown.

I pull back the covers and swing my legs out of the bed, my feet landing inside my shoes. I shuffle over to a chair and wipe at my eyes, trying to wake myself up.

"Can I get you ... can you come with me, please, Ellie?" the nurse asks, and this time there's a kindness to her tone.

I'm mid-lace when I look up to reply, and that's when I see it.

Pity.

Sympathy.

Pain.

My heart lurches. I feel it like a lump in my throat, something I can't swallow.

No.

No.

No, no, no, no, no, no, no, no—

"I need to talk to you outside."

My hands fall limply to my sides. I shake my head. Or, I think I'm shaking my head. On the inside I'm shutting myself away into a place where Joel is well, and we're in love, and we're making love, and we're happy, and *we're not this. We're anything but this.*

I want to just stay in this chair. If I stay here, nothing will change. No one can tell me words I don't want to hear. No one can take him away from me.

But for some unknown reason, my feet thud out of the room after her, shoelaces trailing beside me. I don't look back. Doing that will confirm what I know deep down is true.

I'm not ready for tomorrow yet.

Someone has control of my body and it sits down right in the middle of the green plastic chair in the small waiting room of the ward. Someone has pasted a blank look on my face that's directly at odds with how full of emotion I am inside.

"I'm terribly sorry." The nurse's hand reaches for my own, and I numbly let her take it. She gives it a squeeze and looks me dead in the eyes. "Joel Henley has passed away."

Five small words.

Five simple, small, *life-ending* words.

"He died peacefully, in his sleep," she continues.

I nod, slowly, three times. I take in a deep breath and let it all out, my chest deflating like a balloon.

"Can I get you anything? A glass of water? Tea? Coffee?" The nurse tilts her head to the side, taking her hand back and placing it in her lap.

I shake my head this time, and open my mouth to speak. Words. I need to ... "Has ... does Mr Henley ...?"

"Ms Armstrong has been called, and will be in later. Mr Henley is in with his son now." The nurse confirms, then pushes to a stand. "He's asked for a few moments alone, but if you want to check back at the desk in five, I'm sure you can go in to say goodbye."

She walks back to the desk and I sit there, staring at my hands. This time twenty-four hours ago, everything was okay. Now, nothing is the same.

I was sleeping when he died.

I didn't even realise he'd passed.

For some reason, the thought hits me. It's a stabbing pain aimed straight at my heart and it twists, digging the wound deeper. How could I be so connected to him and not feel him leave? How could I be by his side and not know he'd gone?

That thought is the one that breaks me. My soul tears, and I go from numb to completely shattered. I'd thought sadness was something that hurt you mentally, emotionally. I didn't realise true devastation carries a physical ache, too. I'm so upset, so completely hurt that my pain is a punch in the stomach. It's a wallop to the chest. A knife to the heart. Tears prickle my eyes and then stream down my cheeks. I go from zero to one hundred in a second and lose myself as waves of pain crash over me and pull me under. I gulp for air in between angry, heart-wrenching sobs. My throat stings with each cry and my shoulders shake. I clutch at my stomach and double over on myself as the hurt eats at me with everything it has.

Heartache is so damn ugly. There is nothing beautiful in this moment of grief.

There's nothing beautiful in death.

The nurse rushes over, a plastic cup in her hand. "Here." She hands it over, but I'm shaking so hard I can't keep it still. Water splashes from the cup onto the floor.

"Is there someone I can call, sweetie? Your mother, maybe?" the nurse asks, and it only makes me cry harder. Because I don't want anyone else. I want Joel. He's the only person who can heal the gaping wound inside of me.

I shake my head but don't make eye contact as I try so hard to stop the pain. Slippered feet pad away, and it's just me and my all-consuming sobs.

Some time later—it could be minutes, it could be hours—the nurse is back by my side, one hand on my shoulder. The ache is still so fresh, so raw, and her simple act of affection rubs salt in my wound.

"Would you like to say goodbye?" she asks.

Would I like to say goodbye.

No. I want to scream no with everything I have. I want to say hello. I want to ask how he's feeling and make bad jokes about the nurse who keeps referring to him as 'her poppet'.

I don't want to say goodbye. Not ever.

"Ye-e-es." I manage between sobs.

The nurse nods, and a split second of regret passes over her features before she schools them again. I wonder if she regrets what's happened, or that she offered to take me in.

I choke my sobs back by sucking in deep breaths. It's easier than I thought it would be—probably because my throat is hoarse from crying.

After a few minutes, I swipe my hands across my cheeks and under my nose, then look up at the nurse. My chest still rises and falls at a rapid rate, but I'm containing the monster within.

For now.

"I'm ready," I say.

Liar.

The nurse leads me down the hall, as if I might have forgotten where Joel's room is. Mr Henley stands outside the room. His head rests against the wall, and his skin has an ashen tone to it. His eyes are closed, but he opens them right as we near.

He doesn't offer me his customary smile or his usual polite greeting. Instead, he just shakes his head and shrugs, an apology for the unthinkable. For the death of the man I love.

THE TWENTY-ONE

The nurse opens the door and waits, and I look her in the eye. She has brown eyes, a deep chocolate colour. Her gaze is strong. Independent. Secure.

I wonder what it's like to feel like that.

She gives me a small nod. A *you can do it* stamp of approval.

And I do.

I walk into the room and over to the bed.

Joel looks exactly as he did earlier tonight, or was that yesterday? I've lost track of the time. His eyes are closed, and his skin is that same pale colour. His mouth is open, his lips slightly parted, as if waiting for my kiss. And who knows? Maybe he was.

His chest doesn't rise and fall, though.

The machines don't beat life into him.

The clock on the wall overhead ticks a solemn beat, a funeral dirge for the recently deceased. Once again, I feel as if this can't really be happening. I'm outside looking in.

Things like this don't happen to me.

Not to the man I love.

"Hi," I whisper. He looks so normal lying there—so very much alive. I take his arm and give it a small shake. "Please wake up," I beg. My lips press together to try and stem the emotion that wants to pour out of my mouth. Tears roll down my cheeks again, and I'm almost surprised. I thought I'd have none left to give.

It's all so final. I shake his arm harder this time, and beg again. This can't be it. I won't let it be it. "Wake up, Joel." Denial wraps its way around my heart and consumes me with a passion. He can't be dead. This can't be happening to me. I shake with a vengeance, so hard his body starts to move. He has to wake up. He has to be with me. "Please wake up." *Shake.* "Wake up!" *Shake, shake, shake. "Joel!"*

The nurse sticks her head in the room, but I don't stop shaking him. I can't. Because he's just asleep. He wouldn't leave me. He can't leave—

Cool hand lands on my back, and she rubs a small circle there. "Sweetheart, he's gone."

"No!" I cry, but my shaking slows and now I'm just holding the arm of a shell, the body of a man I thought I'd be with forever. I collapse over the top of his chest, my tears soaking through the webbed blanket, my shoulders heaving. It hurts. God, it hurts so bad.

The nurse's footsteps pad away, and then it's just Joel and me. For the last time.

The last time ever.

I push up from the blanket and look at that still angelic face. He's as beautiful now as he was the first time I saw him. Every time I saw him.

I lean over and kiss him on the lips. They're warmer than I thought they'd be—not the temperature of cool marble, as I'd somehow expected. In that kiss, the press of our lips together, I try and inject everything. All my thank yous for everything he's done. All my sorrys for everything I know I'll screw up in the future.

All my love, for now 'til eternity.

I inch out of the room, walking backward the entire time. I hate this moment, but I don't want it to end. Because once it does, I'm no longer in this limbo of life with Joel. I officially begin life without him.

At the door, I pause, one hand curled around the frame. The sky outside the window has taken on a soft grey hue, as if the sun is just thinking about starting the day. The light softens the overhead yellow one.

A sharp breath shudders through my chest as I look one last time ...

Then I unhook my hand from where it has been holding my body up against the doorframe ...

And I run.

I bolt to the end of the corridor, pushing through the emergency exit door and hurtling down the stairs. I fly around the corners and leap to the bottom landing, clearing steps two at a time.

I reach the ground floor and push through the door, racing through the foyer. From the corner of my eye, I see the café and gift shop have a green hue to them, as if there's a security alarm trigger present.

My feet slam against the tiled floor, echoing through the quiet building, and I run toward the glass doors. They're slow to open, so slow, but then they do, and I stagger to my car. A white ticket is clipped under the windscreen wiper, and I grab it, scrunch it into a ball and shove it deep within my pocket. Shaky hands find my keys and unlock the door and then I drive, tears blurring my vision as I pull out of the hospital. I'm on autopilot. All I know is I need to get away. I need to get out. I have to somehow stop these memories.

Joel and I, holding hands.

Joel and I, laughing.

Joel and I, pushing the limits.

Joel and I, making love.

Now ... it's just I.

And I don't know how I'm going to deal with that.

TWENTY-NINE

I thought I'd grieved before. I'd thought finding out Joel had cancer was one of the worst things that could happen to me.

It turns out, I was wrong.

I guess I'd figured that when it came time for Joel to pass, maybe I'd somehow be prepared for it. Maybe I'd have accepted his fate.

Or perhaps I'd have changed it. Perhaps they'd have developed new technology, and found him a miracle cure.

I didn't expect it to hurt like this.

I didn't expect this pain.

I turn my phone on silent and place it on the hall table, then walk to my room and curl up in bed, darkness coating me in a thick shroud. I don't sleep—my eyes don't want to shut. I want to stay awake. I want it to be this day forever, because right now I can hurt and it sucks, but it still feels as if Joel could come walking down the street at any moment. I try reading, but the words all jangle together in a blur, and my heart doesn't want to hear about other people's happily-ever-afters. It just wants to bleed.

Hope comes in and out, tiptoeing around and offering me food and drink, spritzing perfume as she goes. These are all things I register but I don't truly see.

All I see is Joel.

That face, so still.

Those lips, so warm.

The sun changes intensity, creeping in under my bedroom window curtains. At some point, day turns to night, and I should sleep.

I can't.

The gnawing at my stomach keeps me awake.

At some point, Hope comes in again. She places a peppermint tea on my bedside table and pushes my hair back. She gives me some ibuprofen, as if that will help me heal, but I take it anyway. At this point, I'll try anything,

My eyes are dry from being open so long and crying so hard, but it seems I can't let go.

Not until Hope leaves the room and I remember his shirt in my dresser from camping so long ago.

Feverish desperation takes hold. I can't open the drawer fast enough, and I curse as my hands fumble with the knobs. Finally, I grab the soft blue material, shake it out, strip out of everything I'm wearing and place the shirt over my head. His sandalwood scent floats over me and I close my eyes, relishing the softness and the peace this one simple thing brings.

This time, when I slide back into bed, sleep takes me in its embrace almost straight away.

My dreams are of boys with striking cheekbones and heart-warming smiles, and a life that is completely beautiful.

I cuddle his warmth closer to me, pressed firm against my body. It's so peaceful lying here, the afternoon sun streaming in the window.

I squint open one eye. The second flies open straight after that.

My hand reaches out, stabbing around the bed. Where—

Reality crashes down on me like a strike of lightning.

He's not here.

He'll never be here again.

A fresh onslaught of tears attacks my cheeks, and I wipe them away with the shirt, which makes me cry harder. I can't dilute his scent with my tears. This could be the last thing of his I have.

Like a crazy person, I rip off the shirt and jump out of bed, tearing open the top drawer of my dresser. I empty the socks onto the floor and reverentially place the shirt within, as if somehow having its own compartment will mean it never loses that smell. It never loses its very Joel-ness.

When that's done, I go back to bed. Because there's nothing else I can do. After what happened at Mum's place, I'm not going to work for Colin. I don't have any events to prepare for, or paper bags to stuff.

And I don't have Joel.

I close my eyes and sleep.

This time when I wake, Lia and Hope are in my room. Lia's sitting at the chair to my desk, her long pianist's fingers elegantly draped one on top of the other. There's barely a bump from where Smith broke them. You can hardly tell.

Hope sits cross-legged on my black and white striped matt. Her hands rest on her knees, as if she's about to break into yoga at any moment, and for all I know she could be.

I pull the quilt up closer to my chin. I feel so exposed. Naked, due to lack of clothing and emotional armour.

"Hey hon." Hope reaches up and squeezes my foot through the quilt.

"Hi," I croak, then cough to try and clear the darkness lodged in my throat.

"How are you feeling?" Lia asks. Her face is the picture of concern.

"Y'know ..." I shrug, and trail off. Just peachy doesn't seem to cut it, but I don't know what other answer she's looking for.

Hope lifts my phone up from the floor in front of her. "Joel's dad's been calling you."

My heart twinges. I can't speak to him now. I'm not ready to face him just yet.

"I can't imagine what you're going through, sweets." Lia chews at her lip for a second. "Is there anything we can do?"

There's only one thing that comes to mind. Only one thing that will help me right now. "Yes," I say, my voice clearing as I speak. Tears prickle my eyes as I think of how much love I have for these two girls, these two women who have helped me through so much—who are here for me now, even if I haven't leaned on them as perhaps I should have before. "Please don't die." A sob lurches and tears fall, and soon Lia and Hope are dabbing at their eyes and sniffing.

"Fuck, Ellie," Hope curses on a sob. "We're supposed to be comforting you. Why'd you have to go and ruin it for?" She smiles. Lia picks up a balled up sock from my floor and throws it at Hope's head, knocking her right in the middle of her 50s coif.

"What's with all these socks anyway?" Hope asks, picking up a pair and narrowing her eyes. "Do you want me to put them away?"

I shake my head, mute.

And then, like the good friends they are, they don't question it further. They just let me be.

"So how's Jase, Lia?" Hope asks.

"He's good. Well, not perfect. We're having some long-distance issues."

"What? You only live an hour apart," Hope says.

Lia sighs. "I know, but with him at the bar and me at uni, it really doesn't work ..."

The girls chat for the next hour and I listen, occasionally smiling, occasionally drifting off. Every time my mind thinks of a certain blond-haired boy with chilling blue eyes, I snap back to the present and get lost in the girls' stories again.

And then, once more, I sleep.

THIRTY

On the third day, when I wake the sun isn't shining. It's raining, tears from the clouds battering against the windowpane, and I want nothing more than to stay in bed.

But Joel doesn't let me.

He never could stand for me playing it safe.

Hope deposits the letter on my nightstand and steps back, her arms folded across her chest, her forehead lined with worry. "This came for you."

At first, I don't know why she's so concerned. When I flip the paper, I see the return address. The name printed there in scratchy blue pen.

Joel Henley.

Air is hard to suck into my lungs. It's thin, as if a giant cloud hovers in the air, stifling and choking all the way down my throat. My hand shakes as I pull the envelope to my chest and stare at it for the longest time. I measure its weight with my hand, a little heavier than what I'd expect of a normal letter. I run my hand from one side to the other, noting the soft texture of the cream paper and feeling the little lump in the corner.

The letter is postmarked the 25th. Four days ago.

Back when Joel was alive.

Did he do this himself, or did he have his dad write the letter for him? Does his father have one, too?

Then I don't wonder anymore, because Hope snatches the letter out of my hands. I claw at her but she steps back, and I can't reach her without leaving my bed, which so far I've only done for bathroom breaks and to make tea and toast, bringing it back to eat in the solitude of my room.

"Give." I snatch at the letter, but she lifts it high out of my reach. She's holding my heart out on a limb, and in that moment I hate her with a fierce intensity. "What the hell, Hope?"

She takes a step back and parks her hands on her hips. Her eyes narrow into angry slits and her mouth is a slim line of toughen up. "You listen to me, Miss Mayfield."

The way she refers to me by my surname hurts.

Joel used to do that.

"I know you're going through something incredibly tough right now. I know you're hurting, and sweetie, we love you and we're here for you." At that, Hope softens, and a fleeting glimpse of pain crosses her face. "If I could make your pain go away, I would. Trust me." She inhales, and her chest rises and falls in one fell swoop. "But there is someone else out there who's hurting, too. Someone you've been shutting out." She reaches down and lifts my phone from the floor.

I frown, knowing exactly who she's talking about. Henry. Joel's dad.

"You lost your lover, but he lost his son, Ellie. And he desperately wants someone to share those last moments with." She shakes her head sadly and tosses the cell at the end of my bed. I scramble back to the headboard and hug my knees to my chest, as if touching the phone would be poison. There is too much there I don't want to see. Too much I don't want to do. "He's been calling, Ellie; surely you can at least let him know you're okay. There are also around six missed calls from your sister—"

"Joel would be proud of me for not calling back." I straighten my back, defending myself.

Hope shakes her head. "Joel wanted you to seize the moment; to live in the now and take every opportunity you got with both hands." She gives a small shrug of her shoulders. "Not running to rescue her is a part of standing up for yourself, but ignoring her entirely? I wouldn't be so sure that's what he wanted."

Her words cut me. They're worse than the sadness, the never-ending devastation that's been tearing at my soul for weeks because they're so much sharper. Those words mean I failed him—the one thing I never wanted to do.

She pauses and gives me one long, hard look. "You're allowed to grieve, Ellie; you have to. But right now, you're just denying what's happened. And sooner or later, you're going to have to face the world head on."

She slaps the envelope against the palm of her hand and then turns and walks out of the room. "Letter's on the sideboard in the hall. On the condition that you're showered when you want to read it."

As she leaves with that letter, my mind churns. Guilt batters my soul, and for the first time in three days I wonder about the afterlife. The *what if*s. What if he's watching me right now? What if he sees that I'm not making an effort, and that I'm just ... being?

What if he regrets loving me?

It's that final thought that picks up my phone and reads the texts from Henry, asking me to come and see him. That thought throws the covers from my bed—that thought that twists the mixer tap in the shower—that thought that lathers fresh pomegranate-scented shampoo through my hair, massaging it into my scalp, and then letting it all wash out onto the floor. That thought finds clean jeans and a white tee that smells of soap and fresh and life, and that thought that brushes a little blush on my cheeks to stop the death-white look I have going on.

It's that thought that takes the letter from the sideboard, along with my keys, and yells to Hope as I walk out the door. "Love you!"

"I love you more!" she calls back from her room.

I place the letter on the seat next to me. There's a white piece of paper screwed up in a ball on the floor, and I pick it up, unfolding it.

It's a parking fine from the other day at the hospital. For $554.

"Crap," I mutter, then scrunch it back up again and throw it to another spot on the floor. Who fines someone while they're obviously visiting someone in pain?

An overwhelming sense of helplessness weighs down my limbs again. With shaking hands, I turn the letter over once, twice, as if trying to read its contents without actually opening the seal.

Then I put the letter down and reverse out of the driveway. If this has taught me anything at all it's that the clock doesn't stand still when you want it to. You can't take time out of life just because you're emotionally in need.

You have to tackle it head on.

One hour and twenty minutes later, I pull up outside of the two-storey cream-rendered house that Henry mentioned in his last text. A Jacaranda tree weeps in the front yard, purple flowers littered over thick green grass. Four cars are lined one behind the other in the long, twisting driveway, and there are another six parked flush against the curb, all surrounding his house. I stop my little crap-mobile behind a BMW that has to be worth at least four of my cars. It's for that reason that I leave enough room between him and me to almost park a third vehicle.

The walk up the driveway is like everything else in my life these days—both long and incredibly short. It gives me time to think about what I'm going to say. The sort of condolences I can offer.

So far, my script is shaping up nicely. *I'm sorry for your loss* and *how are funeral plans going* and *is there anything I can do* all feature heavily.

When I get to the front door, I raise my hand to knock. I freeze, my fist balled, ready to make contact with the navy wooden door. I can't do this. Why am I here? I barely know the guy, and he just lost his son. He doesn't need some kid who'd only reconnected with him a few months—

The door flies open before I have a chance to finish that thought. A woman with curly ash-blonde hair stands there, a kindly smile plastered over her face. She looks older than Joel's mother, Ms Armstrong, but still seems very youthful. She's bubbly and effervescent, yet her eyes seem focused and crisp. A champagne of a lady.

"Of course, Ellie Mayfield."

Looking into those crystal blue eyes, so much like *his*, makes my heart pang. It's a hot poker to the soul.

Instead, I look behind her. Women mill around, conversation buzzing between them. There are a lot of champagne glasses and dainty fine china tea cups, and a line of people around five-deep wait by what looks like a table, all with big baking dishes in hand. The scent of pastry and herbs wafts over to me.

Quiche.

That's what you do when you visit someone in mourning. You bring quiche.

My pulse races. The air is thick again, and I pull at the collar of my T-shirt, as if it's too tight. The world is closing in on me, and I have nowhere to run to.

"I ..." I shake my head. "I should have bought quiche."

My hand drops and I back away. I can't be here. I have no place amongst these people.

"Don't be silly, dear. You didn't need to bring ..."

She could be telling me about the quiche ingredients or describing how to do the Macarena. Her words blend into the high-pitched chatter drone going on behind her. I can't deal with this. I can't deal with—

"Hey, Ellie. Don't tell me you're leaving—we just got here."

Warm hands wrap around my shoulders, and I stiffen.

"Sorry." The hands move away, but the friendliness in the voice doesn't. "How you holding up, girl?"

I turn my head to the side. Fiona stands there in a cute denim overalls number. Marc and Kohl linger behind her, both looking even less comfortable than I feel, hands in pockets, eyes averted elsewhere.

"Okay." I shrug, because it's what you do. You lie when people ask how you're feeling after the man you love has died.

"Let's go inside. I'm starving, and there's bound to be quiche in there." Fiona takes my hand and leads me back toward the house.

"There's quiche," I quietly confirm, and Fiona squeezes my hand.

The lady who'd welcomed me is no longer at the door, and we walk straight into the throng of mourners.

"Fiona's here!" someone exclaims, and soon the heads of thirty women flip in our direction.

Questions fly at us in a flurry. They're all concerned for her wellbeing, how she's holding up, how her mother is, was the traffic bad getting here, would she like some quiche. It's like a well-meaning flock of hens all chirruping and bock-bocking at her.

"Where are all the guys?" I ask Kohl, keeping my eyes on the swarm as they walk closer.

"They'll be upstairs with Henry. But there's always more chicks than dudes with this crowd." Kohl shrugs, and a wry smile crosses his lips. "Single dad. Lots of money. I'm sure you can fill in the blanks."

I can now, even if I wish I couldn't.

Kohl taps Marc on the shoulder and they both slink though the crowd, heading for a staircase I hadn't noticed before at the back of the room. Fiona fields questions with ease, and I'm left feeling like I don't belong. I was a part of his new life, not this in between one. Not the one full of people reminiscing about things like his hockey team— hockey?—and the suit he wore when he went to his cousin's wedding.

I shift uncomfortably, and am seriously considering leaving when a hand grips my wrist. "Hurry." Kohl widens his eyes and I scoot along after them, thankful that this invitation included me.

We reach the top of the stairs. The crowd is closer around Fiona now but she's holding court like a pro.

"They like young blood," Kohl mutters. "Freaking vampires."

I turn to see Henry Henley standing to the side of the landing, his thin arms folded across his chest. Deep purple bruises shadow his eyes, and he looks tired, so damn tired.

Maybe he's tired of grieving.

Maybe he's tired of pain.

"I'm ..." He clears his throat and starts again. "I'm glad you came."

The words could apply to all of us, but his gaze focuses squarely on me. Kohl and Marc mutter lame excuses and walk past him toward a doorway where a television plays.

Henry walks alongside me and places his hands on the railing, overlooking the crowd below. He gives a small shake of his head then turns to me again, staring straight into me, just like Joel used to do.

Joel.

A wave of pain washes over me, but I steel myself against it. I can't fall to pieces right now. I just can't.

"This has been the hardest week of my life." He studies his hands. "A parent should never have to lose a child."

I reach out and touch his arm. The contact startles him, but I think it startles me even more. "I ... I can't even imagine."

He gives a low, throaty chuckle and smiles. "Here I am, inviting you here to make sure you're okay and telling you how I feel. Shame on me." He shakes his head. "The thing about grief is it's all relative. You can only compare it to what you know. And I have no doubt that right now, the pain you're going through is the hardest damn thing." He winces and brings his hand to the bridge of his nose, rubbing either side, as if to alleviate some tension. "I know things happened fast during these last few months between the two of you. I just ... I want you to know that he really loved you. Always had. Right from the day you started dating."

It's the validation I didn't know I was seeking. As soon as he says the words, a small knot unfurls inside my heart.

"Do you want to see his old room? Of course, you can take anything you want," Henry says, as if it's a souvenir shop of his son's life. I think of the T-shirt in my drawer and wonder how many more like it I can smuggle away, then give a slight shake of my head. What the hell is wrong with me?

Henry leads me down a long hallway to a room at the very end. He opens the door and steps back, his arms gesturing to the right, as if the room is a prize on *Sale of the Century*. "I'll leave you to it."

"Thank you."

He turns to walk away and then pauses, one finger in the air as if he just remembered something. "Would ..." He turns back around. Doubt clouds his features. "Would you like to speak at Joel's funeral?"

No.

My body seizes, my spine rigid.

I hate public speaking. Right down to my very core.

"I'll leave it open for you on the day." Henry gives a small smile and walks away again, calling over his shoulder as he leaves. "Think about it."

The second I step foot inside Joel's room, his smell hits me. Outside it's all quiche and wine, but in here it's masculine and spicy, and a scent that's so uniquely him. I close my eyes and suck in a deep breath, trying to get as much air into my lungs as I can, trying to make every particle hit every corner of my chest.

When I open my eyes, it takes a few seconds to adjust to the shadows. The room is in darkness, the curtains drawn, all the objects left around just abstract shapes.

I inch over to his bed and sit down on the very edge. It doesn't feel right to be in here without him. It feels as if I'm stepping on private ground. In a place I shouldn't be.

Spying his bedside table, I reach over to open the drawers—

But I can't. My hand doesn't want to invade his privacy like that.

This was a place he never invited me to go. A part of him he didn't want me to see.

Eyeing all the books on the shelf above his bed—*Healing the Natural Way, Coping with Cancer, 101 Steps To A Pain-Free Life*—I can see why. He was protecting me from who he was. The man he thought I'd never love.

It's almost ironic that I've spent the last few months keeping secrets, only to find out the biggest one of all was kept by the boy I'd pledged my heart to.

I'm tempted to look around, to learn more, but it doesn't seem right. Instead, I pull back the covers of his bed and slide my body underneath. It smells so strongly of Joel here. It's a heady cocktail of pain and pleasure, and one I'm not afraid to mix. I suck it back, deep into my body, and I wait for release.

I suck in a deep breath and fall asleep to thoughts of heartache and loss and Joel.

THIRTY-ONE

I sit on the cliff-top, the letter in my shaking hands. Below me, the sea crashes against the rocks, a turbulent relationship based on emotion and solid foundations. Like so much of my life. Like so much of me.

I kick off my flip-flops and dig my feet into the hard red dirt. Small rocks prick at the soles of my feet, and wind whips at my blonde hair, curls flying around my face in a chaotic fury.

I bite down on my lip, thankful that I'm the only one here. That the tourists have taken today off, or that they're out getting bagels and double-shot skinny mocha low-fat fair-trade lattes, or whatever the hell it is they do.

I stare at the white piece of paper, my nemesis. She's been taunting me all week, but I haven't been able to face her. It's a demon I'm not strong enough for. There's so much here in this one little parcel—sorrow, regret, heartache.

But for the first time in a week, I see something else.

Love.

And it's eking out from the seams, clawing its way into the air and sneaking into my lungs with the air that I breathe.

I slide my finger under the seal and push through the resistance, tearing the paper. The letter is thin in my hand as I pull it out. I place the envelope on the ground under a shoe and suck in one last breath for comfort. Because this is it. This is the last time I'll hear from my love.

The last time he'll have words meant only for me.

Tears prick at my eyes as I begin to read.

Dear Ellie,

There's no easy way to start this letter. I've written it a thousand times—drafted the words I want so badly to say to you in my head over and over until they're as trite and cliché as a pop song, as scripted as a Shakespeare play.

The thing is, Ellie Mayfield, you're so far from in the script.

You were never in my schedule. Even though I thought of you often, I didn't think we'd ever reconnect. I think that's why you so completely took my breath away. Why you so completely stole my soul.

There are so many things I want to write—and none of them seem enough. When I fell into you again, it was too easy to pretend that life was like it was when we first met. Once upon a time, I thought we'd get married. I thought we'd buy a house with a white picket fence, and have beautiful little blonde-headed babies who ran around and teased their friends next door for years on end. I know guys aren't supposed to think of shit like that, but I did. I met you and I breathed you in. I couldn't imagine anything without you—the future included. You deserve to be cherished.

That's why the first and most obvious thing I want you to know is, I want you to love again. I want you to have the whirlwind romance of your life. I want a man to sweep you off your feet, to treat you like a princess and to be there for you for every second of your amazing journey—and it will be amazing—and for you to fall head over heels for him. I want you to fall for him so completely that you never even think of me.

Except to reminisce on how my penis size is bigger. Obviously.

At that, I giggle. Or, I try to giggle. Tears flow thick and fast down my cheeks, and it comes out more as a choked laugh, the emotion getting caught in my throat.

The second thing I want to tell you is that you are not a rule-obeyer. This whole time, you've told me how you play it safe, you obey the rules, but you haven't! You've done these things—you've jumped, you've risked, and you've said it's because I've been there to catch you—but it's you. You've always been the one to catch yourself. I've been watching from the sidelines, cheering—and damn, have I been cheering—but that's all I've done. You're the hero in this story. It's time you took the lead.

"You're so wrong," I whisper, but my words are lost on the wind. I pick up a small round stone that was resting innocently next to my right foot and toss it up in the air, catching it with a snap of my wrist on the descent. I've never been the hero. I've needed him to catch me.

Haven't I?

And finally, you are the bravest person I know.

Before you start objecting, know this. You've pushed so many limits with me—not only in those stupid bloody challenges, but in every aspect of your life. You risked everything emotionally, even though we both knew this was never in your plan. You've done so much to protect yourself from hurt, and I'm so sorry I brought that right to your doorstep. I've spent so many nights beating myself up over not walking away, but I couldn't resist you. You're a force greater than nature.

Sometimes, two people have a pull that connects them. It's greater than time, or space, or a single emotion. It's something out of this world. Something truly stellar.

That's what I want you to know.

And even though we're apart right now, even though we're in different times, a different space—I'll find you in the stars.

Make sure you look for me there.

All my love.

Joel

(And I mean all ...)

By the time I read the last line, I'm a blubbering mess. The wind cools my hot tears as they stain my cheeks, and the taste of salt teases at my tongue from the salt air and my own heartache. I press my lips against the letter, as if by kissing it I'm somehow kissing him, kissing Joel, kissing the man who is still managing to break my heart from somewhere out of this world.

I stay like that for hours, watching the waves crash against the rocks, watching the sun turn the sky orange then pink then grey, watching the container ships out at sea go from coloured lumps to lit up mysteries.

I stay until my legs and butt become numb from their rested state, prickles itching at the underside of my body. I give a little shake to try and inject some feeling and healing into my body, dislodging the envelope I'd stowed so carefully. I pick it up, ready to store the most precious thing I own back into it, when I feel something still in there. Something I hadn't noticed before.

Frowning, I pull apart the lips of the envelope. Inside, two items rest—one cardboard ticket, and one glint of gold brass.

I take the cardboard first, pulling it out in front of me. It's a ticket, printed with a time and date three months' from now, and the name of a company.

A very familiar name.

I laugh, and this time the noise carries on the wind, out over the cliff top. Because he bought me a sky-diving ticket. The bastard continues to push me, even when he's not here.

The second thing in the envelope is smaller, and harder to grasp. My fingers fish around in the bottom of the envelope before they finally pull it out.

It's a star, gold, with a small loop at the top to connect to a necklace or bracelet. It says everything and nothing all at once. It says he's with me. It says I don't need him.

It says whatever I need it to say, whenever I need it to say it.

Just like Joel always did.

This time when I cry, it's for how perfect he is. How he's handling his death with as much romantic prowess as he did his life.

How I miss him, so damn much.

And how I'll look for him in the stars.

Always.

Forever.

Eternally.

THIRTY-TWO

The day of the funeral rolls around, and I still haven't come to grips with my grief. It's still too fresh. Too raw. Too absolutely freaking painful to process. But his envelope sits on my bedside table, and it gives me a small eon of comfort. It makes me want to try.

I get up early and take a long time in the shower, washing my hair, shaving my legs. I moisturise my whole body in some fancy lotion Mum got me years and years ago. I choose the pale pink silk dress that glides over my body with the kind of precision I'd use if I were selecting an outfit for my wedding day.

And in a way, it is.

It's my first and last formal event with the true love of my life.

I've texted Mum about the funeral today, but she's only offered up short replies. No doubt she'll have another more important event on that prevents her from attending.

Lia and Hope wait at our front door at exactly ten a.m., two hours before the funeral starts. They're both dressed in black, and both looking solemn, their faces drawn.

We walk to the car together. My two sisters, more my blood right now than my own ever will be, arms linked, faces stoic. It's time to say goodbye.

The trip to Sydney is spent in silence—no loud music, no giggling stories, no *are you okay*s. Just silence. Thinking time. And damn, do I need it to get my shit together.

We pull up and park four blocks from the funeral home. Cars line the street, testimony to the kind of love Joel radiated.

The three of us start the journey to the church. My heels wobble as I pick up the pace. We're so close now, but I can't get there fast enough. Lia grips her hand in mine, and gives me a squeeze. She says everything and nothing in that one small gesture. It's exactly what I need to hear.

There's one door to the church still open, but one has been closed. I sign the register, scribbling my name down, and then take a long, deep breath through my nose and out through my mouth. Calm. I need to be calm. I can't go racing into the church like a grieving bull in a china shop.

"Love you," Hope whispers, and I glance back at her. I look up at the wooden roof of the church patio, as if hoping to find the strength I need there

I'll catch you if you fall.

I roll back my shoulders and walk into the room. Lia, Hope and I stand at the back in amongst tens of other mourners. Up front, Henry starts to speak. We make eye contact, and he gives me a slight smile.

The scent of too much perfume is heavy in the air. Everyone is still, listening as Henry talks about his son. The love of my life.

"He was a strong man. Even when he was a kid, he'd be out to change the world. To improve things. But not just to make things better—to make you feel better about being you. It was never more evident to me just how much he cared when around a week before he died, he told me so. He said 'Dad, I love you. More than anything.'" Henry pauses, and looks up from the piece of paper in front of him. "'But if you don't go home and shower, I'm making Nurse Paige give you a sponge bath.'"

A soft ocean of laughter fills the room. It's the sort of laugh that is quick to come as people search for relief from their pain. In times of trouble, we all need moments like these.

Henry continues to speak of what a great man Joel was. He holds it together, right 'til the very end when a few tears escape from his eyes, and he dabs at them with the white handkerchief he had in his right pocket.

The priest continues the ceremony, and several more people speak. Fiona steps up to the plate, and so does Joel's grandmother, the woman who opened the door at Henry's house when I visited earlier in the week. Henry looks at me, his eyes asking me if I want to go up and speak.

I don't want to.

I hate public speaking.

I can't think of anything worse to do.

But I have nothing left to lose.

One shaky foot steps down the aisle, then another. The sound of my heels on the tile is like a cannon shot in the otherwise quiet room. Heads turn and follow me as I walk, and whispers rustle through the crowd.

When I reach the podium, I clutch at its sides to hold me up. My knuckles are white against the blonde wood.

I look out at the sea of faces—so many of them gathered here to remember the man I loved. They're all ages—young, middle-aged, old—and from all walks of life. Some are all in black, while others have donned vibrant hues of pink and turquoise, as if trying to prove to the world how okay they are. How they're coping fine.

I take a deep breath, and open my mouth.

Nothing comes out.

My knees are weak, and I blink back tears for what feels like the millionth time since this whole journey started. I swallow, then close my eyes for one moment. What would Joel do in this situation? Would he speak, square his shoulders? Make some crappy joke?

He'd tell me he'd catch me. Then he'd kiss my forehead.

I miss you so much.

"Hi. My name's ..." My voice cracks, and I do my best to shake it off. "My name is Ellie Mayfield. And Joel Henley ..." Deep breath, Ellie. You can do this. "He was the man I loved."

A soft murmur goes around the room. Some women shake their heads, no doubt thinking Vanessa had gotten a whole lot blonder and probably a little less into designer threads.

"I met Joel when I was just five. When no one else would choose me to be on their team in school sport—Joel picked me." I pause, looking down. That overwhelming sense of pain crashes around in my stomach. "Joel Henley continued to pick me throughout the rest of my life. When we were fourteen, and he asked me to be his girlfriend. When we were sixteen, and he took me to our school formal." I pause, and swallow the lump of loss that's wedged in my throat. "When we met again, he wanted to choose cancer. And I ... I'm so glad he chose me." I sob, and it echoes around the church courtesy of the microphone. My shoulders cave in, and *why does it hurt so much?* Why hasn't someone figured out how to stop this thing called pain and prevent it from ever happening? "He was the most amazing man I've ever met, and he taught me so much. He taught me how important it is to live—and I'll never ever forget that."

My knees collapse under me. I hold my shins, folded over at the waist. The pain rips through me, tearing me in two. It hurts so damn bad.

"Hey." Henry is at my side, offering that damn handkerchief over, and I nod and gratefully accept it. My vision blurs and when I see a pair of silver stilettos I think I must be imagining them.

Only I'm not.

A warm arm snakes over my back. "You did so well," my mother says.

I look up into her brown eyes, mirrors of my own, and manage a wobbly smile. "I didn't know you were coming."

She takes my arm, and I stagger to my feet. "I love you, Eleanor." She pauses. "I haven't always been there before, but I'm so sorry. And for you, my strong, independent daughter, I will always make time."

And even though I'm in my darkest hour, even though I'm minutes away from saying my final goodbye to the man I love, a small flame of hope ignites in my chest. It's not strong; it flickers dangerously close to winking out of existence altogether.

But this could be the start of something amazing.

And I know Joel would be happy about that.

THIRTY-THREE

We're in the car on the way home when my phone rings. I jump, the noise breaking our silence so harshly. The ringtone is Taylor Swift, and I don't even bother looking at the caller ID. I don't have to.

I swipe across the screen and hold it to my ear. My hand shakes as emotion pours through me. I've never been a religious person, but I sent up a silent prayer.

Dear God, please let this be good.

"Ellie? Thank God you answered," Dani says, her voice high-pitched yet quiet. "I'm in trouble. I need you. Please."

My heart seizes in my chest. The world slows down and for a moment, for a heart-wrenchingly long moment, I consider letting her suffer.

After all, she threw me under the train at Mum's last week. Why should this be any different?

Joel wanted me to stop letting them take advantage of me, to be my own person.

What he didn't realise—what I didn't realise until now—is that me saving her is me being myself. In trying to keep her alive, I'm doing what no one else in my family has done in the last year. *Fight for someone else.*

And don't let them take no for an answer.

"Where are you?"

Hope shoots me a worried look, and gives a small shake of her head.

Dani rattles off an address, and I repeat it in my head over and over, imprinting it upon my brain, before hanging up.

"Sixteen Meleuca Court, Abbottsville," I tell Lia, who taps the address into the GPS without asking anything further.

"Ell Bell, are you really up for this?" Hope asks.

I nod. Because this time, I am.

We arrive at the address Dani gave ten minutes later. Tension is thick in the interior of Lia's Hyundai, and I'm sure it's not just the stifling air-conditioning. Pressure weighs heavily on my shoulders as I stare out at yet another rundown ghetto house. Yet another refuge for my sister's escape.

My sister sits on the porch step, an image I am all too familiar with and all too enraged by. My car door flies open.

This is it.

I'm not letting someone else live this anymore.

I storm across the yard. My shoes smart against the concrete path, slapping sounds that are completely at odds with the fierce anger boiling inside of me.

Dani looks up when I'm a few feet away. Her eyes are red, and her cheeks blotchy. "Thank you," she sobs. She stands and holds her arms out, waiting for my embrace, but I walk straight past her, charging into the house.

"Eleanor!" she screams.

Her bare feet thud in my wake, but I'm inside the darkened shack before she can catch me.

On the couch, three guys sit, ten bottles of beer littered in front of them. One man is covered in tattoos, one is pale and weedy, and one looks as if he could model for Billabong if he tried. They're three complete opposite lifestyle clichés, and I would never in a million years have picked them as belonging together.

The only thing they have in common is danger.

It leeches off them, permeating the air, coating my skin and infiltrating my lungs.

I shake in my stupid shoes, and heat rushes to my stupid made-up cheeks. I can't do this. I can't—

Dani tugs on my arm. When I spin to see her, her face is pure panic—completely stripped bare. The strap of her tank falls down her shoulder, a reminder of how skinny she's become. It exposes a bruise, green and purple, that runs around the base of her neck. In her eyes, I see a wild fear I haven't seen before. I see terror. "El, let's go."

I know what I should do. These three men are bigger than me, stronger than me, and I have no doubt about the damage they could do to those who got on their wrong side.

But that's the thing about hitting rock bottom. You have nothing left to lose.

And this is a gamble that I'm prepared to take.

"Who the fuck are you?" Tatts asks.

I glare at him. Heat coils my muscles into springs. It balls my hands into fists. "None of your fucking business."

Surfer God laughs, only it's a chilling, cruel sound, as if he knows something I don't. As if he could slice me in two. "Get out of here, little girl."

With that, I snap. I pick up the closest beer bottle and I slam it against the ground with all my might. Brown glass shards fly everywhere. Three men look at me with widened eyes.

"She's fucking on a trip," Pale and Weedy says, his eyes flitting from me to the floor and back.

Tatts stands up. He's six-foot-something, and as he steps closer, I fight every instinct I have and hold my ground. I don't run, despite how much I want to. Despite how much better that would be.

"Leave her alone." My voice tremors as the words come out, but I stand my ground.

Tatts steps closer, and I bite down hard on my lip. Fear courses through my body, and I hate it and relish it all at once. I hate it because it turns my blood to ice; it freezes in my veins.

I relish it because I *feel*.

"We can leave her alone, little girl," Tatts seethes. He pushes at my shoulder, and I stagger backward into the wall. The salty taste of blood fills my mouth and I swallow it down. "It's her who can't leave us."

"Well this time, she doesn't have a choice." I move to step around Tatts and reach for Dani's arm, but he blocks me. Without laying a finger on me, he's asserted himself as able to crush me like a fly. It's in the cold onyx of his eyes.

"D ... Dani, get in the car." I swallow, struggling to control the tremors in my voice. My hands grip onto the edges of my skirt.

Tatts steps closer again. A whiff of smoke chokes my throat. "She doesn't want to leave."

"She was begging to stay last night," Pale and Weedy pipes up.

I swallow down the excess saliva that has somehow appeared in my mouth. Taking money from Colin for a little heavy petting is one thing. But she's not ... she wouldn't ...

"That's right, little girl." Tatts smirks. "Your sister *fucks* us to get high."

I shake my head. Tears glass over my eyes as I try to make contact with Dani, but everything's a blur. How can things have gotten this bad? How can she have fallen so far, so fast?

"Every few nights, she comes back. Spreads her legs, and in return …" Surfer breaks into a laugh. "Well, we show her a good time."

"She never sleeps with me," Pale and Weedy mutters, but it hardly seems like a saving grace, given the circumstances.

I seek out my sister's eyes and hold them, brown eyes so like my own. All I want is for her to deny it. To say that she never did any of the things they're implying. "Is it … true?"

Torture is watching a heart break in front of your eyes.

Dani shatters in front of me. She sways, and for a brief moment I think she's going to pass out. Her face pales to an ashen colour.

"We're leaving." I push forward to go to my sister. To save her.

But Tatts wraps a firm hand around my upper arm, and my heart leaps to my throat. His grip is so tight it crushes my skin, and I think of the bruise around my sister's neck. I jerk back against the wall, but he doesn't let me move. Flat eyes bore into mine, a staring match that I know I'll struggle to win.

For the first time since arriving, I wonder just how smart this idea was after all.

"I'm not a slut."

Her voice is small, but audible. Pale and Weedy snorts. Tatts doesn't batt an eyelid.

"I …" Her voice breaks. "Ellie, let's go."

Tatts gives my arm one more squeeze, then releases his mammoth fingers with a sneer that has blood pumping fast through my veins. "I ain't gonna keep her here if she wants to leave. But she'll be back."

I grab Dani's wrist and try not to run out of the house.

"See you soon, whore," Surfer calls as we hasten out the door.

As we head to the car, no one follows us. No one seems to try and slow us down.

"Ellie, I—"

"Save it," I whisper. Tears glass over my vision and I wonder when it's going to end. When I can catch a damn break.

"No." She stops still on the patchy lawn, and I turn to look at her.

"So help me God, if I have to carry you to the car—"

"I didn't … I didn't know." She shakes her head, and fat tears swim down her cheeks. "I never meant to … I'm not a whore."

I take two steps forward and wrap my arms around her. Even though she's out of that house, she still needs saving.

Maybe she always will.

We stand there for a moment, until she looks up at me with a smile fighting her wobbling lower lip. "Let's go home."

I open the door and shove her across the back seat, then hop in beside her. Lia and Hope are silent while I click Dani's belt buckle, and minutes later, Lia pulls out of the drive and heads toward the main road.

"You guys look like you're going to a funeral or something," Dani says, giving a short laugh at her own joke.

"We just did," Hope seethes.

Dani's eyes widen. "Shit," she breathes. Another tear creeps down her cheek. "Sorry."

I turn to face her. My shoulders stiffen. "No."

Her cheeks pale, the red blotches popping even more. "No?"

"You don't have to be sorry. It's because you're going to rehab, Dani."

She reaches for the door handle, but Lia pops the child lock. Dani is stuck here.

She's stuck facing her problems.

"Don't make me, Ellie. Please, don't make me." Her fingers claw at my skirt, pulling it to her as if that will make a difference. As if that will change the way I feel.

And even though this knowledge clouds my heart, even though it's a heavy weight blinding my soul, for the first time in years I see clearly. And I see the truth.

"Dani, you need to get help. I can't force you to do that, but if you don't, I'm not going to be here for you anymore. I want out. I don't want to be put through this—this saving you, week in, week out. I want to be able to love my sister. To know that when I wake up in the morning, she's going to be there." I suck in a shuddering breath. "That she's not going to die just like Dad did. Just like Joel."

I swipe at my eyes and the stupid tears that gathered there. It hurts so damn much thinking of what I've lost. I hope against hope that I'm not about to lose my sister, too.

The words hang in the car between us, and for a few moments I wonder if I was wrong. If maybe my threat isn't enough.

"No."

I lean closer to hear the word, unsure if I heard right.

"I won't be like Dad, Ellie." Frail fingers reach across the back seat and wrap around mine. "I don't think I can stop. But I'll try."

I pull my hand closer to my chest, hers still wrapped up in it. "I'm going to need more than try."

She levels me with her gaze and bites down on her lip. "I'm going to do more than that." Her voice wobbles. "I'm going to want to."

Want. It's the one word from her I never thought I'd hear.

Sometimes you have to reach rock bottom to be able to swim to the surface. That's how I feel as Mum and I check Dani into rehab one week later at Sydney's most exclusive private facility.

She hugs us both at the door as she goes in, but I know it won't be easy. She's only there because she wants to be. Who knows how long that want will last?

Still, as I twist the pendant Joel gave me on a chain around my neck, I hope. Because if there's one thing all this has taught me, it's that people can change.

"You did good, Eleanor." Mum smiles at me. Her dark sunglasses reflect my own back at her against the bright summer sun. "Thank you for keeping my daughter safe."

Her words are not enough. It's going to take a long time to mend the relationship between my mother and myself.

But for now, it goes a long, long way.

Three weeks later
The headstone looks the same as it always has—brown, gold-embossed marble marking out his name. Only this time, everything is different.

This time, my mother and sister are here beside me.

We're not fixed. I'm no longer the girl who believes in happy endings, that everything will work out okay.

But we're trying.

And that sure as hell has to count.

"Hi," I whisper, crouching down to trace the all-too-familiar name on the tile.

"Do we have to talk to him?" Dani asks. She scrunches up her nose, but she schools her face immediately upon seeing my look.

"No."

"Sorry." Dani's hands go up in defence. She's on day release from rehab so we could all be here together. "You do your thing."

And even though my grief used to be a private thing, even though it was mine alone to bear—I do.

"I miss you." I look back at the stone and offer up a smile. "I know I'm missing Joel now too—God, I miss him so much. It's crazy how one guy can have such an impact on your life."

I swallow down the sob that threatens to choke my throat and continue. "But … but I'm trying. I applied for uni. I'm going to study. I'm going to …" I blink back tears. It's stupid, but a part of me hates the idea of being anything but the girl I was when he died. Because this means it's over. That I'm moving on.

I steel myself against the doubt lingering in my head. Moving on doesn't mean letting go. I have to keep telling myself that.

I open my mouth to find the words to finish my sentence, but I don't have to.

Mum's hand lands square on my shoulder as she says "She's going to make something of herself."

My heart warms, and I look up at her.

"You would be so proud of her, Ian. She's done exactly as you asked." She pauses. "She's kept us girls safe."

And even if it took me stepping away to do that, even if I had to expose my sister's secrets and hurt my mother's heart—I'm glad I did.

Because the best things in life are never easy.

Joel Henley taught me that.

EPILOGUE

Time passes, and it's not easy. It never is. Life doesn't put itself on hold while you bleed. It doesn't stop while your soul spills onto the pavement for everyone to trample on, to smother with their boots and sharp high heels.

It goes on, and on, and on.

The worst is laughing. It's feeling happy. It's being with friends, achieving, feeling good.

Because at the end of that, you remember. And nothing hurts like that reminder that everything isn't as perfect, as shiny as you thought it was. Nothing hurts like waking from a dream. Nothing hurts like the guilt that gnaws and chews at your stomach, your heart, your mind when you realise you've just laughed, you've just enjoyed a moment completely and thoroughly—and he's still gone.

You can't stop those moments from washing over you, no matter how hard you fight them. Sometimes, you just have to let the hurt in.

And that's what I'm doing today.

I press my eyes shut, trying to push back the salty sting that needles at my eyes. I can't get emotional now. Not at this moment. Not when there's so much to lose, and so much to gain.

The roar of the plane blares constant and unyielding, a powerful machine. It's hard not to clap my hands to cover my ears to protect them from the sound.

Still, there's something so sweet in pain. Because if this is as bad as it gets, shit could be a whole lot worse.

I shuffle against the wall behind me, wanting to press myself against it as the door opens. The roar becomes all-consuming, everything I hear, think, feel. It's loud, so loud, and I don't know if I can do this.

It was Joel's dream for so long—but it was his dream. Not mine.

Not the girl who is so afraid to jump. Who is so afraid to leap with no one there to catch her, especially now that her lover has passed away. He isn't coming back.

The instructor, Eric, makes a signal to me, asking if I'm okay, and I do what any idiot in my position would do. I grin and nod as fast as I can, as if I can somehow convince the both of us that I got this.

Eric completes the prep for our jump, and we inch toward the opening. My heart races. Blood pumps through my body like the bottom line in a drum-and-bass track. My pulse roars in my body, a thunderous rush of blood somehow heard above the noise coming from the machine floating way too high and yet way too close to the ground for my liking.

"Ready?"

I don't know if I hear or just see him ask.

All I know is that it's time.

And I have to choose.

Now.

Sometimes in life you choose to take the risky path. Sometimes you choose to push the limits, to see just how high you can go. Taking chances won't guarantee you any safety—but neither will following the rules.

And isn't it better to have pushed yourself hard, to have stretched as far as you can, and know that you tried?

It's that thought that resonates in my head, in my heart, in every damn cell of my body as I give the thumbs up to Eric.

He doesn't need to be told twice, even when I have a slight twinge and wish he did. He gives my shoulder a friendly squeeze ...

And then we fly.

The plane was loud, but this is louder. I hurtle toward earth, toward land. Everything is so fragile in this moment—life, love, death. I scream, and it's gone before I can truly embrace the sound. My heart sticks in my throat and panic blossoms in my chest. This is too fast, too high, too long, and I know with an unwavering certainty that something is wrong. This isn't happening the way it's supposed to.

I'm going to die.

I fight. I grab for Eric behind me, I push against the air holding my limbs out, and I fight, I fight with everything I have to stay alive. Because I want to live. Damn, do I want to live.

Fire burns within my chest as I realise the truth in those simple, easy words.

I want to live.

Damn, do I want to live.

And then, everything is right.

Time slows in a rush. I change from a catapulting ball of death to a dandelion floating on the breeze, a daydream of sweet release.

I'm safe.

Everything is fine.

And in that moment I finally hear Joel's truth. He was always there to catch me, and I'll forever be grateful for that. Yet the real rush is in falling, whatever the consequence. In not knowing the outcome. In that moment where you've risked it all, you've laid everything on the line, and it could go either way.

It's what I did when I jumped out of a plane today.

And it's what I did when I gave Joel my heart.

As we float gently down to earth, Eric laughs and yells, "How was it?"

The scent of eucalyptus wafts toward me as. To the left, I see the hot-air balloon field, the multi-coloured balloon shining tall in the morning light. To the right, I see forest, houses, and then the endless blue of the ever-powerful ocean, stretched out as far as the eye can see.

In the sky above me to the left, a single star winks. It's bright, unnaturally so against the pale pink of the dawn sky.

"It was everything," I yell, and Eric gives a bemused laugh.

To the star in the sky, I add, *and it was enough to help me see what you wanted me to see. To know that I can do it. Taking the risk is half the achievement.*

Half an hour later, I'm out of the equipment and taking a moment on the green landing field.

"Come on, Eleanor," Eric calls from the shed, and I look back over to him and smile. He's kind of cute. He has a shock of black hair and a winning smile that melts from head to toe. He's also completely and utterly not my type.

But I'm proud of myself for noticing anyway.

I run my hands along the side of my head, pushing back my curls, and take one last look up at the sky. A fiery orange strip of sun has burnt its way along the edge of the horizon, casting a warm yellow glow over everything.

My star is no longer there. Now it's just me and this brand new day, full of life without the man I love.

And tinged with hope.

Because for the first time in three months, I hope for something more.

My feet move of their own accord, heading toward the office building Eric disappeared into. Just before I go too far, I turn back. A hot-air balloon rises in the sky in the distance, the balloon gay in the morning breeze. That scent of eucalyptus and saltwater and *home* infiltrates my nostrils, and I smile.

And it feels good.

I press my hand to my lips, ready to blow a kiss. "I'll find you in the stars," I whisper, then press my lips to my hand and blow.

And I know my love will carry on the breeze, through the trees, and it will find him somehow. I know that he will look out for me, no matter where I am.

Always.

Forever.

Eternally.

ACKNOWLEDGEMENTS

Thank you so much for buying this book. It means so much to me to know that you took the time to read something I created. If you would like to keep in touch, please sign up to my e-newsletter, join my reader group on Facebook, Lauren's Foxes, or simply follow my facebook page. I'd love to connect with you.

Of course, I need to thank my talented cover designer, Kim, for the beautiful job she did on this cover. It's yet another gorgeous piece—thanks so much, lovely!

My beta readers, you're all amazing! Simone (I can't believe you read it twice!), Stace, Carmen, Jenn and Kristine—I can't release a book without you. You're all so talented and kind, and I am stoked to call you guys friends. Also, to the lovely ladies at Hot Tree—your words make my words better! Thanks for your time.

The gorgeous Sali, you helped talk me off the ledge and introduced me to Voxer. Oh yeah! And you made this story a zillion times more than it could ever have been without you. Thanks so much for all your help.

To the fabulous Kylie, Beth and the Give Me Books team, you always nail my promo and I love you so much for it. Thanks for your professional work.

Every blogger who takes the time to read and review, I salute you! I'm honoured that you've chosen to read my work. Thank you once again.

Finally, to my gorgeous family and friends, with a special shout-out to the coolest doctor in the land, Ms Whitfield, and of course my sexy husband. You're my greatest love story.

ABOUT THE AUTHOR

Lauren K. McKellar is the author of romance reads that make you feel. She lives by the beach in Australia with her husband and their two dogs. Most of the time, all three of them are well behaved.

Website: www.laurenkmckellar.com

Facebook:
https://www.facebook.com/LaurenKateMcKellar

Instagram & Twitter: @LaurenKMcKellar

BOOKS BY LAUREN K. MCKELLAR

CRAZY IN LOVE

#1 The Problem With Crazy

#2 Eleven Weeks

#3 The Problem With Heartache

EMERALD COVE

#1 How To Save A Life

#2 The Twenty-One

NOT LIKE THE MOVIES

#1 FAME

#2 FORTUNE (coming soon)

THE PROBLEM WITH CRAZY

Book one in the *Crazy in Love* series

The problem with crazy is that crazy, by itself, has no context. It can be good crazy, bad crazy ... or crazy crazy—like it was when my ex-boyfriend sung about me on the radio.

Eighteen-year-old Kate couldn't be more excited about finishing high school and spending the summer on tour with her boyfriend's band. Her dad showing up drunk at graduation, however, is not exactly kicking things off on the right foot—and that's before she finds out about his mystery illness, certain to end in death.
A mystery illness that she could inherit.
Kate has to convince everyone around her that her father is sick, not crazy. But who will be harder to convince? Her friends? Or herself?

The Problem With Crazy *is a story about love and life; about overcoming obstacles, choosing to trust, and learning how to make the choices that will change your life forever.*

Praise for *The Problem With Crazy* ...

"Heartbreaking, life-affirming—one of my all-time favourites." Glass Paper Ink Book Blog

"This story is beautiful, heartbreaking and will leave you thinking about it for days to follow." A.K.A. The Book Harlots Review

Read a sample of

THE PROBLEM WITH CRAZY

ONE

The problem with crazy is that crazy, by itself, has no context. It can be good crazy, bad crazy … or the kind that makes you turn your head and avoid eye contact, even though you know you shouldn't.

Sometimes it can be thrown about with vicious intent, like when my mum used it against my dad.

"I am going to go crazy at your father, *if* he eventually decides to grace us with his presence," Mum hissed at me. I say 'at' because even though her eyes were darting to all four corners of the full-to-exploding hall, spit still landed square in the middle of my left cheek.

"Mu-um." I sighed. I was pissed, too, though. I could accept his missing my birthday and Christmas last year, after he'd run out of our lives without a trace, but come on; what kind of father calls to say he's coming, and then is late to his only daughter's graduation?

"Kate, it's the least he could do," Mum mumbled. She was taking huge strides down the side of the hall, scanning the hordes of seated parents and students for an empty chair. Other parents and graduates-to-be milled around, a buzz of excitement filling the auditorium. Up on stage, our principal, Mr McDonald, was speaking to a few class captains. *Suck-ups.* "I've not had a cent from him in more than a year, and now he thinks he can just walk back into your life to play father at your graduation? If that drunken idiot thinks I'll sit next to him when he finally does get here, he is going to be sorely mistaken."

"I doubt he thinks that," I breathed. Recounting my father's sins, both on the phone to him and in my presence, was one of my mother's favourite activities since he'd left.

"There. There's a seat." Mum extended a maroon-painted talon toward an empty chair in the front row. It matched her freshly pressed suit-dress perfectly. The talon, that is; not the chair. "It'll be a better view for my photos, anyway." I cringed. It was bad enough she was taking photos, but front and centre? Really?

I racked my brain, trying to come up with a contingency plan to get me out of this mess when I felt a cool pair of hands close over my eyes.

"Guess who?" a deep voice asked from behind me.

"Dave!" I spun around to greet him, planting a tiny kiss on his cheek.

"Hey, Kate. Mrs T." He nodded in Mum's direction.

"Hi, Dave. You look just lovely," Mum swooned at Dave's tucked-in white school shirt and firmly fastened navy-blue tie. Even his hair was slicked up into neat little spikes, a change from the usual scruffy mess I loved running my hands through.

"Thanks. Hey, I'm sure my folks would like to sit with you, if you're trying to find a seat." Dave pointed his delicate musician's finger toward an empty seat three rows behind us. His parents waved with fervour, and I said a silent prayer of thanks. "They're just over there."

"That is so kind of you to offer. I'll go on and find them. You two kids get backstage—oh! Mr McDonald has turned on the microphone. They must be about to start."

I turned toward where she was pointing and saw our school principal had indeed gripped his hand firmly around the microphone. The lights dimmed and the audience slowly hushed. I grabbed Dave's arm and we raced to the door on the left hand side of the room, the one that would lead us to the wings.

Compared to the silence of the hall, backstage was chaos. The other 163 members of our school year milled about, a sea of navy check and white, all talking far too loudly with the exuberance of the released. This was it. In approximately sixty-four minutes, if the dress rehearsal was anything to go by, we would all be officially finished school. And I, for one, couldn't wait.

"You guys! Can you please get into alphabetical order?" Stacey whined from her position at the top of the stairs. Her blonde ponytail bobbed up and down she brought her fingers to her temple. No one seemed to be listening. Apparently, graduation was the one time she couldn't make our entire year stand still and take notice.

"Oh, Kate. Good, you're here." She bounced over to my side, blue eyes sparkling as she scanned me up and down. "I was getting worried. What took you so long?"

"You know … She couldn't decide what to wear." Dave joked.

"But—it's school uniform today." Stacey tilted her head to the side. I sucked in a breath and ignored the elbow to the ribs Dave gave me. Sometimes, I wondered how Stacey had gotten through high school alive.

"Well, helloooo Stacey." Michael came up from behind, giving her a skirt a quick tug as he scooted his way into our circle. Stacey gave his puppy-dog eyes a quick glare, her hands quickly smoothing the material back down and making sure her assets were firmly covered.

That was how, I reminded myself. With a body like that and eyes that could kill, Stacey had done more than attend high school. She veritably ruled the school.

"Dave, man, how you doing?" Michael asked, clapping his weathered hand on my boyfriend's shoulder.

"I think I'll be better in an hour or so."

"I know what you mean."

"Not to interrupt your male bonding session, but can you please line up in alphabetical? It's im*por*tant," Stacey pleaded, her hands clasped in front of her.

"Your wish is my command." Michael bowed.

"Right." Stacey narrowed her eyes at us, gave a sharp nod, and then spun on her heel. "I'll see you when we're graduates, Kate." She threw one hand up in the air and charged to the front of the line.

"Man, when is that chick gonna notice I'm alive?" Michael turned to watch her go. "Sometimes I think she'll date anyone but me."

"When we're on tour with Coal she won't be able to help but notice you," Dave said. His green eyes came alive, widening at the thought of their upcoming tour.

"You know it. This will be our time to shine." Michael nodded. "It's a good thing your girlfriend is so good at organising things. We'd never have made the tour if she hadn't hit them up."

"It was nothing." I felt the heat rise in my cheeks.

"Yeah, it's not like she wrote the songs." Dave stroked the back of my hair, bringing shiny brown strands of it to rest over my shoulder. "It was probably just seeing her face on our album cover. She's too pretty to say no to."

"Dave." I slapped him playfully across the chest, unsure if it was an insult or a compliment.

"Hey! I'm not saying you weren't part of the reason we got the spot." His hands were up in the air in defence. "And when we're famous rock stars, you can live a life of luxury as payment."

"I can't wait," I whispered, turning to him. He stood deliciously close. He wrapped his arms around my neck and I inhaled his scent—exotic, spicy, and loaded with cologne.

"I can't wait for the first night of tour," he spoke into my hair. "For *our* first night." His words were loaded with meaning. I felt his hands travel a little lower, skimming over the curves of my hips. My school skirt suddenly felt very thin, and very short.

"Guys, get a room," Michael said. I pulled away, my face hot for the second time that day.

"We will. On tour!" Dave laughed, and threw his hand up in the air. Michael laughed and high-fived him right back, and I pretended to ignore their stupid boy banter. Nothing makes a girl feel special like a joke about losing her virginity, made by her boyfriend.

It was lucky I loved Dave—because sometimes he could be a downright jerk.

"Everybody, please line up NOW. They have STARTED ALREADY." Stacey's hands were on her hips as her blonde hair tossed from side to side.

"She's so cute when she's mad." Michael smiled.

"Good luck." I leaned in and kissed Dave on the cheek.

I made my way to my spot in line, leaving the two boys to walk to their allocated places in alphabetical order. They were next to each other, Belconnen and Belmonte. They'd actually met in roll call one year; funny to think they were now co-founders of one of the biggest on-theverge bands today. I grinned a smug smile. Thanks in part to me, no matter what Dave said.

A blanket of silence settled over the line and I chewed my lip. I wondered if Dad made it, then hated myself for doing so. I hadn't needed him for the past year, and I didn't need him now. Mum and I did just fine without him.

The line shuffled forward and I felt the butterflies kicking around my stomach. This was it. I was going to graduate. My whole future was ahead of me, planning tours and events for the band, spending time with Dave, visiting different countries world over and—

"Tomlinson." Mr McDonald's voice boomed through the microphone, echoing backstage. I looked up. Front of the line already. I smoothed my hands down my blue-plaid skirt and plastered a smile on my face. Father or no, I was really doing this. I was finally going to graduate high school and go on the road with Dave—far, far away from here, from the memories that haunted our two-storey wooden house and this small, seaside town.

I strode out of the wings. In front of me, hundreds of parents gazed up at the stage, expectation written all over their faces. I swallowed. I'd never been great with crowds.

"A reminder that we'll hold all clapping till the end of each letter," Miss Lucas, the assistant principal, disciplined the parents as I crossed the stage to their side. *Because nothing disrupts a school assembly like unruly clapping.*

"Kate Tomlinson," Mr McDonald said. I walked up to him and shook his hand, ignoring the stench of stale sweat seeping from his shirt. I took the certificate from Miss Lucas and stood front and centre on the stage, right in front of the photographer to get my formal shot. On the left-hand side of the floor in front of me, three quarters of my year lined up, holding their certificates, too. Sometimes, being almost at the end of the alphabet was a blessing. At least I had a reprieve on smiling from letters A to S.

"Okay, taking your photo in three, two—"

"Yyyyyyes! That's my daughter!"

The voice came from the very back of the auditorium, accompanied by over-enthusiastic applause. My heart stopped beating for several seconds, stuck somewhere in between my throat and my chest.

What.

The.

Hell.

"Good job, Katie! Good—yob." I hadn't heard it for more than a year, but the voice was easily recognisable. It was my father.

My "dad".

I scanned the room till I spotted him. He was pumping his hands together, standing in the doorway, his mouth slack-jawed, eyes alive with enthusiasm. His voice was slurred and loud, too loud. When he'd left home, he'd been drinking a bit, and Mum and I had hoped his absence would have toned down his boozing.

Clearly, it hadn't worked.

HOW TO SAVE A LIFE

ONE

I remember in primary school we learnt about alliteration. You'd have to think of an adjective starting with the first letter of your name that truly described yourself.

I'd been upset, because Laura took "lovely", but eventually, the teacher helped me settle on "ladylike". Ladylike Lia. It felt like the only one left.

Now, though? Now I'm spoilt for choice.

Lonely Lia.

Little Lia.

Lia the Liar.

Lia the Lost.

My name is Lia Stanton. And this is my story.

I flick through the book, searching for something, anything. Anything to help drown out the wallow of loud music coming from the living room downstairs.

The words, though? They don't want to cooperate. They're blurring into one another faster than a steam train, creating a page that feels less like a history book and more like some kind of dot art by Lichtenstein, minus the colour.

"I ... will always love you ..."

I bring my hand to my temple and wonder if I press hard enough, if I can knock myself out. If I have to listen to her singing that damn Whitney Houston song one more time, I think I'm going to use this text book as a weapon and bludgeon myself to unconsciousness. It'd be a hell of a lot easier than asking her to stop.

"Will-alwaysssss ... love yiew ..."

Yep. She's getting progressively worse as the song goes on.

Focus, Lia. F-O-C-U-S.

Once again, I start to read, and I don't know if it's the volume from next door or the fact that I've been using my phone as a torch, but I'm not able to concentrate. I could turn on the light, but there'd be every chance that she would see. They say misery loves company, and my mother is living proof of that.

I glance over to the poster on the back of my door, shining my phone's torch toward it. With a grin, I jump from my bed, snagging the red marker from my desk on the way. When I get to the chart, I make a big red cross through number 154. *One down, way too many to go.*

This is undoubtedly the best part of my day. When I cross off one more number on the poster. When I officially mark my life as one step closer to freedom, one step closer to leaving Emerald Cove and starting my new life in Melbourne. Away from the memories that haunt me around every corner. Away from the strange looks that I still get. The whispers that follow.

And as much as I hate to admit it, *away from her.*

"You ... ooo ... ooo ... oou," she warbles, her voice tremoring as she climaxes over the high notes.

Although freedom will never happen if I don't finish reading this history text.

"Damn it," I whisper, then march over to my bed, grab my book and slide my phone into my pocket. I turn and open the door, walking out to the living room where she has the wine bottle as her microphone and the photos as her audience. They're scattered over the coffee table, their glossy sheen reflecting the candles burning on the mantel. The smell of wine mixes with the candles' scents of vanilla and some kind of pungent tropical flower, and my stomach roils.

"Duet?" Mum's head lolls to me, and her eyes, chocolate mirrors of my own, don't seem to focus—instead, they gaze glassily over my body.

"Maybe later." I smile, and take my coat from the old rack near the door, tossing my long brown hair over my shoulder. "I'm going out."

"On a school night?" She frowns.

"Not a school night, Mum."

It's totally a school night.

"Oh. Haf fun," she says, and skips over to her iPod to start the song again. It's odd—when she sings, her heart bleeds, but in between tunes, she can be oddly cheery. I feel for my keys in the pocket of my jacket and shut the door behind me, just as the serenade starts again.

Sometimes I feel guilty for lying to her like that. But when she makes it so easy, it's hard not to use it to my advantage. Because sometimes, I just have to leave.

Leave. Leaving is easy.

Leaving is all I want.